# Wizards of the Apocalypse

# Wizards of the Apocalypse

## The Hidden Wizard

X. Zombie

# Praise for
## *Wizards of the Apocalypse: The Forgotten Prophecy*

"A great fantasy read for both younger and older audiences."
- Amazon Review

"*Wizards of the Apocalypse: The Forgotten Prophecy* was a unique read unlike most books on the market. X Zombie's debut provides a unique blend of horror, fantasy, whimsy, and friendship that's great for both younger and older readers."
- Amazon Review

"I fell in love with the characters and the illustrations were such a fun addition. I'm super excited to read the rest of the story!"
- Amazon Review

"You will be taken into fantastical kingdoms with wizards, dragons, elves, and zombies that talk. As you journey through this fun adventure you will not want to put it down."
- Leah Ann Brown, author of *Chronicles of the Hidden Realms*

"A fantastic adventure with a clever twist on a zombie apocalypse!"
- Stephanie Cotta, author of *The Conjurer's Curse*

# HAUNTED LANDS

# UNDERWORLD

OCEAN OF SOULS
BASALT WASTES
SHADOWBLOOD FORTRESS
HIGHBORN DEMON TERRITORY
MOUNT ONYX
WYVERN STABLES
MOUNT IGNEOUS
NOVA
SHADOWBLOOD OUTPOST
HALL OF BLACK MIRRORS
OBSIDIAN RANGE
LAKE MAGMA
GLASS BEACH
RIVER OF FIRE
SCARLET DUNES
INFERNO MOUNTAINS
BURNING PEAKS
LOWBORN DEMON TERRITORY
SULFUR RIVER
SEARING PENINSULA
MOLTEN OCEAN
N
W
E
S

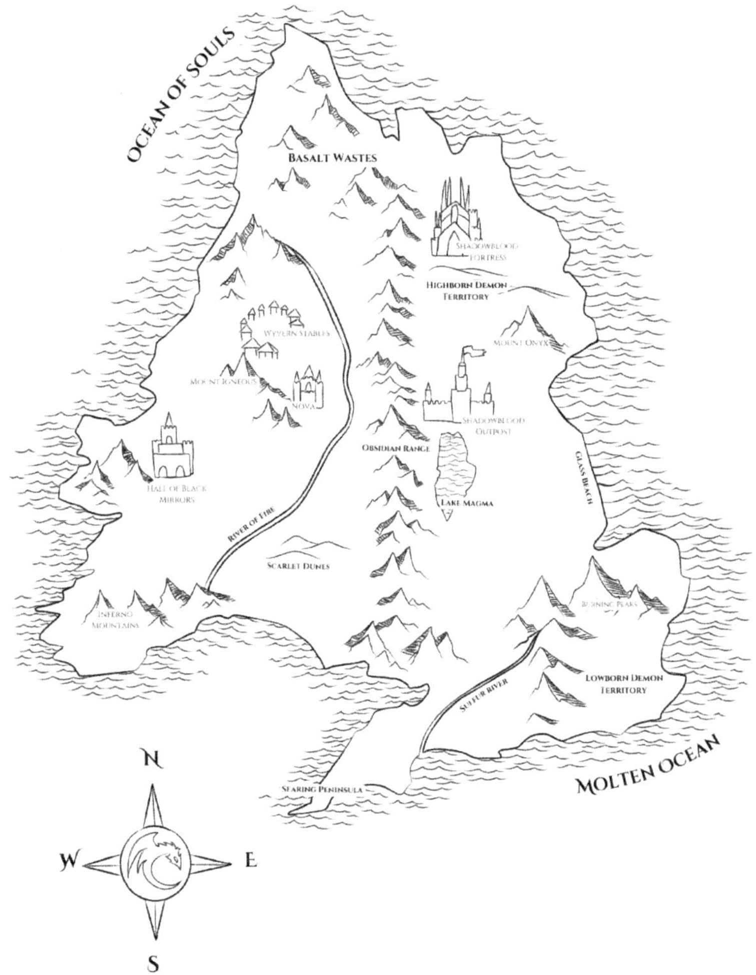

# Chapter One

It had been a week since Blanchett's wizards ensnared Malice in the Otherworld, shattering the zombie king's chances of conquering Skeletonia. Zokar stood alone in his quarters. The room was large and bare. No flowers, no curtains or decor save for an armor stand—just bare stone and a few brackets carrying unlit torches.

His room had a hearth, across from it stood a four poster bed, without a canopy and covered in tattered, white sheets. The furniture was scratched and broken; a chair sat in the left corner with a broken leg—broken in a recent fit of rage. The posts on his bed boasted deep claw marks. Being paranoid, Zokar hardly slept, often spending most of his nights sitting in bed and clawing at the oak posts with his overgrown nails, expecting someone to barge in and murder him.

The zombie king growled at his reflection in his cracked mirror. Unbridled rage covered his face, which was normal, but today, it was mixed with the bitter taste of defeat.

Zokar in no way enjoyed having Malice around. He counted down the days until he had enough magic to overthrow the demon. The problem was the zombie king needed Malice to gain said magic. Without her, the zombies were on their own, left to fend for themselves the same way they did after losing the first war.

*There has to be a way to release the Shadowblood from the Otherworld,* thought the zombie king. *I hate admitting this, but maybe Marcus knows of a way.*

Zokar brought his rotting hand to the ugly stab wound in the center of his chest—courtesy of Skeleton's head knight. The zombie king ran his fingers across it, feeling the rigid tissue. His magic expedited the healing process, but it was still scarred. Most zombies took pride in their scars. Zokar didn't; to him, scars evoked thoughts of defeat.

Magic tickled the back of the zombie king's mind, yearning to burst out like a relentless storm. Zokar pinched his lips together as he quickly pulled on his faded-blue linen shirt. He snapped at one of his servants to help him don his armor.

A small zombie sidled over, carrying his new breastplate. It resembled his previous one, except this one was polished and free of bloodstains. Zokar belted on his dagger with a flick of his wrist. He scowled at the lone blade.

*If that infernal knight hadn't flung my dagger into the lava, I'd have joined the power of both. One will have to do.*

Rising sunlight glinted off Zokar's crown as he placed it on his head. After looking in the mirror one more time, the zombie king exited his quarters and headed for the throne room. Zombies in leather armor ambled around the corridor, saluting the zombie king as he passed by. The perpetual fear in their eyes lifted Zokar's spirits. He didn't need Malice's magic to maintain authority over his subjects.

Zokar listened to the soft click of his boots on jagged stone as he descended the winding staircase. The zombie king had Marcus scour the Zombieshire castle library for anything that might aid in releasing Malice from the Otherworld. With each passing day, Zokar pressed his second-in-command to find information before Blanchett's wizards grew too powerful. So far, his efforts had turned up nothing.

The only good news was that Zokar had bought the zombies some time. He recalled the moment he bit

Sir Emerson. He remembered his teeth sinking deep into soft flesh. Since Malice gave him magic, Zokar hadn't needed to bite. If he wanted someone dead, he'd whisper a spell, causing his enemies' necks to break or their heads to explode. So biting Emerson wasn't something Zokar planned; it was just fun. Now, as he traversed these halls, the foolish knight was succumbing to the zombie infection. He'd become a zombie soon enough. Skeleton would have to kill his friend.

A cruel smile played on Zokar's face. *Perhaps that infernal knight will turn and infect everyone in Skeletonia. Wouldn't that be fantastic?*

At the bottom of the stairs, Zokar took a right and approached the door to the war room. Turning the brass handle, he opened the door to find Marcus standing at the table. A map of the Haunted Lands lay unfurled on the oak wood; an open ink well with a quill sat beside a few candelabras sitting at the table's edges, casting a warm yellow glow on their surroundings. The walls were plain save for the huge poster detailing the anatomy of a dragon, which was a guide to obtaining unfathomable power.

For decades, Zokar had wanted to gain control of the Dragon Isles and access dragon magic. Dragons were the most powerful beings in the Haunted Lands, and though there was no record of the scaly beasts succumbing to the zombie infection, that wouldn't stop Zokar from trying. A virus that transformed its victim into a flesh-eating monster combined with something as large and formidable as a dragon would surely bring the wizards to their knees.

Zokar blew out a long breath. *Malice could help us with that.*

"Find anything?" Zokar asked Marcus.

The second-in-command stood upright, his spine straightening with too much confidence. Confidence that made Zokar's lip curl.

"I did, sire," the captain answered. "I think I found someone who can breach the pathway between the surface world and Otherworld."

Zokar eyed Marcus dubiously. "You know that's impossible. Even on Samhain, when the portal between the worlds is the thinnest, no one can escape the Otherworld, not even the elves or the dragons. It's too deep into the Underworld. It's the lowest layer, you moron."

The second-in-command said nothing and slid a large tome across the table. It was a thick book, not as thick as the Apocalypse Grimoire, but thick enough to house a lot of information. The title read: *History of the Sorcerer Tribes*.

Zokar's brows rose. He flipped open the book and was greeted with worn pages. The edges were frayed and ripped, entailing ages of being read. The text was luckily not written in the ancient wizard tongue. The zombie king brought his gaze back to his right-hand man.

"Sorcerers are going to help us?" Zokar said in disbelief.

Marcus nodded. "Their magic is supposedly strong enough to break the barrier between realms. They can help us free Malice."

Moving the book, Marcus pointed to a part of the map where a cluster of mountains was illustrated with *White-Talon Range* written above it. "There's where we have to go. I read that's where the last sorcerer tribes reside. The Silver Flame Tribe, to be specific." Marcus flipped the page. There was the introduction. Though Zokar could see the same page Marcus did, the second-in-command felt the need to read it out loud.

"Sorcerer territory was composed of three tribes:

the Blue Moon Tribe, the Silver Flame Tribe, and the Solar Flare Tribe. The land was ruled by a triumvirate; they lived in harmony for many years until Queen Cressida Moonwatcher of the Blue Moon Tribe died; the Silver Flame Tribe queen, Meredith Argent, claimed she was the rightful queen of all three sorcerer tribes and disagreed with the triumvirate and wished to create her own dictatorship," Marcus paused and cast a glance at his king.

Zokar had heard of the Sorcerer Wars the same way he learned about the Elf Wars: through Malice's teachings. But all she taught him was the basics. The zombie king didn't learn further. Whenever he asked for extra information, Malice shut him down, claiming, "Zombies should remain limited in their knowledge of magic." Her explanation always rankled Zokar. His face heated just thinking about it. *She'll pay for how she belittled and underestimated me.*

Turning to a page he had bookmarked, Marcus continued reading. "Argent turned to dark magic to ensure her victory. She and her tribe collaborated with the demons—specifically Shadowbloods."

The second-in-command glanced at the zombie king again, determination dancing in his lone eye.

"They're the key to Malice's emancipation."

"How can a sorcerer free a demon from another realm?" Zokar asked, his voice dripping with impatience. He braced his arms on the worn table, saying with agitation, "Shadowbloods are the most powerful demons, and Malice was trapped by a measly group of wizards. When are you going to get that through your thick skull?"

Marcus pulled the book back and flipped through more of the pages. He shoved the book in Zokar's direction. Folding his arms, Zokar glared down at the page and read it before returning his gaze to Marcus.

"They worked closely with Malice; they have the magic it takes to release her," Marcus replied. The torches cast ominous shadows over the captain's face. A shiver rattled through Zokar.

Arms still folded, Zokar leaned against the wall behind him. His armor scraped against the hard stone.

"How can we be sure the sorcerers won't just betray us?" *I already have to worry about you betraying me.* "They will. We must ensure the zombies have the upper hand in this."

Marcus rolled his eye and stood up straight. "You can't think like that. Without Malice, the zombies are as good as defeated. And after seeing what Skeleton and his friends can do, we don't stand a chance. We need all the allies we can get—especially other magic-wielders."

Zokar kept his frown, jaw clenched. "No, we need allies who fear us!" He slammed his fist on the table, rattling its contents. His magic bubbled near the surface. Marcus took a step back, but his features remained composed, unafraid.

*Curse him! I can't even scare the captain anymore. He's getting too good.* "Fear is how the zombies secure their power." Zokar pinched the bridge of his nose. "If we act friendly to everyone we meet, they'll use us. We'll storm the Silver Flame Tribe and force them to submit." Zokar made a fist, and tight veins popped out on his knuckles. "And we'll eliminate those who stand in our way."

"You're not going to obtain that power if Malice isn't here," Marcus said calmly. His voice slid like oil, causing Zokar's skin to prickle. "Besides, if Malice realizes *you* gathered fellow magic-wielders who practice dark magic to free her, I think she'd forgive you." The captain placed his hands behind his back in that confident manner Zokar hated. "Our main goal is to free Malice. If we don't, the Haunted Lands will never belong to the zombies. Is that what you want?"

Silence fell over the war room. Zokar chewed his lip in thought, listening to the soft crackle of flames. *Working with sorcerers would mean more people for me to keep an eye on. More people who could contest my power and dethrone me. On the other hand, if I rally them to free Malice, that should reconcile our feud. I'll take credit, and she'll have to forgive me. Maybe even grant me more magic as a reward. Once I have all her magic, it won't matter what the Silver Flame Tribe does. I'll be too strong to stop. I just have to bide my time. Befriend the tribe, pose as an ally, and bring them under zombie authority when their backs are turned. My authority.*

Zokar's limbs tingled, a sick smile splitting his scarred face. He locked eyes with the second-in-command and gave a curt nod.

"It's settled. We'll recruit the Silver Flame Tribe," said Zokar. *For now.*

Marcus sighed audibly through his nose. *Gods, why is Zokar so stubborn?*

The zombie king's paranoia made convincing him to take action nearly impossible. Even mere suggestions would trigger Zokar's paranoia; some days, he was so obstinate that it made Marcus want to slam his head into a wall. If the second-in-command hadn't reminded Zokar of his and Malice's feud, he'd never have gotten through. Too often, catering to the zombie king's ego was how Marcus got his attention.

The zombie king moved to the war room door. "We leave tomorrow for the White-Talon Range." Then, he slammed the door behind him.

Stone pressed into Marcus's back as he leaned against the wall; the coolness of the bricks seeped through his doublet. Goose flesh stippled his arms. Marcus rubbed his forehead, eye heavy. Days of scanning the library archives for anything regarding the Otherworld left Marcus sleep-deprived. But in the end, it would all be worth it.

Once Malice was free, Marcus would continue pledging his loyalty to her. The Shadowblood wouldn't bestow the title of zombie king on just anyone; Marcus would have to prove himself. Continue proving his worth. Marcus was serious about making allies with the Silver Flame Tribe. That would have to make Malice proud. Bringing her powerful allies with a similar goal? What could be better? Once he was the zombie king, he'd unite the undead, bring Skeletonia under their rule. No killing or slaughter needed.

*I saved Zombia from that fireball. I will not allow more killing. Not under my watch. Zokar's plagued Zombieshire for too long.*

A lightness filled Marcus's chest. He inhaled a new, cleansing breath and faced the war room door. In the distance, he could hear Zokar bellowing orders at his guards and servants, followed by hurried, panicked footsteps. Marcus narrowed his eye and shook his head as he made his way to the door. He placed his fingers on the handle and paused.

*Soon enough, Malice will be free,* thought Marcus. *Soon enough, the zombie throne will be mine.*

# Chapter Two

*I'll get through this. I'll survive. There has to be a way to cure me of this infection.*

These are the phrases Emerson had been repeating to himself for the last week. He said them under his breath as he dipped his hands into the basin beside his bed and splashed his face. The cooling droplets slid down his forehead and cheeks, doing little to mitigate the sweltering heat.

A fever had gripped Emerson by the time he and his friends returned to the surface world. At first, he convinced himself that the rise in body temperature was the heat of the Underworld. After reaching the coolness of the forest, Emerson hoped his temperature would decrease. It didn't. Tears prickled Emerson's eyes, blurring his vision. When Zokar's filthy teeth broke the skin, he knew his fate was sealed. No amount of convincing himself he'd be okay would change it.

Blinking them away, the knight dried his face

with a linen towel and turned quickly away from the mirror. Emerson couldn't bear to look at his reflection. He didn't want to witness the zombie he was becoming. Glancing down at his arm, he peeled off the bandages concealing his bite mark. They came away coated in red. He winced as the dried blood tugged uncomfortably at his flesh; the bleeding had stopped, thankfully, but the ugly ring of tooth marks stared back at Emerson—a constant reminder of his impending fate.

The skin was puffy and dauntingly discolored. Purple-brown splotches encompassed the ring, flecked with hints of green. Nausea washed over Emerson. *I'll turn soon.* Grabbing fresh bandages from his satchel, he dressed his wound and sighed. *My friends can't find out. They'll have to kill me. Tristan would never be able to do it. None of them could, but especially him. And if they don't kill me, I'll become a threat.* Emerson stole a glance at the bandages through blurry vision. *I can't become a threat to the ones I love.*

After slowly donning his armor, Emerson belted on his sword. The crystal blade weighed on his hip more than it should. He tugged at the collar of his armor. The past few days, everything felt heavier and more constricting. In fact, everything was sore, his joints and muscles alike. Nonetheless, being a knight was a duty unto death, and Emerson was determined to spend his last days fulfilling the oath he had taken long ago.

Taking a cleansing breath, Emerson pushed open his door and started down the castle corridor. The sun shone through the high windows, glinting off the crystalline surface of Emerson's armor plate. Fellow soldiers waved and greeted the knight. Emerson frowned, kept his head down, and sped up his gait, not wanting to speak to them. Ignoring his fellow soldiers-at-arms pained him, but he couldn't risk exposure; he knew his countenance would betray his fear. They'd know something was amiss. So, Emerson drowned out any greetings by listening to the rhythmic click of his crystal boots on the castle floors.

"Em! Emerson. Wait for me!" came a voice the knight usually loved hearing. But today, he wasn't in the mood for it.

First came racing footsteps. Then, Cameron materialized in Emerson's peripheral vision before intercepting his path. His friend wore a dark-gray leather apron, black gloves, and his trusty goggles were perched on his head of messy, raven-black hair. Emerson groaned and rolled his eyes, pain shooting through his skull.

"What is it, Cameron?" asked Emerson with a listless tone.

"Would you wanna head down to the fishing hole later? Me and some of my friends from the guild are going." Cameron's emerald eyes were wide and pleading.

Emerson didn't hesitate. "Sorry, I'm working late today." He crossed his arms, cupping his shoulders with his hands, unease and guilt warring within.

Cameron looked taken aback. When Emerson began walking, his friend intercepted him again, causing the knight to sigh through his nose.

"You've said that all week," said Cameron. He folded his arms. "You haven't come to visit me in my shop, you haven't met me for lunch, and it's been *ages* since you've invited me to come watch you at jousting practice. Are you okay, Em? You can talk to me."

*Don't tell him you've been bitten,* thought Emerson. *I don't need another person worrying about me.* His stomach churned at the thought of ignoring Cameron when he only wished to help. The past week was excruciating, physically and mentally.

"I'm fine." Emerson tried not to meet his friend's

gaze. The knight walked briskly, and when he reached the corridor leading to the sparring room, he felt a tug on his right arm. The arm Zokar bit.

"Talk to me!" pleaded Cameron. "We're friends, what's wrong?"

Emerson tore his arm out of his friend's grasp and flared his nostrils. "Nothing is wrong! I've already told you I'm fine, Cameron." The knight's voice echoed off the walls more than he intended.

The guildmaster backpedaled, eyes wide, mouth open. "Em?" His voice came out as a squeak, which flooded Emerson with guilt. *Gods above, I didn't mean to yell at him.*

That's when Cameron's gaze fell on the linen wrapped around Emerson's bicep. "What happened here?" he asked.

Before Cameron could grab him again, Emerson responded in a low tone, "Leave me alone." Regret struck again when moisture clung to Cameron's eyes. Quickly, the knight turned and focused his gaze on getting to his destination.

Emerson's chest felt tight as he walked to the war room. Guilt gnawed at the back of his mind since being bitten, and only mounted after his argument. Honesty was the backbone of his oath. Of friendship. *Without honesty, wouldn't that make me deceitful? I can't be deceitful toward my friends—or my king.* Emerson knew withholding the truth from his friends would be for the better. Rounding a corner, the knight descended a flight of dreary stone stairs, leading to the subterranean war room where Tristan decided would be the best secret place to practice. The clash of metal and cheerful shouting reached his ears.

Emerson blew out a breath. *All I have to do is continue serving at Tristan's side until I can't anymore. At least I'll die knowing I fulfilled my duties.*

Tristan stood in the castle's subterranean war room, face to face with Cerys—a fledgling wizard and his mentor.

Though Tristan wished he was in the sparring room, he knew that would be a huge risk. Soldiers used the sparring room daily; there was no way to practice magic without getting caught. All their sessions with Cerys and reading the Apocalypse Grimoire were kept under wraps since Tristan and his friends returned to Skeletonia.

So, Tristan figured underground would work

best. He had a war room that matched the size of the sparring room save for the large table and chairs set in the center. Sconces were artfully placed, shedding light on every surface of the room, even reaching the furthest corners.

After Tristan, with his friends' help, managed to levitate the table to a far side of the room, leaving the floor open for sparring, Radius brought down a few weapons' racks from the sparring floor. Tristan didn't ask for much—just a few spears, poleaxes, and daggers. The walls were thick, capable of canceling any noise from crashing spells and incantations. The war room wasn't ideal, but it would have to suffice. Comfort and familiarity could be exchanged for safety.

Tristan clenched his fists, feeling fiery magic vibrate through his bones. At first, Cerys was hesitant about allowing him to transform, but she agreed he needed to balance his shape-shifting while maintaining the rest of his magic.

"Are you sure you want me to do this?" asked Tristan. "What if I hurt you?" Tristan was in skeleton form, so very little could harm him. His bony fingers clenched and unclenched on his bow's handle.

"Yes!" Cerys said, exasperated. "You ask that

whenever you spar with one of your friends. It's getting on my nerves." She pointed to three spears hanging in the weapons rack Radius brought down. "Shoot arrows from your bow at me after setting them on fire."

Tristan hesitated, gulping nervously. What if the spell went awry, and he impaled his friend with a fiery arrow? On the other hand, with every spell he practiced, Tristan improved. And having the Apocalypse Grimoire had been a huge boon in sharpening his wizard skills. Why should this be any different?

The king smiled and glanced at the spears. Closing his eyes, he reached for his inner magic. Tristan pulled back the string on his bow; three arrows materialized in the string. Tristan drew the rune for fire and placed it on the magical arrows, setting them alight. Turning to Cerys, he shot three arrows her way.

The mage did a graceful flip over two of the flaming projectiles. The third one she kicked with the heel of her boot and sent it into the wall, in between the bricks. Cerys landed on her feet with a huge smile plastered on her face. Tristan watched in awe, the tightness in his chest loosening. His cheeks reddened a little.

*Well, I worried for nothing. How embarrassing. I*

*need to grow more comfortable with practicing my magic. I can't afford to hesitate. Malice wouldn't, so neither should I.*

Clapping erupted from the far side of the room. Tristan grinned over to his sister. She and Zombia sat in oak chairs that were already in the war room; the Apocalypse Grimoire sat between both girls, allowing them to study. Cerys had roused her apprentices at dawn.

The sun had barely reached the lip of the castle wall when she woke them and dragged them down to the bowels of the castle. The birds hadn't even begun their morning melodies, but the mage had insisted the wizards practice from dawn to dusk. Honing their magic skills required much practice; no time could be wasted. They didn't have much to begin with. Tristan would have liked to continue training the day the wizard returned to Skeletonia, but hiding their magic was paramount. So, they had to sacrifice a whole day to finding a secret place to practice and revamping the war room to match their *needs.*

"Do more of that, and we'll send Malice running for the hills," laughed Tibia.

Snapping his fingers, Tristan switched back to human form. Fire rolled through his muscles, his body already beginning to ache. Maintaining his skeletal form *and* using his magic wasn't easy, but it was necessary. The first time Tristan tried balancing the two, his skeleton form failed mid-fight. Though it merited a laugh from his friends, Tristan remained determined. Nights of reading the Grimoire and practice served him well. A week later, the wizards had improved immensely.

"Cerys, are we going to practice more healing spells later?" asked Zombia. Her hazel eyes flashed with anticipation. Tristan couldn't help but grin at her. *The Haunted Lands would be far better if more people were like her.*

The mage looked at her, grinned, and nodded. "Absolutely. Those spells are just as pertinent as the dangerous ones."

Tibia rolled her eyes. "The dangerous ones are what we need. Healing spells won't stop Malice. She needs to be destroyed."

"And she will be once we procure the dragon-claw dagger," Cerys answered. "But your wizard training is important. Malice isn't just waiting around for a dagger to enter her heart. We'll have to fight her, and such a fight would require a lot of healing."

He and his friends barely escaped the last time. Fighting Karneleth using the zombie-controlling staff, meeting the Firebournes, and trapping Malice in the Otherworld. Tristan's stomach churned at the thought of fighting Malice again. Upon arriving home, Tristan wrote to Faye, filling her in on what transpired. He even added that he'd appreciate it if Faye gave him and his friends some magical advice. Elven magic wasn't too different from that of regular magic-wielders. When Tristan reached the end of his letter, he asked for the dragon-claw dagger. Once he dispatched the letter, Tristan and his friends played the waiting game, training in the meantime.

Tristan understood Faye had her own queendom to run. The Dragon Isles had their own governments and cultures, entirely separate from the rest of the Haunted Lands. While the dragons worked as excellent zombie repellent, conflict still occurred. Maintaining peace within the elf tribes was no trivial matter. More conflict in the Haunted Lands was the last thing he wanted. Weeks ago, Faye said she'd convince the Icebloods and Moonbloods to fight alongside her and Skeletonia. Hopefully, she accomplished that.

Cerys broke the silence. "Tibia, your turn."

Tibia looked up from the Grimoire, nodded, and stood. Her crimson cloak with a raven stitched into the fabric flowed behind her like a bloodied wave. She pulled her crossbow from her back and let her magic fit the bolt. She flashed her friends a smirk. "Now, teach me a spell that will make the undead quake in their boots."

The next ten shots fired rapidly as magic reloaded the bow. Some bolts were imbued with fire, others had ice. With each one, Tibia's smile grew wider and wider. Eventually, it made Tristan shake his head. Pure laughter escaped his sister.

When it was Zombia's turn, she controlled her powers and channeled the elements nicely. Using her glaive, she batted away the brimstone Cerys summoned upon her, scattering stray fragments all over the war room.

Her favorite element to work with, Tristan learned, was water. Cool, refreshing, and nearly harmless, yet mighty. It truly suited her demeanor. Zombia managed to channel water through her glaive. She sent the water over to the smoldering pieces of brimstone. By the end of her lesson, everyone was soaked. Tristan's white locks were stuck to his face from unbridled water. He couldn't help but laugh.

After that, Cerys had her wizards line up along the sparring floor straight across from her.

"It seems you've grown quite accustomed to using your weapons to channel the elements. Well done," the mage said. Her arms were folded behind her back, her green eyes stern. "Now, imagine your enemy has stripped you of your weapon. The good news is that you can still fight without it. Observe."

Cerys waved her hand and chanted a spell. She wrote another rune in the air, which looked like the letter H. At the same time, the mage said, *Hagalaz.* The golden rune warped and took the form of a sword. It looked exactly like a real sword, except it was transparent with a sunflower-yellow sheen.

Tristan took a sharp breath, unable to pry his eyes from the luminous blade.

"We're going to learn how to do that?" Tibia asked in awe. Her sapphire eyes rounded.

Cerys bowed. "Well, you're going to try. Copy what I did. Push yourselves."

Tristan reached deep within himself and drew his magic together. Tapping into his magic had become easier. In the beginning, drawing out his magic was like trying to penetrate a steel door with a stick. Now, it was as simple as opening a door and walking through.

He delicately wrote the same rune and spoke the same word. He wished for a bow and then made his affirmation. In seconds, bright gold magic slithered between his skeletal fingers  and  took the form of Tristan's preferred weapon. His breath caught in his throat when he saw the shimmering bow, and it resembled his real one, except this one was transparent and coated in an ethereal sheen.

It felt as heavy as his real one, despite not being made of anything but magic. He pulled on the string; it felt like a regular bowstring. To his surprise, an arrow appeared in the bow. He aimed and fired, sending the shaft into one of the stones.

"Look at this!" Zombia squealed, her eyes gleaming. "Isn't this incredible?"

Zombia's enthusiasm was contagious. Soon, all three wizards were enveloped in fits of laughter, immersed in practicing with their magic-made weapons. Tibia summoned a shield, which enabled her to deflect her brother's arrows. Heat rose to Tristan's face when Tibia jumped around in victory; her crimson cloak spun around her in an arc.

By the end of the rounds, Tristan's energy was depleted. His head spun, vision going white momentarily. A wide grin flitted across his face. He looked at his friends. Zombia held a broadsword crafted from bright green energy. Tibia held two daggers; their energy glowed a deep indigo blue. Creating weapons from pure magic awakened new emotions Tristan hadn't expected to obtain from doing magic: confidence and a sense of belonging and purpose.

The last time he truly had these feelings was at his coronation. He was obligated to protect the kingdom, his people, and his friends. It was an honor, and it was all he ever wanted. When Tristan was just learning his magic, he feared it would hurt his friends; now, he saw it as a boon. But that didn't mean he'd allow it to go awry. He'd use anything and everything to protect the ones he loved—magic wouldn't be any different.

Quickly, he snipped the tethers of his magic and watched the weapon vanish into mid-air. Zombia and Tibia did the same. Their faces were flushed; their breaths came out short as they rested. When Tristan reached for his canteen, he found it empty and laughed, remembering Zombia had used all the water in the room to douse the brimstone and them.

"Sorry about that. Maybe we should do water magic outside near the garden fountain," Zombia said, rubbing the back of her neck. She tucked a strand of damp brown hair behind her ear and smirked.

"The downside of constructing weapons from your magic is that it exhausts the wielder's magic faster," said Cerys. Her voice lowered, taking a serious tone. A shiver skittered down Tristan's spine, and it wasn't from the water. "Pay special attention to your magic when creating these weapons."

The three wizards nodded in unison. Tristan exchanged wary glances with his friends.

"It seems your magic skills are improving."

"We'll kick undead behind twice as hard," affirmed Tibia, pumping her fist in the air.

"What is it with you wanting to fight all the time?" asked Zombia, making a face.

Tibia snorted. "Isn't that our job as the Wizards of the Apocalypse? Fight the undead and save the Haunted Lands."

Tristan raised a brow with a smirk. "You've given us a title?"

His sister nodded, shoulders pulled back with pride.

"I never considered giving ourselves a name," said Zombia. She rubbed her chin. "But that has a nice ring to it."

The king's sister beamed, and she extended her arm in a mock flourish. "I figured we needed some sort of title; since we are wizards and our job is to end the Apocalypse, I saw it as a good fit."

Tristan rolled his eyes, but couldn't stop the smirk pulling at the corners of his mouth. *I find titles unnecessary and a bit silly, but I commend her for the creativity. The title does suit us.*

Heads turned to the door, and Tristan found Emerson standing there, arms folded behind his back. Every muscle in his body appeared tense, as though he were a criminal awaiting execution.

"Morning, Em," said Tristan in a cheery tone. The king tried keeping his voice positive, but the truth was Emerson had been off lately. He was more taciturn, listless, and overall distant from his friends. Tristan missed the friend he used to know. The knight barely talked to Cameron. He didn't visit the guild hall. There was no mention of Blaster inviting him to the fishing hole. After a day of guarding, Emerson retreated to his quarters, closing out the world. And he was constantly jumpy about being touched, always backing out of someone's grip as though their touch was like fire.

A cold chill settled over Tristan like a leaden blanket, slowly driving away all his warmth. *I hope it's not what I think it is.*

Tristan knew of the natural plagues that invaded society, but he knew what Emerson had wasn't one of them. He saw the knight's eyes. The blue and green were fading as angry red stormed across his irises. Emerson's tan melted away, leaving him looking pale and ill. Sweat glistened on his face, gluing his chestnut hair to his forehead; overall, he appeared disheveled. Tristan swallowed hard.

"Are you all right?" he asked. He extended a hand to place it on Emerson's shoulder, but the knight briskly pushed the king's hand away.

"I'm fine," Emerson said curtly.

"You don't look fine, Em," Zombia said. She placed a reassuring hand on her friend's shoulder. "Why don't you take the day off? I'll go get the apothecary."

The knight shook his head vigorously. "When is Faye arriving?" Emerson asked, completely ignoring Zombia's suggestion.

"This afternoon," Cerys answered. "But really,

you don't look well." Her hand neared Emerson, and he batted it away like he did with Tristan.

"Really, I'm—" Emerson's words were cut off by a series of violent coughs. Each one racked the knight's body, doubling him over. They deepened and became all-consuming. Soon, he was hacking like something was lodged in his airway.

Tristan bent down to steady his friend. "Emerson!"

Bright-red blood dripped through the knight's lips. Scarlet splotches decorated the floor and the front of Tristan's navy-blue tabard. The knight collapsed to his knees. His coughs continued. More blood dripped from his mouth in little red rivers.

"I'll get the apothecary." Tibia sprinted out of the war room.

"Dear goddess," said Zombia. She crouched beside her friend; her hand rested on his back. Emerson continued resisting her help even as she placed her shoulder under his arms, bringing him to his feet. "Look at his eyes."

Tristan did and felt even sicker. His friend's eyes were tinted scarlet red. Emerson's coughing stopped; his breathing was labored, making an awful wheezing sound as he leaned into Tristan's chest, eyes closing.

"Let's get Emerson to his room," said Tristan. The warmth of Emerson's blood threatened his gag reflex. *Don't let this be the zombie infection.* Tristan's thoughts were merely wishful thinking. The symptoms of the zombie virus were evident.

# Chapter Three

Tristan's breath was quick and shallow. Panic clouded his mind. *No, no, no, this can't be happening!*

Tears stung the king's eyes as he held Emerson's shaking form in his arms. He felt his friend's blood sticking to his clothing—blood Tristan would never have thought he'd see. Since he was a squire, Emerson fought with the prowess of a fully-fledged knight. His tenacity knew no bounds. He'd fence and spar from dawn to dusk.

After meeting Emerson in the village when he and Tristan were children, he knew Emerson would make an excellent knight one day. Not once did Tristan imagine he'd be cradling his friend's ill form in his arms. When Emerson did fight zombies, he moved with a cat's agility, dispatching the undead before they could even touch him.

The castle walls were a blur as Tristan sprinted to the knight's chambers. Zombia ran past him and threw open the doors. The morning light spilling in through the window highlighted the green tint in Emerson's flesh.

"Here." Zombia pointed to the four-poster bed.

Tristan set Emerson on the navy-blue sheets gently. "Hold him up," Tristan said to Zombia. "I'll remove his armor."

Cerys closed the door behind them before racing to Zombia's side.

Together, the mage and Zombia supported the knight's shoulders while Tristan unfastened the straps that held his armor on. Carefully, he lifted his breastplate, revealing sweat-stained clothes beneath. Moisture glistened around Emerson's chin and neck. The knight's breathing became easier, but not by much. Once Tristan removed the last piece of Emerson's armor, Zombia released her hold, letting Emerson lay back on plush pillows with a deep groan. When he fell back, some of his hair swayed to the side, exposing his ears. His ear's helix wasn't round—it had a delicate point. Tristan backpedaled. Zombie ears. *There's no mistaking he got bitten.*

"Look for bite wounds," said Zombia.

Tristan scanned his face and neck for them. A

lump formed in Tristan's throat. *Emerson has been hiding his arm!* His gaze turned to the crisp-white bandage wrapped around his friend's right bicep. Peeling back the linen, Tristan learned the severity of the wound after a rotting stench walloped him in the nose. Then, he saw the bite marks.

A disgusting ring of holes decorated Emerson's bicep. Purple-brown splotches mottled his entire upper arm; the green tint stretched down to his fingers. The same color covered Emerson's face, devouring any vestiges of the knight's humanity. Breathing suddenly became difficult for Tristan.

*Zokar must have bitten him. He was the last zombie Emerson fought.* Blood roared in the king's ears. *It should have been me fighting the zombie king. Me who got bitten. Not Emerson.*

"Let me heal him," Zombia said firmly. Her brows knit with determination.

"Your healing can only go so far, Zombia," warned Cerys. "The most you could do is hinder the infection. Not cure it."

Zombia pressed her lips together and nodded. "It's better than nothing." The wizard placed her hands to Emerson's forehead and began whispering a spell.

Tristan recognized it as one of the many healing spells

in the Apocalypse Grimoire. Cerys required all three of them to learn multiple new spells a day, in addition to more history of the magic world. Tristan had grown to enjoy his daily reading sessions.

When the spell was done, Zombia stepped back. "That will halt the zombification process."

Some human color returned to Emerson's complexion, but it warred with the green. Emerson's body shook as though he was in the Ice Queendom, groaning all the while. "It's better than nothing."

"Much better than before." Tristan blew out a breath.

"Is there anything in the Apocalypse Grimoire for curing the zombie infection?" Zombia asked nervously.

To Tristan's horror, Cerys shook her head. "That's the one thing Blanchett didn't write in the Grimoire. She's still looking for a cure herself. She has yet to update it."

Footsteps approached, then a knock, and a moment later, Tibia entered the knight's chambers with the apothecary in tow. The apothecary was one of Tristan's own, a skeleton by birth. Tristan and Zombia backed away from the bed.

Tibia looked between her friends with rapidly

blinking eyes. She clenched and unclenched her fists; her posture was as rigid as a board. "So, is it true? He was bitten?"

Tristan swallowed nervously and nodded. Tears threatened to break free, but now was not the time for them. He heard the apothecary mumble to himself as he took Emerson's vitals. Potions and salves hanging from his belt jangled like wind chimes. On any other day, it would have been a lovely sound. But today, they might as well be the peal of a funeral bell.

"Zokar was the last zombie he fought," Tristan said to Cerys. "He must have bitten him." The king clenched his fists, rage burning in his mind. Tristan focused on his boots, needing a distraction. He didn't want to believe Emerson was bitten. But with the pointed ears and green coloring, it was obvious. Emerson would turn soon. His magic rumbled beneath the surface. But he couldn't free it. Hiding his magic was hard enough when Tristan *wasn't* angry. Since he wasn't in the underground war room with a few feet of stone between his magic and the ears of the castle guards, growing too angry wasn't a good option.

Zombia grabbed the king's hand. While his worry abated a little, her touch didn't soothe the guilt swirling inside him—guilt over what happened to Emerson and concealing his magic from his kingdom. Tristan led his companions near the door, giving the apothecary and Emerson some room.

Tibia stared out the rectangular window. "It's almost noon. When Faye arrives, we'll ask her what to do. The dragons have to have some sort of zombie-reversing magic."

"Remember what Cerys said," Zombia said with a choked voice. "There isn't a cure. She said even Blanchett never experimented with dragon magic due to losing so many of them in the war."

Darkness clouded Tristan's mind. *I don't want to shoot Emerson. I couldn't.* The king looked to Emerson, who lay helplessly in his bed with the apothecary hovering over him, probably giving the knight the inevitable news that he already knew. *I know Blanchett never tried using dragon magic, but what if...*

Tristan's gaze darted to the mage. "Did Blanchett ever make a potion? A tonic or anything that could cure the zombie infection other than dragon magic?"

Cerys clutched her wand and nodded. "Blanchett has an elixir. Seeing the dwindling number of dragons, she spent countless nights experimenting with various herbs and potions during the war until she found a cure. Then, she found it. Whenever people in her army got bitten, she made them drink her elixir, which improved within days. The bad part is the elixir won't cure someone that's already turned."

"Great, we just need to go find her!" Tristan said gleefully. *Blanchett had an elixir? For how long? When was she going to return and distribute it?* He'd ask those questions later. But now, there was a more pertinent one. "I assume you know where Blanchett's new location is, right?"

"I do, and I can take you there," Cerys said with a sad smile.

"You know where her new location is?" pressed Tibia.

Cerys stroked her braid. "I grew up in her new citadel, not the Crimson Citadel. I was trained under her, remember? She'd already fled her former home when she rescued Ingrid and me. She lives under the White-Talon Range far north of here."

Tristan's blood boiled. *The Cadre forced Blanchett and her people underground. How despicable. And for what? So they could be the most powerful? Lie to the people, tell them magic is evil, then kill off any possible competition. Sounds like a typical dictator.*

"It's settled then." Tibia straightened her back. "We go to Blanchett's new hideout."

"But we have to hurry. Zombia's spell won't hold too long," warned Cerys. "Also…" The mage hesitated, wringing her hands. "Zokar has black magic; that too was transferred to Emerson. The dark magic will expedite his transformation. We have less time than if he were bitten by a regular zombie."

Tristan's hands went clammy. He desperately wiped them on his black pants. *Hang on, Em. We'll find a cure.*

"Traveling on foot wouldn't be a good idea, then," posed Tristan. "We should head out as soon as possible. We'll leave as soon as Faye returns with Shadowstalker." Tristan had missed the elf's trusty dragon companion.

"Sire," the apothecary said.

Tristan whirled around. Judging by the hollow look in the apothecary's eyes and stiff posture, Tristan could tell he and the apothecary shared the same emotions.

"I changed the wound's dressing, but sure enough, those lacerations are a zombie bite. I also gave him some ginger for the fever and chamomile tea to help him sleep, but he'll turn soon." He cleared his throat. "You might want to consider—"

Tristan put a hand up, stopping the apothecary's words. He didn't want to hear the end of that sentence. He knew there were only two solutions. Shoot Emerson in the head or exile him to the Zombie Forest. Those had been the only two solutions since the Apocalypse began. Some people released their infected loved ones into the forest, not having the heart to kill them. Tristan didn't have the heart to kill someone either, but releasing sick people into the forest would increase the number of zombies. So, killing was a safer, more humane action. It was barbarous and made Tristan's stomach wrench, but it was the reality of living during the world's end.

"Thank you for your help," Tristan said to the apothecary. He kept his voice level. "You're dismissed."

After a curt bow, the apothecary exited, his long white robes trailing behind him.

Emerson groaned, drawing Tristan's attention. He, Zombia, and Tibia approached the bed. The knight looked terrible. His pale skin slowly turned green, and sweat soaked his pillow.

Tristan pressed the back of his hand to Emerson's forehead. It felt like fire surged beneath his skin. He cracked his eyes open a smidgen.

"I'm sorry I didn't say anything, Tristan," said Emerson. The only movement his body allowed was a slight lifting of his chin.

Tristan placed a calming hand on Emerson's forehead. "No, don't be sorry. Rest. We'll find a cure. I promise."

Emerson managed a small smile. "I truly owe you."

Powerful, rhythmic wingbeats echoed outside.

"Faye is here," Zombia said, turning back to the mage.

"Let's go greet her," said Cerys. With a whisper of her cloak, she was gone.

Sighing, Tristan turned to Zombia and Tibia as the three made their way out into the castle hallway.

"It should have been me," Tristan muttered under his breath.

"Don't say that," Zombia reprimanded her friend. "This isn't anyone's fault but Zokar's."

Tibia cracked her knuckles. She looked ready to punch something. "I'll tear that zombie's head off. First, we need the dragon-claw dagger, and now, we need to save Emerson. Why can't those infernal zombies let up?"

The Skeleteria queen began pacing; her black heels thudded against the stone floor. She didn't cry or even appear sad. Her face reddened with anger.

Tristan blinked away the tears in his eyes and pressed his palm to his forehead. "I was supposed to fight Zokar. He was after *me*. But Emerson wanted to fight the zombie king in my place. I shouldn't have let him."

Zombia wrapped her arm around the king, leaning her head against his chest. Tristan rested his chin on her head. The scent of roses caressed his senses, doing little to ease his nerves. "You can't control Zokar's actions. Or Emerson's." Releasing her embrace, Zombia grasped her friend's gaze. "Emerson wanted to save you, Tristan. He wanted to fulfill his oath as a knight. To serve you. To die for you."

"He's my friend too," said Tristan softly. "And I stood by and let him get bitten."

"That's not true," said Zombia. "It was only after an honorable battle that Zokar used a lowly sneak attack in his evil ways." She grasped Tristan's hand. "He came out of the darkness and bit Emerson from behind. No one could have prevented that.

"Zokar's responsible for infecting him," Zombia continued; her brows turned downward with fury. "You. Are. Not!" She tapped Tristan's chest for emphasis. The king sighed and nodded.

"We'll cure him, Tristan," Tibia said, nudging her brother's shoulder. "If Blanchett truly is the High Wizard, she'll be able to fix this."

Zombia squeezed the king's hand, giving him a reassuring smile. "Together, we'll cure Emerson; we'll find the dragon-claw dagger."

Tibia raised her fist in the air. "And I'll kill Zokar."

Movement caught Tristan's attention. Looking out one of the castle windows, he spotted a recognizable black dragon flying toward Castle Skeletonia. Red, orange, and yellow leaves fell from the trees as they swayed from the wind caused by Shadowstalker's powerful wings. Their beats resounded off the castle walls. Zombia released Tristan's hand. He wished she didn't.

Tristan, Zombia, and Tibia turned down the corridor leading to the great hall. Guilt crawled up his throat. *I'm not going to let you die, Emerson.*

# Chapter Four

Shadowstalker's huge form blocked out the sun, casting shadows on Tristan as he crossed the threshold. The dragon stood in front of the opened portcullis; his wings were tucked in at his sides. Tristan tried not to gawk. The dragon had grown a lot since the last Winter Solstice, and he still wore the silver collar Faye gave him when he first hatched. It was with magic that the accoutrement grew with Shadowstalker.

Tibia, Zombia, and Cerys fanned out behind Tristan, their eyes glued to the marvel of shimmery scales and teeth. The dragon bowed his head, greeting them. Tristan laughed and patted the dragon on the forehead, careful of his sharp, curved horns.

*Greetings, Tristan.*

The words tickled the back of the king's brain like a feather. The king faced the dragon with a smile. *Hi, Shadowstalker.*

Dragons talked through telepathy. From what he

read and remembered his parents telling him, Tristan knew dragons used telepathy after the Cadre took power. To remain inconspicuous, the dragons opted to speak through people's minds. It made Tristan frown.

*Someday, I do hope magic becomes legal again. I hope people realize how helpful it is. After we defeat Malice, we have to dismantle the Cadre.*

"Thank you for coming," the king said, breaking away from his thoughts. Tristan always greeted Shadowstalker out loud despite the dragon reading his mind. The dragon grinned, and his scaly cheeks dimpled. Dimples weren't common with dragons due to their rigid cheekbones; but Shadowstalker was the only dragon Tristan had seen that had them.

The dragon nodded, then cocked his head, his eyes creasing with sympathy. *Something's perturbing you, Tristan. What is it?*

The king swallowed hard, fighting back the tears already welling. "It's—"

"Hi, everyone!" Faye peeked out from behind Shadowstalker's horns and slid down his shoulder. Landing perfectly on both feet, she approached her friends, gripping her trusty dragon-eye staff. She wore a violet surcoat, with a dragon in flight stitched on the

front. Her lilac hair was pulled into a tight bun. Sunlight glinted off the teal dragon eye dangling from her choker, and to tie the whole ensemble together, a pair of purple-leather goggles hung around her neck. Tristan had seen her wear them from time to time. Whenever he visited the Dragon Isles, he saw everyone in Faye's army wear them.

Faye wrapped her companions in a warm embrace. "Thank you for allowing me to teach you elven and dragon magic." Faye's lilac eyes flitted to Cerys. The mage grinned. "I truly look forward to it"—Faye produced a sheathed dagger from her belt—"and I have something for you."

*The dragon-claw dagger.* Tristan took the dagger from his friend's hand. There it was, the only weapon in the entire Haunted Lands capable of Malice's destruction. The weapon felt heavier than a real dagger. Power pulsed through the leather sheath, surging into Tristan's hand.

"Thank you, Faye." Tristan shoved the dagger into his belt. "But we have a problem. Emerson was bitten."

"That filthy, decomposing zombie king bit him!" blurted Tibia. Her face was red now.

Faye's palm shot to her mouth, her cool-gray skin blanching. "Moon above, how'd it happen?" Her eyes focused on Tristan's clothing, on Emerson's bloody bile soaking his front.

Tristan itched to change into his armor, nightshirt, or anything else but this soiled tabard. He didn't want to think about what his friend was becoming. Taking a deep breath, Tristan explained everything. It was all he could do to keep from yielding to his emotions.

"And we didn't discover it until today." Zombia stepped forward. She wrung her hands. She leaned into Tristan, needing as much comfort as he did. "Zokar has black magic, which Cerys mentioned would expedite the zombification process." She shuddered. "We don't have much time. We need to go to the White-Talon Range, where Blanchett currently resides. She has an elixir that cures the virus."

Cerys gave an affirmative nod.

Faye nodded as she climbed into the saddle, resting between Shadowstalker's shoulder blades. "Let's go; I'll give us all a ride. It's a three-day flight from here."

"We can practice magic along the way," Cerys added with a grin.

Tristan smiled. But what else was he to do? He didn't want to think about more wizard training. How could he when his close friend and the best knight was dying? Wizard training had to continue, or the Haunted Lands would perish at Malice's hand.

Tristan began climbing Shadowstalker's arm when he saw recognizable black and white banners parading through Skeletonia, heading straight for the castle. A knot formed in the king's stomach; his foot slipped on Shadowstalker's scales.

*The Cadre is doing their monthly visit.*

"Cerys, get inside," Tristan told the mage.

"Give me your weapons; I'll hide them with me," Cerys replied. After Tibia, Zombia, and the king handed her their weapons, the mage bolted through the castle door.

Tristan turned to Faye and Shadowstalker. "You need to leave now, before they see you. This is your chance." The king knew the Cadre despised dragons, since they were massive vessels of magic.

Faye threw her head back and laughed. Tristan furrowed a brow. "No one on the Dragon Isles fears the Cadre, just like we don't fear zombies. If the Cadre threatens us, I'll have Shadowstalker set him on fire."

Tristan knew why the elves didn't fear zombies—zombies fear dragons. But the Cadre was another story. While it wasn't his place to tell a queen of another entire nation what to do, he felt he should warn her as a friend. "Faye, maybe you want to—"

The achromatic banners drew closer to the gatehouse. Tristan tried his best not to look or act suspicious. All this wizard training kept the king and his friends so preoccupied that the Cadre's monthly crusade across the Haunted Lands slipped his mind. The faction had been inspecting kingdoms and queendoms for as long as he could remember. He often wondered how his parents hid their magic twelve times a year. Radius helped keep Tristan and Tibia out of trouble by repairing broken items shattered by Tibia's rage and rounding up all the frogs Tristan spawned in the pond.

*Gods bless Radius for getting us this far.*

Hinges screeched, and the portcullis lifted, revealing several people sitting atop black horses arranged in a diamond formation. Each Cadre member wore a black, double-breasted button robe trimmed with silver. Under their helmets, Tristan glimpsed green skin.

*What in the world? Are there zombie Cadre*

*members?* Their shields bore crossed war hammers. It matched their banners, which sent chills over Tristan. The king's mouth pinched shut. He knew why they chose that as their heraldry. The hammers represented "crushing" magic once and for all.

The man at the formation's head turned Tristan's blood to ice. He'd never forget the Cadre leader's winter-gray eyes, the same eyes that visited the castle every month since he was a child. The eyes that belonged to someone who killed thousands of magic-wielders: Kieran Bennett.

Kieran's square chin was turned up as he peered down the bridge of his nose at Tristan. That's how Kieran looked at everyone. He observed the king as though Tristan and his friends were objects meant for dastardly experiments.

Dismounting, Kieran approached his silver-trimmed robes sweeping ominously across the stone floor. He took great care in surveying all of the king's friends as though he were sniffing out the magic like a wolf hunting prey. Tristan's posture stiffened.

Kieran was a tall man with cropped dark brown, almost black hair and deep sun-kissed skin. His face was as rigid as granite. Muscles rippled beneath his robes, manifesting his strength. Kieran looked at Shadowstalker and Faye with pure disdain. "Dragons and elves. Sickening, lowborn creatures," Kieran muttered under his breath. "Still working on how to rid the Haunted Lands of you." Kieran made sure to say that loudly, earning himself a scowl from both Faye and Shadowstalker.

Tristan clenched his fists. *What does he mean by that? Still working on how to rid the Haunted Lands of dragons and elves? Is Kieran building some kind of secret weapon? Is he assembling a huge army? Dragons weren't easy to vanquish, but knowing the Cadre leader, I suspect he has something vicious up his sleeve.*

Kieran pivoted from the dragon and elf to face Tristan. "It's good to see you've been tending to your kingdom rather than following in your parents' *magic* footsteps, sire," he said slowly, making sure to spit the word *magic* as if the word itself was poisonous. "To do otherwise would be an act of sheer folly."

Tristan tried not to flinch. He kept staring at the Cadre leader head-on as he inhaled Kieran's scent—sea salt. Perfect for repelling magic, Tristan had learned.

"Get what you need done and leave," the king said flatly. *If the time was right and my friends' lives were not at stake, I would put an end to the Cadre.*

Kieran clasped his hands behind his back. "I'm here for a different reason, *sire.*" He said the word sire with derision rather than respect. The title didn't matter to Tristan; it was how he said it. Kieran used people's titles and names with mock benevolence. In a broken world of zombies, the Cadre had to play heroes.

Zombia and Tibia bowed a greeting to Kieran. The look on their faces said it all. They, too, were eager for the Cadre to leave.

The Skeleteria queen folded her arms. "If you're not here to do your dumb inspection, why are you here?"

Kieran nonchalantly reached into his satchel and produced charred flower petals and dead leaves. Goose flesh stippled Tristan's skin. *Those charred petals and dead leaves are from Malice's trek to the Fortress of Portals; he'd found them! He won't trace them back to us, right. We haven't practiced black magic.*

"Magic destroys the good, carving a path for malevolence," Kieran said. Tristan scowled, wanting to slap that smug grin off the Cadre leader's face. Zombia looked at the floor. Tibia rolled her eyes, arms still folded. Kieran loved to quote his own mottoes he'd written for the faction.

Tristan ground his teeth. *Narcissistic churl.*

Kieran began pacing in the too-quiet courtyard; his black cloak followed him like a shadow. "We have been finding patterns of magic evidence all over the Haunted Lands. Charred foliage and magic-wielder sightings have grown prevalent. Also, the Fortress of Portals has been recently used. Our only problem is we can't find who or where the wizards are."

The Cadre leader stopped pacing and whirled on Tristan. "We think it's time for another inquisition and purge. Stay vigilant. If you suspect someone you know is using magic, it doesn't matter if they're a friend or family; you are to report them. Understand?"

Tristan held his breath to avoid inhaling that dreaded sea-salt smell and nodded. Usually he loved the smell of the ocean, but not when it radiated off someone who plagued the Haunted Lands. Kieran mounted his horse and threw the burnt petals at the king's feet. "Magic is chaos, sire. Remember that, and the Haunted Lands will forever be safe."

Together, the Cadre exited in a series of hoof beats. Once the faction disappeared, the king turned to Zombia and Tibia. His throat closed up.

"How in the Underworld does Kieran know we're magic?" Tibia hissed though Kieran was outside the gate. "We've been so careful."

"He said that magic has resurfaced, Tib," Tristan replied. "He doesn't know it's us."

"It's a matter of time until he discovers our powers," Zombia said in a melancholy tone. "Who do you think told him?"

Tristan sighed. "Maybe the zombies. One of the Cadre had green skin."

"But that doesn't make sense." Tibia folded her arms and furrowed her thin brows. "The zombies *want* magic. They wouldn't collaborate with a syndicate that worked so hard to abolish it."

The king pursed his lips. Tibia had a point; why would the zombies risk exposing their own craving for magic by telling Kieran about Tristan and his friends? Stumped, Tristan sighed and said, "Who knows."

*What are you up to, Kieran?*

Tristan glanced into the sky and frowned. Though not even an hour had passed, it was still time Tristan and his friends could've used. Every minute that passed, Tristan was closer to losing a friend.

"Get Cerys, finish packing, and let's ride!"

shouted Faye from atop Shadowstalker.

Tristan and Zombia raced up the castle stairs to look for Cerys; all the while, the king's head buzzed with questions as uncertainty crept in.

*How did the Cadre learn of magic resurfacing so fast? I thought we had more time.* But if the zombies had begun spreading the word of what Tristan and his friends did to Malice, and their magic, their days of keeping it hidden were numbered.

# Chapter Five

While Zombia looked for Cerys, Tristan headed to his room to change into his armor. Closing his door, he pulled off his soiled tabard and threw it on the chair next to the unlit fireplace.

Frowning, he made a mental note to burn it later, for Tristan never planned to wear it again. Yes, water and soap would clean the blood, but the memory was indelible. Even without the stains, Tristan would always remember the zombification slowly consuming his friend.

Blowing out a long breath, the king donned his armor, feeling a little better not having Emerson's blood on his front. Instinctively, Tristan ran his thumb over his gold cuff, unable to shake the Cadre's visit from his mind.

*The Cadre knows about us,* thought Tristan. *Well, they know magic has resurfaced and they're hunting for it. Knowing Kieran, he won't rest until he's eradicated every last drop of magic. I can't put my friends in danger. He can burn me; not them.*

Tristan pushed his thoughts aside and replaced his soft-leather boots with iron greaves. Approaching the bed, the king dropped to his knees and dragged out his satchel, which held the Apocalypse Grimoire. Cerys required her three apprentices to read a few chapters and learn at least one new spell or potion every night. He put the satchel over his shoulder.

Tristan sighed and shook his head. *And after today, we have even less room for taking chances. I can't risk my friends' lives. Though I'm a wizard, I'm still king of Skeletonia. It is my job to protect them.*

Tristan was still getting used to the Grimoire's weight. He grunted as he stood, the strap of his satchel digging into his shoulder, but it wasn't just the leather and paper. A deep sense of responsibility added a few pounds to the already heavy book. Before leaving, Tristan glimpsed *Translating Runes*, resting on his pine desk. He reached for it, but since Faye was joining them on this journey, Tristan decided against it. Besides, his Dragonblood friend taught better than any book could. Plus, she was fun when giving lessons. Her peppy yet serious attitude was a great combination. After grabbing his cloak from the foot of his bead, Tristan made for the castle gardens. His gait was brisk but not with excitement. He grew pensive, nearly drowning in guilt with each step.

Tristan tried not to tremble as he traversed the breezeway leading to perfectly trimmed hedges. The bushes were a lush green, complimenting the sky's vivid blue. White and red roses bloomed on the thorny masses, emitting their sweet scent. Birds chirped merrily as they flitted around; some took a respite to splash in the birdbaths.

The king was about to embark on yet another journey. He would leave Skeletonia in Zombie's hands and owe his friend another false reason for doing so. He hated hiding his magic from his best friend. Since childhood, Tristan and Zombie had told each other everything. Tristan remembered he had swiped two apple tarts from the baker's window ledge. He and Zombie had run to the castle stables and ate them, promising not to tell their parents. That cheeky endeavor had remained a secret ever since.

But this was different. Magic was way more dangerous than swiping apple tarts. Magic would alert the Cadre.

Tristan pulled his cloak tighter around himself, feeling the frigid bite in the autumn air. Orange, red, and yellow leaves blew in the soft breeze, vibrant against the clear sky. It was a shame winter approached; the flowers would die soon.

*Just like Zombie's and my friendship, if I don't reveal my magic to him soon*, thought Tristan. *His palms grew clammy. But would that be a good idea?*

At the center of the vast garden, in front of the granite fountain, Tristan found Zombie. Daisies, poppies, irises, and flowers were nestled into individual beds, creating a menagerie of color. Zombie knelt over a patch of dirt, planting a batch of green onions for the winter. Before the king uttered a word, Zombie turned around and peeked out from under his straw hat, brown eyes creased with concern.

Tristan hesitated but smiled, trying not to look suspicious.

"Hey, Tristan. What's going on?" asked Zombie. His voice was as friendly as ever. Placing his trowel in the dirt, Zombie stood and embraced his friend. The tenseness in Tristan's chest relaxed.

"I need you to watch the castle again with Radius. I'm sorry, but..." Tristan paused and bit his lip, wondering if he should say why he was leaving. "It's Emerson. He's very sick, and we need to get an elixir for him."

Zombie's jaw slackened. "I'm sorry. Of course! I don't mind at all. Mind telling me what's made him sick?"

Tristan looked to the side for a moment; the rose bushes suddenly became more comforting than looking into his friend's face. "He got...p-poisoned. During the journey, he was cut with a poisoned blade, and we need to get an antidote." This was a half-truth. The zombie illness was like poison. Tristan felt sick lying to his best friend, but it was better than revealing everything about his magic. He knew keeping his magic a secret from Zombie was to protect him. Keep him out of the Cadre's path. The less he knew, the better. *Some day, I'll tell him everything. I just hope it won't be too late.*

Zombie nodded but folded his arms. A frown crossed his face, making Tristan tense. "Is everything okay?"

Tristan nodded. "Y-yes, why do you ask?"

Zombie raised an eyebrow, smirking. "I know when you're lying, Tristan."

Tristan's cheeks reddened, and he held his breath.

His eyes darted from side to side.

Zombie snickered and elbowed the king in the ribs. "You always stutter when you're lying, or something's on your mind. Do you want to talk about it? I'm listening."

Zombie's voice sounded genuine this time. Tristan bit his lip, thinking about how to tell the truth without revealing too much.

"A zombie bit Emerson," said Tristan. That was true.

Zombie's face turned a pale shade of green. "Oh, no! By whom?"

Tristan hesitated again, wondering if he should tell him it was Zokar. He remembered Zombie didn't know about the zombie king's powers, and telling his friend who it was would be safe enough. He would refrain from mentioning Zokar's magic.

"It was Zokar."

Zombie clenched his fists. "That's terrible!" Warm arms wrapped around Tristan. He leaned into Zombie, thankful he got by with a half-truth, but he still felt an undercurrent of regret and disgust with himself. Zombie deserved to know the whole truth. However, it was too risky—for now.

"We need to—"

The king pulled away from his friend and stood tall. "Please keep an eye on Emerson; get him anything he needs."

"Will do. But, the zombie virus has no cure," replied Zombie. "You realize what that means?" His friend's voice lowered, and his brown eyes darkened.

The king rubbed the back of his neck, nerves jittery. "I know. But...a new friend we met on our last journey told me there's a cure. A possible cure. I'm going to search for it. I won't let Emerson die while I'm still alive." *I'll find Blanchett and retrieve her elixir. I'll do whatever it takes to save him.* Tristan's chest ached at the mere thought.

Zombie sighed and folded his arms, maintaining that calm expression as his eyes and brows twisted with worry. "Why put yourself in danger? What if it doesn't work? The virus is incurable, and the chances of becoming a demi-zombie are rare." Zombie sighed, unfolded his arms, and placed a calm hand on Tristan's shoulder. "You're risking a lot when there's no guarantee it will work."

"It's worth a try. I don't care if we have to face an army of zombies; I'm going to do this for Emerson. All of us. Zombia agreed to it as well, and she wants to save him too."

Another protest formed on Zombie's lips, but Tristan silenced him with a tenacious gaze.

"He's my knight. He swore fealty to me to protect and serve by my side until death. He's done that and more." Tristan swallowed hard. "I owe him my life, Zombie."

Tristan paused and listened to the buzzing of

bees and smelled fresh roses, allowing his mind to ease. Though, not for a moment did his eyes leave his friend's. Zombie tugged at his gloves. He clearly didn't want Tristan going on this journey. The side-glance Zombie gave him told Tristan that he was suspicious. How long could he conceal his magic?

He had two choices: reveal his magic and risk the Cadre pursuing him, or keep it a secret and damage his friendship with Zombie. A friendship that began in childhood. Zombie was there for Tristan when the village kids bullied him; he was there to discuss regal duties and join him on hunting trips. Zombie's love for gardening was why Tristan gave his friend the job of tending to the castle gardens when he and Zombia escaped from Zombieshire. Tristan wouldn't relinquish those memories for the world.

A few moments of silence trickled by before the king said firmly, "I'm going."

"Good luck, my friend," Zombie said, squeezing Tristan's hand. Uncertainty danced in his eyes as he shuffled his bare feet in loose dirt.

"Thank you. I'll be back soon." Tristan smiled, but the sick feeling returned when he turned his back. He felt as evil and deceptive as Zokar.

By the time Tristan reached the courtyard, he had found Zombia, Cerys, and Tibia, each in armor and carrying their weapons. Faye still sat on Shadowstalker's back, waiting patiently. Sunlight spilled down on her lilac hair, making it appear a pastel shade.

The king reached out, thanking Cerys when she handed him his trusty bow. A jolt of magic sparked through Tristan's fingers. He slung the bow over his shoulder and faced the mage with a raised eyebrow.

"Where did you hide?"

"In one of the castle library passages," answered Cerys. She smirked at Tristan, proud of herself. "The Cadre does check passages, but not without getting lost in them. I can't imagine how many members they'd lose if they checked secret passages. That's why they rely on people reporting other people."

"That was a wise choice," Zombia said, throwing Tristan a rueful glance. "We might need a better hiding place than the war room to practice magic. Now that they know magic has resurfaced, Kieran's visits will increase."

"I have no doubt they'll expand their security and inspections of known magic areas," Tibia added, shaking her head. She headed for Shadowstalker and began climbing before Faye touched her elbow, forestalling her.

"You might want these," she said. From her satchel, she produced a set of flying goggles, enough for everyone.

"Oh, I like these," Zombia said, grabbing a pair and pulling them over her eyes.

"These look like the ones Ghist and Blaster wore," said Tibia. She grinned at the black goggles Faye handed her.

"We could have used these when we rode wyverns." Tristan pulled his goggles over his eyes, and tapped the glass with his fingernail.

Faye nodded, and with Shadowstalker's help, she climbed into the saddle.

Tristan, Zombia, and Cerys followed her. The saddle rested comfortably between Shadowstalker's wings, down the back of his serpentine body. Tristan settled in behind Faye.

Faye glanced over her shoulder. "Ready?"

All her friends nodded.

"Hang on."

With her heel, Faye tapped the dragon's scales. Shadowstalker spread his massive wings; sunlight shone through the thin gray membrane. With a mighty leap, he shot into the sky.

# Chapter Six

After packing supplies, the two zombies left Zombieshire, heading north for White-Talon Range. Zokar and Marcus rode their war horses through the colonnade of pines. A chilly, late-autumn breeze swept by; Zokar pulled his cloak tighter around himself and pulled out a map of the Haunted Lands.

A perpetual frown was chiseled on the zombie king's face as he watched the second-in-command ride beside him; Marcus sat with too much confidence. The setting sun beamed through the treetops, giving him a surreal, omnipotent glow. It made Zokar scowl.

*I know Marcus will dethrone me the second he gets the chance,* thought Zokar, gripping the reins tighter. *When we bring Malice back, and she gives me the power I need, I'll kill her, and as well as Marcus is serving me, I'll have to dispose of him too. He could be as dangerous as he is smart.*

If he was going to trick Malice into trusting him

again, he'd have to prove it. Prove he was more suitable than Marcus. The zombie king rubbed his sleep-deprived eyes. *Dictators can't afford to close their eyes for too long. The minute you turn your back or close your eyes, someone could have a knife to your throat, ready to end your reign with one slice.*

The sun began dipping below the horizon as crickets and other nocturnal creatures emerged. Whenever a deer or any other denizens crossed the gravel path, Zokar growled at them like a wild animal. Magic amplified his vocal cords, allowing his voice to echo and send the creatures fleeing into the trees. Shadows danced on tree trunks, making Zokar smile. Zombies loved shadows. In the shadows, they could sneak up on unsuspecting victims and bite them, adding them to the undead army.

The forest began thinning out. Leaves and branches became few and farther apart until the zombies were deposited in a small clearing. A single stone tower stood there, surrounded by a stockade. Tiny yellow dots marked the torches and lanterns held by patrolling guards moving back and forth.

After the Apocalypse began, the undead designed outposts to keep watch as the zombie nation rapidly expanded. These outposts forced villages to spread far and wide, providing difficult connections and increasing the chances for successful zombie attacks. The zombie king grinned, flashing his stained, pointed teeth. Zokar only traveled this far north to visit this outpost—to assess the soldiers and eliminate any possible coups, if needed.

"We'll rest here," Zokar said to Marcus. He folded the map and tucked it into his armor.

The second-in-command gave the king a perfunctory nod. Zokar wanted nothing more than to find the Silver Flame Tribe and bring Malice back. *Then force the sorcerers under my rule. But if I want to do it well, I need rest. Not sleep; just rest.*

Zokar dug his heels into his horse's flanks; the animal broke into a gallop straight for the outpost.

Peachy colors streaked the sky as the sun bid the day goodnight. Zokar moved to the front, lifting his head, so the guards saw his golden crown—so they knew who he was. His lips pressed into a thin line when the portcullis didn't budge. Perhaps it was too dark, and the zombies couldn't tell their king was standing, waiting at the gates.

Seconds ticked by before the gates yawned open, the scrape of metal screaming into the night. Zokar and Marcus rode inside, listening as the gate crashed behind them. The outpost was a simple square courtyard with four watchtowers. Oil lamps lined the walls, giving the place a foreboding light. Stairs led to numerous storage rooms and the barracks; however, most of them led to the watchtowers. Zombies in black and brown leather armor patrolled the courtyard, each wielding sharp spears with swords belted at their hips.

Zokar and Marcus dismounted before another zombie in civilian clothing took the reins and led their horses to the stables.

Footsteps clicked on the floor, making the zombie king and Marcus turn around.

A zombie in dark-brown leather armor and a cobalt-blue cloak approached them. Her left forearm and hand were missing, exchanged for a cauterized stump. Zombies losing limbs was common; whether it was from fighting other battles, decomposition, or wolves, zombies got along well without them. In rarer cases, zombies could survive being severed at the waist, earning them the term crawler. Though Zokar preferred intact zombies, Marcus suggested otherwise. They couldn't wield weapons or run, but they were still deadly and worthy assets to the army. "Biting unsuspecting people on the legs or ankles still spreads the infection," the second-in-command had said.

Zokar recognized the zombie by her perturbing copper eyes and dark-green hair tied into a tight bun. Her name was Wren, and she commanded this outpost. She was a short but very muscular zombie. Zokar held his chin high, asserting his dominance.

Wren dropped to one knee and clapped her fist to her chest.

"Welcome, my king," Wren said before lifting her copper eyes to Zokar. "It's an honor to have you here." The outpost leader's voice was respectful with an undertone of trepidation. A smile pulled at the corners of Zokar's mouth—which was rare.

"We're staying for the night. We are heading to sorcerer territory tomorrow, and we need to rest," said the zombie king.

Wren's face darkened. "That place is teeming with dangerous spells." The outpost leader's voice took on a wary tone. "Is that wise, sire?"

Zokar contemplated delineating his reason for entering a perilous land, but he opted not to. The more information he gave, the more ammunition the zombies around him gained.

*The less they know, the better.*

"It's official business," said Zokar.

Wren cleared her throat. "Sire, we'd be glad to have you stay, and I'll have a room arranged for you and your second-in-command."

She barked orders at a few of her soldiers, sending them running to the barracks to prepare rooms for the two officials. Zokar grumbled. He glanced over his shoulder to see Wren whispering into Marcus's ear. Zokar narrowed his eyes. The second-in-command nodded his head, silent as the soldier's lips moved. Her copper eyes flitted to Zokar for a second before returning to Marcus.

Zokar's chest clenched, and his jaw tightened.

*What are they saying? I'm going to have to keep a closer eye on him. He is a great captain, but he raises a suspicion that leaves me severely disconcerted. He's threatening my reign!*

By the time Zokar finished his thought, he had

arrived at the mess hall. He eyed Marcus wearily.

"Care to tell me what that was about, Marcus?" Zokar demanded.

Marcus adjusted his eye patch. "We are planning a hunting trip tomorrow."

Zokar stopped in his tracks. "What? Why? You know we have a mission!" Zokar hissed through gritted teeth.

"Listen, the zombies here wanted to arrange something special in honor of the king of Zombieshire visiting. We don't often come this far north."

Zokar shook his head. "Listen, you fool. The longer we wait to find the Silver Flame Tribe, the stronger Blanchett's wizards get."

Marcus placed a hand on Zokar's shoulder. Zokar's crimson eyes widened, and his green face flushed with outrage. No one dared to touch the king; Marcus was the first.

"This is something they're doing in honor of you, my king. We should take a small respite before jumping back into the war. Besides, you can practice with those enchanted knives of yours."

Zokar shrugged off his second-in-command's hand and paced, his soft boots clicking anxiously across the floor. Freeing Malice was the paramount task at the moment. However, he had to admit that this was a celebration for him. And there was nothing he enjoyed more than people singing his praises. Besides, it was only one day. They'd stay one more night, then head for sorcerer territory.

Zokar stopped pacing and sighed. "It's done, and we'll partake in the hunting party." The zombie king flicked his scarlet cloak behind him and sashayed for the mess hall, his stomach crying in hunger.

*Wren and the rest of the soldiers here want to kill Zokar?* Marcus thought as he entered the mess hall. While Marcus liked the idea, killing the zombie king and claiming it was a hunting accident still seemed suspicious. Besides, what would he tell Malice when she returned? Wouldn't Zokar dying on Marcus's watch make him look worse?

Marcus's thoughts were scattered by the din of voices. Soldiers cheered and laughed around long, oak trestle tables, drinking tankards of cider and eating assorted meats. That was all zombies ate—meat, preferably human, but truly, animals sufficed. Luckily, the hall smelled of roasted duck. Marcus gagged whenever he smelled cooked human flesh. Zokar told him that made him less of a zombie. And Marcus was fine with that.

Sighing, Marcus made his way to the table where Wren and her crew sat. One of the monsters pushed a plate of food toward him. Politely, Marcus sat back and folded his arms. His stomach was empty, but his mind was too full. Marcus gazed at the soldiers; some smiled at him, others complimented his prowess in battle, and others asked him questions about his time in Zombieshire. A few made crude jokes about Zokar, and Marcus couldn't help but crack a smile. He couldn't laugh outwardly, since Zokar was at the head of the table. It often vexed Marcus that Zokar always sat at the head of the table, but this time, he welcomed it. His absence allowed for him and Wren to conspire about the zombie king's downfall.

Marcus turned back to Wren.

"If you put the arrow through his skull," said Wren, "I'll handle the cover story."

"Shouldn't we try something more...covert?" said Marcus.

Wren set her jaw. "The hunting trip *is* the cover-up.

Hunting accidents are so common, and you'll become the new zombie king. Wouldn't you want that?"

Marcus looked down at the table, suddenly finding the grooves in the wood fascinating. Becoming king was what he wanted, but what if this wasn't what Malice wanted? What if she still had a use for Zokar? Then again, the Shadowblood expressed her own qualms about Zokar as king of Zombieshire. Zombieshire would function more efficiently without a power-hungry ruler, making decisions based on his own desires rather than the needs of the entire country. *On the other hand, killing the zombie king would make me just as treacherous, wouldn't it?*

"How about this," Marcus began, nervously tugging at his eye patch. "You kill Zokar, and I'll handle the cover-up?"

Wren shrugged and splayed her green fingers. "That works too. Whatever it takes to get Zokar off the throne. A dragon can eat him for all I care."

Marcus blew out a breath and nodded. He peered over his shoulder, seeing Zokar still gnawing away on what remained of the duck's wing.

*This is a much better idea. Zokar will be out of my way, and I won't be at fault for it. And Malice will have no choice but to crown me king of Zombieshire.* Marcus's muscles relaxed as he turned to Wren.

The outpost leader narrowed her eyes at the zombie captain. "So, do we have a deal?"

Marcus set his jaw and nodded. "Yes. Let's do it."

# Chapter Seven

Tristan was thankful he and his friends rode wyverns in the Underworld. The experience left him more prepared for Shadowstalker. Dragon scales were rough and rugged. The king only received a cruel reminder of their sharpness after scraping his hand. If it weren't for the thick saddle, Tristan's legs would've been lacerated. Wyvern scales were sharp, but Shadowstalker's were sharper and larger.

Tristan watched as the ground shrank until the great Castle Skeletonia was no more than a tiny gray dot surrounded by a blanket of green. Wind buffeted the king's face; he had to keep one hand on his crown, or it would be whisked away and plummet hundreds of feet.

Glancing over his shoulder, he saw Zombia gripping nervously onto his shoulders. Tibia sat behind her; Karneleth's staff rested in her lap. That weapon had come in handy. Guilt still slithered into Tristan's head each time he used it. And near the back, Cerys sat, gripping onto one of the dragon's dorsal spines.

Instead of using reins, Faye steered using Shadowstalker's horns. Tristan only used horse reins. He wondered what steering would be like using horns. The Firebournes had reins for their wyverns. But wyverns were smaller dragons with smaller horns. He assumed it would be the equivalent of gripping his horse's ears and pulling. But Shadowstalker didn't seem bothered.

Before long, the sunset painted the luminous sky shades of pink, yellow, and orange. Tristan inhaled the evening air to calm his nerves. It did little, though. Seeing Kieran before they left still petrified him. It was only a matter of time before his magic was discovered. Before, he and his friends would have been bound to stakes and burnt.

Faye shouted something, but her words were eaten by the wind. Right as a "what" formed on Tristan's tongue, the elf tilted Shadowstalker's horns down gently.

Tristan's stomach lurched as the dragon began his descent for a copse of pines. Green needles and shrubs blurred by as Shadowstalker made his landing. This clearing was smaller than any of the previous ones, but at least Shadowstalker could fit. Surprisingly, his landing was smoother than the wyverns. Tucking his wings in at his sides, the dragon ducked his head, allowing his passengers to dismount. Zombia slid off but wobbled. Tristan offered her his hand. Her skin was warm despite just being at a high altitude.

"Thanks," she said with a small smile. "I guess I'm still getting used to flying."

"You and me both," the king said with a laugh.

"Flying takes practice," said Faye, popping in between Tristan and Zombia. She grinned from ear to ear. A few strands of her long purple hair had been whipped from her bun, neatly framing her angular face. "Elves are paired with dragons at birth. I've been flying almost as long as I've been walking. You'll get used to it eventually."

Tristan nodded and grinned, pulling his goggles off his eyes and allowing them to hang around his neck. *I'll admit flying has been fun. The world looks so neat from a bird's-eye view. More like a dragon's-eye view.*

While Tibia and Faye went to gather wood, Tristan and Zombia decided to make the fire pit. Two armfuls of logs and a hint of Cerys's magic later, a warm campfire burst to life. Pale orange light splashed against tree trunks and drove away the shadows. The sun had sunk fully, pulling its golden light from the world; the stars were out, turning the sky into a deep-blue shimmering blanket. Once everyone found a rock or soft patch of grass, dinner began. Shadowstalker sat next to Faye; his tail curled around his talons neatly. For a massive beast, the dragon managed to look composed and rather becoming.

"Thanks for the dragon-claw dagger, by the way," Tristan said before taking a bite of dried meat.

Faye took a sip of water from her canteen before saying, "Who am I to deprive a friend of something they need? Also, we can't have Malice roaming free in the Haunted Lands, can we?"

Carefully, he pulled the dagger from the sheath, revealing a curved white blade. All eyes swiveled to the dagger—the key to Malice's defeat. The hilt was crafted from the finest obsidian, and the pommel had a lavender glass dragon's eye. Firelight glinted off the pristine claw, giving it an eerie sheen.

Cerys held her hand out; Tristan gave the dagger to her. The mage looked the blade up and down, running her fingers along its flat side. "Only dragon magic can withstand black magic. After discovering that, Blanchett began collaborating with the Dragonblood

Tribe, making weapons and armor from dragon scales." Turning the dagger, she handed it back to Tristan, hilt first.

Faye finished her piece of bread and nodded. "And before you ask, we don't take scales by force. We wait for them to shed." She gestured to the dagger. "Same with their claws."

The muscles in Tristan's shoulders eased. He guessed Faye wouldn't deprive a dragon of their scales by force, but the slight possibility rattled him. *I'm sure Malice wouldn't think twice about poaching dragons for their scales.*

Tibia tapped her fingers along Karneleth's staff. "Do you ever worry about the zombies or the Cadre invading Elandorr or the Dragon Isles? I know you've said the dragons keep the zombies at bay, but do you ever worry the undead will find a way to invade?"

Faye's brows pulled together. "Before Malice, I didn't worry about the zombies or the Cadre. A few of my scouts reported zombie sightings, but they barely made it past the shore before a dragon swooped down and devoured them; we never had Cadre sightings, thank the gods. Mostly, my focus has centered on the Elf Wars, especially stopping the Moonblood conquest. But now that Malice has returned, my worry has increased. Gods know what dastardly plans she has up her sleeves. Once she's conquered Skeletonia, I'm sure she'll pursue the Dragon Isles.

"Malice must be stopped before she gains access to the dragons. I'm doing everything in my power to unite the tribes in case the zombies and Malice drag the war to our doorstep, but we haven't gotten far. Nothing more than a ceasefire. The Moonbloods still threaten expansion and annexation of the Icebloods and Dragonbloods."

Faye paused before her eyes drifted from her boots, to the dagger, finally locking onto Tristan's gaze. "My people are in grave danger, Tristan. If Malice lives, the war will only spread until the entire Haunted Lands is enslaved to her dark powers. For the good of the Haunted Lands, plunge that dagger deep in the Shadowblood's heart."

Tristan swallowed, his palms clammy and slippery as he shoved the dragon-claw dagger back into its sheath on his belt. It felt as if an anvil had been placed on Tristan's shoulders, crushing his bones to dust. Though the Dragon Isles weren't under his jurisdiction, he still felt responsible for them—for stopping Malice before she reached his friend's home. Another promise he had to keep. Save Emerson, then kill Malice.

Tristan looked to Shadowstalker, who was curled up behind Faye, gnawing on a large slice of dried beef. Once it was devoured, Shadowstalker rose and shook out his massive wings.

*I think I'll go hunting. I'll return soon.*

Faye patted her dragon between the horns. "Sorry I couldn't pack more food, Shadowstalker. We have to travel light. Stay safe and unseen."

Shadowstalker grinned, his scaly cheeks dimpling, before he turned and vaulted into the sky. His wings blocked out the moon, casting a dragon-shaped shadow over Tristan and his friends.

Tristan marveled at the dragon. Having felt Shadowstalker's scales, he understood how the dragon and elf tribes survived this far into the Apocalypse. Their mysterious magic kept providing extra strength and allowed them to outwit the undead at every turn. It also helped that they couldn't contract the zombie virus. At least from what he'd read. That didn't mean someone—like Malice—wouldn't use magic to alter the virus. Manipulate it, cause it to mutate so it could infect elves. *"All magic is chaos,"* Kieran had said. *"We must not allow magic to mutate the zombie infection. All the more reason to eradicate it."*

A jolt of cold shot through Tristan. *Hopefully, it stays that way. I don't know what we'd do with zombified elves. Gods above, zombified dragons!*

"How long do we have until Malice returns?" asked Tibia, pulling off a piece of bread and taking a bite.

Cerys's emerald eyes darkened as she frowned. "Soon. Very soon." Her body tensed. "The Hall of Black Mirrors will only hold the demon for so long."

"I'm sure the zombie king's working on freeing her as we speak," said Zombia. She finished off an apple and chucked the core into the bushes.

Tristan swallowed nervously. "When I checked the casualties in the Hall, I didn't see Zokar or Marcus among them." The king shuddered, his eyes downcast, remembering the death and destruction brought by this war. "They're probably doing everything in their power to release Malice."

"Well, we should continue practicing then, shouldn't we?" Tibia said, shooting to her feet, ready for a fight before Cerys placed a hand on her arm.

"Not until we've rested," said the mage. "Read

more of the Apocalypse Grimoire instead."

Groaning, Tibia sat down and clutched her crossbow. Tristan reached into his satchel and pulled out the Grimoire. Grabbing the red ribbon of a bookmark, he opened it. Zombia, Tibia, and Faye gathered behind the king, their legs crossed and their eyes glued to the worn pages.

"The Art of Cloning and Illusion" the title read.

Wingbeats echoed around them and the trees and grass swayed as Shadowstalker returned with his kill—two large stags. Plopping down behind Faye, Shadowstalker curled his claws around his dinner before tearing into it rather noisily, drawing a snort out of Tristan and his companions. Turning back to the Grimoire in his lap, his eyes lit up. For the next hour, he immersed himself in the rich history of magic—of his and Tibia's lineage. And for the next hour, he forgot about the Cadre.

Tristan's mouth remained agape throughout the entire chapter, as did Zombia and Tibia's. "The Art of Cloning and Illusion" discussed how a wizard could make clones of themselves to trick their assailants. They weren't *physical* clones; they were illusions.

"I can't wait to try this," said Tibia enthusiastically. "Why not play a prank on the zombies before making them meet their doom? Sounds like fun to me."

"Tib, war isn't supposed to be fun, remember?" said Zombia. She side-eyed her friend with a frown.

"Whatever," Tibia responded, wrapping herself in her cloak; her eyelids began to droop.

Tristan's thoughts about the Cadre crept in again, driving away any fatigue. He stared longingly at the weathered page with detailed potion recipes. What if he and his friends were caught by the Cadre? He'd hoped to defeat Malice and then get his magic under control. He'd reveal it to Zombie. The king hoped his best friend would understand, and he'd help the wizards conceal their powers until they could undermine the magic-loathing faction. After Kieran's visit, Tristan realized he and the wizards were running out of time. Time wasn't on their side in regard to Kieran or Malice.

*I know how you feel.*

Tristan recognized Shadowstalker's telepathic voice. The words came soft and gentle. He locked eyes with the dragon.

*You do?* Tristan almost said the words out loud but remembered at the last minute that Shadowstalker

Wizards of the Apocolypse

could read his thoughts.

The dragon nodded his massive head. *I do, Tristan. With the Cadre around, life hasn't been simple for the dragons or elves.* The crackling fire filled the silence, splashing Shadowstalker's horns in gold and orange.

Tristan furrowed his brow. But the Cadre never ventures into the Dragon Isles.

Shadowstalker's eyes narrowed; smoke curled up from his nose. *Did you know that people don't trust dragons anymore? They think our magic is malicious. They don't think about the trials we endured with our attempts to find a cure for the zombie virus. But that doesn't deter them from defaming our kind.* A loud breath escaped Shadowstalker's nose as more smoke wafted out. *If dragons weren't social pariahs, we could collaborate with people and possibly discover a cure. The Apocalypse could end!*

Shadowstalker's mouth twisted into a sneer, flashing his serrated teeth. *Of course, the Cadre doesn't care about what's just. They want to be the ones praised for ending the Apocalypse. They want to be the heroes. Duplicitous, manipulative heroes.*

Tristan stared into the dragon's eyes, growing pensive. The dragon looked at Tristan, his golden eyes sparkling with wisdom. Being this close to Shadowstalker sent Tristan's magic into a frenzy. Little bits of electricity flitted through him like wild fireflies. A low hum buzzed in the back of the king's mind, tickling his brain. No wonder the Cadre feared dragons. They weren't just marvels of beautiful scales and sharp teeth, but also inscrutable magic. Shadowstalker did understand. The Cadre was so caught up in eradicating magic from the Haunted Lands that they hindered any fight for a cure. *Their rules against magic are an attempt at a power grab.*

Shadowstalker let more smoke curl out of his nose before his eyes filled with determination. *Bring light magic back to the world and drive away the darkness. That's another part of Blanchett's prophecy.*

Tristan stared at the dragon, biting his lip and listening to the fire crackle. Was it possible to overthrow the Cadre? The faction wouldn't be easy to debase with their claws so deep into the public. But if bringing magic back could end the Apocalypse, it was worth doing, and Tristan would accomplish it with his friends.

"Hey, little brother." Tibia tipped the log Tristan was sitting on, heaving him onto the ground.

"Why?" the king responded, rubbing his backside

and shooting his sister a vexed glance.

"When you're done daydreaming about Zombia, could you take first watch?" A smirk played on her crimson lips.

Redness flushed Tristan's cheeks. "Will do. You could have just asked, you know."

Tibia laughed and shrugged. "This was more fun."

Tristan stood and brushed dirt from his kilt. "And for your information, I wasn't daydreaming about Zombia, I was talking to Shadowstalker."

"Sure you were," responded Tibia sarcastically. She leaned into her brother's ear. "You ought to tell her how you feel sooner or later." That part didn't sound sarcastic, which caught Tristan off guard. Heat rose to his face. *I do want to tell her how I feel. I just...need to find the right time.* Tristan opted for an eye roll instead of words, which drew a snicker from Tibia. She continued smiling as she curled up under her cloak.

Cerys and Faye followed suit, but Faye chose to sleep in Shadowstalker's tail. It coiled around her like a constrictor, but instead of suffocating her, it looked protective. Faye looked comfortable. She wrapped her violet cloak around her and Shadowstalker's tail, making Tristan wonder how his friend slept against those rough scales. Silence filtered through the camp save for crickets and the occasional owl. The king kept his eyes and nose alert for zombies.

After a while, Tristan sat next to Zombia, who sat by the fire, wrapped in her forest-green cloak. The dimmed light backed her hair, giving her a halo. Tristan smiled.

"You know, you didn't have to pretend you were talking to Shadowstalker," Zombia said, inching closer to Tristan. He smelled the unmistakable scent of fresh cut roses. "I think it's sweet you were daydreaming of me."

Heat rushed to Tristan's face. "I wasn't lying. Remember, dragons speak through telepathy."

Zombia blushed. "Right. It's because of the Cadre, isn't it?"

Tristan nodded and frowned. "If Kieran wasn't a threat, the dragons might speak outwardly. I've always wanted to hear a dragon talk."

"I've wanted that too."

Zombia leaned into Tristan; in return, he rested his chin on her head. *Should I tell her how I feel? Is this the right time?*

"Do you think the zombies told the Cadre about our magic?" asked Tristan.

Zombia shrugged. "Who knows. I don't see how that would benefit them. Zokar wants more magic; the last thing he'd want to do is get Kieran hunting magic-wielders again. If he were intelligent, he wouldn't do that."

Tristan's mouth went dry; his shoulders tensed despite the warmth of Zombia leaning against him. "That's what worries me. Zokar's prowess lies in brutality, not intelligence."

Zombia reached to hold Tristan's hand, but suddenly drew back and gasped. "What happened to your palm?"

"Oh, it's nothing," Tristan responded with a chuckle. "I scratched myself on Shadowstalker's scales."

"Let me heal that."

"No, Zombia. Don't waste your power."

Gently, she took the king's palm and dragged her fingers across it, drawing the rune for healing.

"*Uruz*," Zombia whispered. A soft golden glow enveloped his hand. Instantly, the pain evaporated; the skin sewed itself back together.

Tristan flexed his fingers. "Thanks. But you

should conserve your magic."

Zombia shrugged and looked toward the forest, tugging at her sleeve. "I need to practice. Besides, I like healing people. It fills the void left from escaping Zombieshire. I swore I'd free the rest of the zombies one day. I hated myself for leaving them." Zombia frowned, eyes gleaming in the firelight. "Healing others is the best I can do for now, and it's the best I can offer in hopes of making the Haunted Lands a better place. After we finish Malice and this undead blight is over, I want to become a professional healer."

Tristan's heart felt full. He reached out, taking Zombia's hands in his. Her cheeks tinted red. "That's great! We could always use more healers, Apocalypse or not."

Zombia gave a curt nod and strong smile. "Exactly. Once Malice's defeated, I can focus entirely on helping others." Her fingers intertwined with Tristan's, sending sparks shooting through his chest.

"I could even have Emerson take over your paperwork, if you want to be a healer full-time." *If he survives,* the king thought ruefully.

"Oh, thank you, Tristan." Zombia threw her arms around the king. "But, I'd still want to be queen! I just want to use my powers for others. It would be something I did on the side. But I appreciate the offer." Tristan's heart swelled. This was one of the many reasons he loved Zombia. Her unwavering kindness would bring peace from all the queendoms and kingdoms of the Haunted Lands.

"Magic on its own is neither good nor bad; it depends on the wielder. The sooner the Cadre understands that, the better off we'll be."

Tristan stared into the fire. He agreed. It wouldn't be fair to punish every wizard, witch, mage, and sorcerer for the few evil ones. Someone like Zombia wouldn't wreak havoc. They wouldn't burn buildings with enchanted fire, nor would they use telekinesis to tear their victims in half. Someone like Zokar would. Yet, the Cadre's sole goal was to eradicate every magic-wielder in the Haunted Lands. Tristan thought changing the Cadre's mind was impossible. But if he and his friends defeated Malice, a highborn demon, then maybe they could enlighten Kieran.

In the back of Tristan's mind, a little voice told him the Cadre might have a point. Though Kieran's narcissism churned Tristan's stomach, what if eradicating magic was the right thing to do? Without the Cadre, all types of magic would be free—including dark magic. What if more people dabbled in dark magic? Like Malice. New threats could emerge with magic's unguarded existence. All this time Tristan spent reading the Grimoire and practicing magic had been enjoyable. He learned more about his powers within a few months than during his childhood. However, was freeing magic worth unleashing new perils?

On the flip side, Tristan had yet to see Kieran's plan to eradicate magic come to fruition. He'd burnt thousands of magic-wielders, yet Malice and Zokar were wreaking havoc with their dark powers. Even eradicating every dark magic-wielder, the threat would live on. Evil would forever exist; banning magic wouldn't solve that. And right now, the Haunted Lands needed light magic more than ever.

Tristan sighed deeply and wrapped his cloak around himself. "Goodnight, Zombia, sleep well." Love you. Tristan thought the words, but never said them.

Clutching his bow, Tristan sat in the grass and looked up at the masterpiece of the stars against the dark blue sky. The moon climbed higher, washing the treetops with silver light. Tristan's eyes felt heavy, but his mind buzzed like a million angry hornets.

*Can we save Emerson? He's my friend. I can't imagine a world without him. I can't even begin to imagine how Cameron would forgive himself if his best friend turned. I couldn't forgive myself.*

Eventually, those thoughts put aside, Tristan drifted into a restless sleep.

# Chapter Eight

It didn't take long for Tristan to realize he was experiencing another dream—no, a nightmare. The king found himself standing behind a pillar in a vaulted room packed with zombies and demons. Through the sea of green, Tristan saw an onyx throne in front of lavender-colored curtains bearing a dragon with its wings spread in flight.

Unlike a regular throne room, this one resembled a cavern with high ceilings. He wrinkled his nose as he inhaled the sickening scent of sulfur. The curved basalt walls, obsidian pillars, and lava-filled lanterns revealed his location.

Tristan was in Castle Elandorr, Faye's queendom. But, if that was so, where was she? Why was her throne room packed with zombies instead of Dragonbloods? He glanced left and right in an attempt to leave his hiding spot. When he touched the pillar, his hands passed through it. There was no way he'd fight that many zombies and win, not in just a kilt, tunic, and cloak—and without a weapon.

Tristan ducked behind the pillar just in time. The heavy iron doors swung open as two burly zombies trudged through, carrying someone. Their boots clicked across the black marble floor; both monsters wore full iron armor, which was rare for zombies. Most of the undead could scarcely afford leather.

Curiosity nagged at Tristan, coaxing him to the front. Tristan glanced down at his hands and looked to the throne. *I wish I were invisible in dreams. But then Blanchett wouldn't have seen me.* A thought formed in Tristan's head, causing him to purse his lips. *Can I get hurt in dreams? Even if they do see me? I don't think I should take a chance.*

Tall, sitting dragon statues caught Tristan's eye. There was one between every set of pillars leading up to the throne. *Perfect, I can hide behind those.*

"Thank you for coming here, comrades," called a voice. It was slick as oil, menacing and coaxing, all at the same time. A chill settled in Tristan's chest, heavy as a boulder. He recognized that voice from anywhere.

Malice.

When everyone's attention turned to the throne,

Tristan saw his chance. He darted for the closest dragon statue, waited a few seconds, and jumped behind the one left of the dais. He could see clearly, and what he saw stopped his breath.

Faye knelt before Malice, clothes torn and her face bruised, between the two robust zombies. Her pointed ears folded back with anger; her lips pulled into a scowl. She jerked to the left and right, strong enough to nearly pull one of the zombies over. He grumbled and tightened his grip on the chains. She was drenched in what looked like water, but the dark pink staining with black patches on her clothing told Tristan it wasn't water at all.

What covered Faye was a solution of crushed calcite and obsidian. He learned that was tantamount to acid to Dragonbloods. It devoured their skin like flesh-eating bacteria.

Tristan ground his teeth.

*They must have tortured her using this solution,* thought Tristan. He clenched his fists. *Is this how Malice gains power over the dragons? By torturing Faye?* Nausea churned through Tristan's stomach.

The king peered around the stone dragon's wing. Malice stood on the dais, shoulders back, chin up, and jaw clenched. Zokar and Marcus were behind her, hands behind their backs as they watched whatever was about to unfurl.

"Their magic will withstand your foul spells," said Faye. "You'll never have my dragons!" She struggled in the chains, a scowl twisting her lips.

Malice folded her arms. "I don't have the Apocalypse Grimoire. Dragons are my next option."

Faye jerked at the chains around her wrists, her teeth bared. Tristan wasn't used to seeing his friend this roused. She was usually bubbly and winsome, though he knew she was also the queen of dragons. Elven magic was more complex than anything Cerys taught them. Tristan had seen it in the Grimoire, but fell asleep reading it. He'd been meaning to ask Faye more about it.

"My dragons will never listen to you!" Faye spat. "A dragon and rider's bond goes beyond training. It's solidified at birth."

Malice stepped down from the dais, her navy-blue robes whispering behind her. Her sharp claws caught the dimmed torchlight. She grabbed Faye's chin, staring her in the eyes. Tristan fought the urge to jump out and throttle the demon.

"I don't need your dragons to listen to me," said Malice. Her every word was laced with vitriol. "I want them to listen to you. Because you're going to give them my orders."

Faye blinked but didn't get to utter another word. Malice grabbed Faye's throat but didn't appear to be choking her. Rather, she just had her fingers cupped under her chin. An incantation flowed from the Shadowblood's lips. Tristan strained to hear it. She spoke in the old wizard language. The spell ended, and black veins cracked down Faye's pale gray skin. Her lilac eyes melted to inky black as veins crawled up her cheeks. Horrible screams punctured the atmosphere as Faye writhed in the zombie's iron grasp. Tristan fought the urge to race from behind the pillar and help his friend, but he knew this was a dream. None of this was really happening. *But it feels so real.* Faye clawed at Malice's wrists to no avail. With each scratch, the Shadowblood's skin repaired itself.

Tristan covered his ears and gritted his teeth. He didn't know what spell Malice had cast; all Tristan knew was that he couldn't bring himself to watch. Faye's screams ended abruptly. Peeking through his fingers, Tristan saw Faye hunched over, on her knees, before Malice. Her breathing was labored. Faye rose to her feet and looked up; her tangled lilac tresses fell from her face. And what Tristan saw made him gasp, so loud he nearly gave away his hiding place.

Black veins cracked down her cheeks from her eyes. They, too, were pools of ink—emotionless and cold. More veins popped from beneath Faye's sleeves and onto her fingers. Tristan held his breath, fingers trembling. This wasn't his friend anymore—this was something else: a creature transformed by black magic.

"Welcome to my army," said Malice. "Now, I have a mission for you." The throne room fell silent.

Faye nodded; her jaw and fists clenched.

Malice's scarlet eyes darkened. Shadows from the lava fell over her sharp-angled face. "Gift the dragons with my magic. Once done, order them to attack every village in sight. Raid their supplies." Malice turned to Zokar and Marcus. "Once they have nothing, bite them. Expand the army."

The two zombies nodded; Zokar appeared more enthusiastic than his second-in-command. Tristan narrowed his eyes. *I still don't understand why Marcus chose to save Zombia. If he truly wants to convert, then why does he continue serving Malice?*

"Go and don't fail."

The zombies cheered; some banged their swords and spears on their shields. Those with metal armor bashed them against their chest plates. Faye marched off the dais and out of her throne room, presumably for the dragon stables.

Tristan's knees weakened. So that's how Malice gained control over the dragons! By possessing Faye. Tristan's knowledge of demons was limited, but what he did know was they were capable of possessing souls. They could bring them under their control for as long as they wanted. Would goddess water free those ensnared by demonic hold?

The morning was near. The surroundings flickered; Tristan would wake up soon. *I know this is a dream, but why do I keep having the same one—where Malice has ensnared the dragons? I have to ask Cerys if these dreams are just bizarre nightmares or premonitions. I should warn Faye too. If these are premonitions, she'll need to know.*

The king's surroundings flickered again, this time going black.

# Chapter Nine

Emerson felt abnormally hot. Radius had opened his bedroom window, yet the cool night breeze did little to quell his rising temperature. Laying in bed wearing a sweat-stained nightshirt, Emerson stared at the ceiling, pensive.

The knight and Cameron had never had a fight before. Well, the usual quarrel, yes. The time Cameron hid Emerson's helmet and blamed Tibia for it, or when he started a huge food fight at his knighthood ceremonial dinner—those were times his close friend ruffled his feathers, resulting in the regular quibble. But what had occurred, the undead rage pulsing through him, might have ruined Emerson and Cameron's friendship for good.

Emerson didn't mean to shout at Cameron in the hallway that morning. Cameron was concerned for him, leading to a bombardment of questions. While his friend's incessant questions grated on Emerson's nerves, he knew Cameron's heart was in the right place. But when Cameron grabbed Emerson's wounded arm, fear flooded him, spurring him to act before thinking. Cameron hadn't visited Emerson since.

Erratic anger was another side effect of the zombie virus slowly dominating Emerson's body. Regret flooded him.

*I can't believe I did that! Moon above, I'm horrible. Cameron can irk me at times, but I'd never take it to heart,* thought Emerson. *I have to apologize.*

He sat up, body aching. He rubbed his eyes. His stomach growled. But roasted pork and garden vegetables weren't what he craved. Whenever he saw a human servant, he couldn't help but stare at their skin. Biting them sounded good. But it was wrong. Those were people. Emerson groaned and placed his hands on his temples. *This isn't me.*

Emerson swallowed down rising bile. Well into the night, a knock rapped at his door. Seconds later, the door opened and Cameron peered into the room. He cast his friend a conciliatory smile. His face and gloves were covered in wood chips and soot; he lifted his goggles, exposing round imprints near his eyes. "Hi. I know I can be annoying, but usually it's Tibia who yells at me. Not you."

It felt like a dragon was sitting on Emerson's chest as he rose. "No, I'm sorry. I—I don't know what came over me." *I know exactly what came over me; I'm turning into a zombie.*

"I'm sorry if I bothered you, but you usually enjoy my company"—his eyes shifted to Emerson's bandage—"that wolf must've done a number on your bicep."

Emerson rubbed his face. There was no way in the Underworld he could tell his best friend the truth. So, a wolf bite was the better option. But was it? It was a lie. *Should I tell him now or allow him to find out when I become one of the undead?* Sooner or later, Cameron would know. *Might as well tell him now.*

The knight's shoulders slumped. Pain radiated from his bicep and out his fingers. "I have something to tell you, Cameron."

His friend stepped through the threshold and stood at the foot of the bed. His bright green eyes widened, brows furrowed. All the quirkiness faded—Cameron truly looked serious. That made him a good friend; though his gags were irritating, his people skills were phenomenal.

"What is it, Em?"

Emerson sighed and rolled up his sleeve, revealing the bandaged zombie bite. His arm looked more green than tan. He brushed his hair away from his ears. At first, Cameron squinted, then he backpedaled, his gloved hand going to his mouth in terror.

"You were bitten by a..."

A sigh escaped Emerson as he nodded. His eyes welled with fresh tears; his vision blurred. "It wasn't a wolf that bit me. I didn't tell you because I didn't want to worry you." He looked to the open window. "But it doesn't matter. My fate is sealed."

Cameron removed his goggles and began pacing. "I can't *believe* you didn't tell me! We could've done something. You have to tell Tristan when he returns!"

"He already knows," said Emerson plaintively. "He and the rest of our friends know too. That's why they departed earlier."

"What do they plan to do? There's no cure." Cameron's voice cracked at that last part. The guild leader's pacing quickened as he placed his goggles on his head. Emerson had never seen his friend this upset; the pain in his eyes was palpable.

"They're out trying to find a cure..." The knight rubbed the back of his neck, deciding whether he should tell Cameron where Tristan really went. *Then, I'd have to reveal their entire adventure. Tristan, Zombia, and*

*Tibia being magic prodigies. How Malice was granting the zombies dark magic. How Zokar, who possessed black magic, was the one that bit me, causing my friends to search for an ancient wizard who may or may not have a cure.*

Emerson looked down at his hands woefully. He didn't think Cameron would tell the Cadre on purpose, but it was hard for his friend to keep secrets. If Tristan did return with the cure, Cameron would know where his friends truly went. In the barrage of questions that would follow, Emerson would end up telling his friend everything.

*Might as well tell Cameron what's been happening before I turn.* From start to finish, Emerson explained what had occurred within the past month. Cameron quit pacing and sat on the edge of the bed, eyes hardened, lips sealed, not cracking a single joke. He nodded, listening to every word Emerson said. The tightness in the knight's chest abated. His nerves calmed, knowing he had a confidant beneath that skilled craftsman and jokester.

"I truly wish I had told you sooner, Cameron," Emerson said, pulling his knees up to his chest. "I can fulfill my knightly duties until I turn. But after that—"

Cameron shot to his feet. "Tristan *will* return, and you *are* getting cured, Emerson! You're not turning into a zombie by all the gods and goddesses. I'm not allowing it." His friend's hands were fists, his brows downward and creased. "And don't tell me not to worry about you! I can worry about you if I want to. You're my best friend; I'd even stay by your side after you turn." Cameron snorted. "Well, maybe behind a fence, over six feet away, while I hold a sword."

Cameron and Emerson both laughed. Even in dire situations, Cameron still found a way to remain jovial.

More pain laced down Emerson's arm, nagging and dull. He ground his teeth; his fingers clenched as though that would halt the agony.

Cameron frowned and headed back for the door. "I'll call for the apothecary to bring you some more chamomile tea and maybe some beef stew. You're not becoming a zombie on my watch." The craftsman disappeared down the hallway. Emerson listened to the tools on Cameron's belt rattle as he sprinted.

Groaning, Emerson leaned against the plump pillows and stared at the ceiling. A cool fall breeze blew through his window, doing little to help his fever. His mouth was dry; his stomach growled, but it wasn't the chamomile tea he wanted. It wasn't the beef stew he wanted.

A soon-to-be-zombie craved live human flesh.

Light from the waxing crescent bathed Zokar and the hunting party in a silver glow. The smell of pine was thick as they rode deeper into the woods, their red eyes peeled for nocturnal game. Anything from jackrabbits to an unfortunate human wandering alone in the Zombie Forest would do. One of the benefits of being undead was their remarkable night vision. Like cats, zombies could see in the dark. Therefore, they hunted in the dark. It was a perfect combination: the ability to see in the dark and green skin, allowing them to melt into the forest shadows.

Zokar looked at Marcus riding adjacent to him. His back was straight as he held three lifeless squirrels in his hands. Moonlight cast eerie shadows over the second-in-command's face, catching his prominent cheekbones the same way it did for Malice. It wasn't the frigid air that sent a chill skittering down the zombie king's spine.

Marcus would ride close to Wren as she whispered something into his ear. Zokar's fists tightened on the reins, his lips pulling into a sneer. *What is he planning?*

When the party reached a small clearing, the bushes rustled. A massive stag emerged from the foliage. Zokar nocked an arrow and took aim. He ground his rotten teeth; he knew he wasn't a precise shot like Tristan. As much as Zokar loathed the Skeletonian king, he envied his archery skills.

The stag blinked at the zombies for a brief moment before prancing away. The zombie king smiled and didn't give the animal a chance. The first arrow soared over the deer's head, between its antlers, making Zokar swear under his breath in frustration. Pulling back another, he let the arrow fly. This time, the barbed shaft punctured the stag's hindquarters, sending it to the ground. The wounded animal turned to the zombie king, its eyes pleading as it tried to rise.

Zokar fired another arrow, puncturing the stag's neck. It collapsed at his horse's hooves. Quickly, Zokar lifted the deer onto the back of his horse and remounted. To his left, he watched Marcus fell a squirrel. His arrow went clean through the creature's skull, before dropping from the branch. The second-in-command retrieved his kill and brought it back, all with a smug grin on his face.

Another rustling sounded in the bushes.

Zokar turned in time to see an arrow fly his way, directed at his forehead. Summoning his magic, he spawned a protective rune. It flung out in a bright-red tendril, grabbed the shaft mid-air, and snapped it in two. The broken arrow fell harmlessly into the grass.

The horses bucked and neighed in fright at Zokar's magic. Surprised grunts echoed from the zombies thrown from their saddles. Narrowing his eyes, Zokar scanned the hunting party, then the forest behind them. Then he saw him: an armored zombie ducked behind the trees, wielding a longbow. Jumping down from his horse, Zokar marched to the bushes and grabbed the zombie by the front of his chest plate.

"An assassination attempt?" said Zokar, staring into the frightened zombie's eyes.

The smaller monster squirmed in his grasp; magic formed in Zokar's free hand. "Shouldn't have tried that on a zombie with dark magic."

The orange embers in Zokar's hands grew, lighting up their entire surroundings.

The horses bucked again, throwing off some of their riders. A few galloped into the woods. Brighter and brighter the embers grew before the zombie in Zokar's palm ignited in flames. The monster burnt until he was reduced to a pile of ash. His last scream ricocheted into the night, sending an owl and a flock of birds fleeing for their lives. Zokar let the chest plate drop in the zombie's charred remains when the flames ceased. He whirled on the rest of the riding party, his eyes narrowing specifically on Marcus.

*He knows something about this. He has to; that would explain why he was secretly talking to Wren.*

The captain locked eyes with the zombie king.

"Did you know about this?" growled Zokar.

Marcus put his hands up calmly. "I didn't, sire. Your magic was fortuitous." The second-in-command looked at the charred zombie's remains. "I'll find the culprits."

Zokar's ears twitched, keeping the rest of the hunting party in his peripheral vision. The way Marcus sounded lacked enthusiasm or any genuine will to protect his king. The idea of killing his second-in-command came and went, but Zokar had to admit having Marcus around, especially his intelligence, was a boon to the zombie army. He was the one that suggested finding the Silver Flame Tribe.

Zokar went rigid. *But that intelligence could be my downfall too.* Luckily, Zokar and Marcus retained their mounts. But the rest of the hunting party would be walking back to the outpost on foot. Not that Zokar cared. Morning would arrive soon. The moon sank lower, just above the tree line. Kicking his horse in the side, Zokar made for the path leading back to the outpost. Marcus rode behind him, staring off into the distance.

Sweat coated Zokar's palms as he gripped the reins. *Once Malice returns, I'll decide what to do with Marcus.*

# Chapter Ten

A chilly morning breeze kissed Tristan's nose. His eyes shot open; he expected to see a sky filled with Malice-controlled dragons. The morning sun greeted him to the king's relief as its light spilled through the treetops. Bolting upright, Tristan rubbed his forehead. Sweat drenched his skin as he took quick breaths.

Tristan glanced around the camp to see his friends snoring soundly, huddled under their cloaks. Shadowstalker had fallen asleep curled into a spiky ball. Now, he was lying on his back, talons up in the air and tongue hanging out the side of his mouth, drooling. His snoring rattled the whole forest, drowning out the birds' morning songs.

The sight of a revered dragon in a goofy sleeping position made Tristan smirk.  Faye leaned against him, her chest rising and falling soundly. Tristan chuckled, wondering how she slept so well against a wall of sharp scales and resonant snoring.

*I need to find out why I've been having all these dreams,* thought Tristan. *I know Cerys had said Blanchett spoke to her wizards in their dreams, but that doesn't explain my recurring dreams with Malice controlling Faye's dragons. These nightmares are no coincidence; they're messages. Could I be...clairvoyant?*

As a child, Tristan heard his parents discuss clairvoyance. While mages and most wizards couldn't see the future, a select few were born with the power. Clairvoyance would be a boon to the Haunted Lands. But Tristan didn't learn much more, courtesy of magic being prohibited.

A sick feeling bled through Tristan. *The Cadre hates us. There really is no place for magic-wielders anymore, is there?*

Rubbing his eyes, Tristan reached for his satchel, which lay propped up against the log he sat on the previous night. He pulled out the Apocalypse Grimoire. Though the leather tome should've gotten lighter each time he picked it up, the weight of responsibility didn't allow that. Tristan folded his legs and set the book in his lap. Makeshift bookmarks were wedged between the pages, courtesy of the three apprentices hopping around the Grimoire reading new spells daily.

Tristan opened the index and traced his finger along the weathered parchment until he found the chapter he needed. He turned to the right page. Grabbing *Translating Runes*, Tristan decoded the writing. The runes translated to "The Mystery of Clairvoyance."

Taking a sharp breath, Tristan read the first paragraph.

*Clairvoyance is rare among magic-wielders. Usually, only one wizard is bestowed with clairvoyance per generation. Mages can't read the future at all. However, wielders born with partial clairvoyance are more common. Their visions will come in snippets of the future—both advantageous and premonitions. Ashley Blanchett is the only wizard who's held complete clairvoyance.*

Tristan's breath caught in his throat. *That dream with the dragons was a premonition, just as I suspected. So, I'm partially clairvoyant. Malice will obtain dragon magic. Though, I don't know how she does that or escapes the Otherworld, I still have to tell my friends, especially Cerys. She'll know what to do. And if she doesn't, I hope*

*Blanchett does. She must.*

Swallowing nervously, Tristan turned the page to read more when he heard one of his friends yawn. He smiled as he watched Zombia shift under her cloak and turn toward him.

"Good morning, Tristan," said Zombia as she rubbed her tired eyes.

"Morning," the king replied, looking up from the Grimoire. After stretching her back, she sat closer to her friend. Tristan's face heated. That warm, fuzzy feeling blossomed in Tristan's chest and stomach. He wished he could stay this close to her forever. It was one of his favorite moments. It brought back feelings of when Tristan and Zombia first met. It reminded him of their picnics in the forest and their hunting trips. She was a ray of sunshine in a dismal world.

"What spells are you reading?" Zombia asked, peering over the king's shoulder.

"They're not spells," said the king. "I'm reading about clairvoyance." He paused, pondering how to phrase what he would say next. "You know those dreams I've been having?"

Zombia nodded, her brows knitting.

"I had another one last night." Tristan stared

at the grass beneath him, needing a small distraction. "This time, Malice escaped the Otherworld and gained control of Faye's dragons."

Zombia's eyes widened as her hand shot to her mouth. "Oh, no! Was it just Faye's dragons, or did she infiltrate the Icebloods and Moonbloods?"

"So far, it's just Faye's dragons. That doesn't

make it much better, though." Tristan rubbed the back of his neck. "It wouldn't surprise me if she went after all the dragon tribes once she's freed. Perhaps even seek out three-headed dragons." *Gods above, Malice and three-headed dragons.* Tristan's stomach clenched at the thought.

Zombia tucked a piece of brunette hair behind her ear. "Do you know how she escapes?"

Tristan shook his head. "I don't."

Tristan looked into her eyes, observing her frown. He wondered how she felt. She was so composed most of the time, same as him. But deep down, there must've been a swirling storm of dread, fear, and uncertainty. Being rulers, Tristan and Zombia had to maintain composure. It was their obligation to protect Skeletonia. The people relied on them. They couldn't afford to run around like decapitated chickens. Even if he and Zombia shared the same fear as those around them, it was their job to protect and lead. At least they could share their emotions with each other and decide what to do next.

"I think...I think I can see the future," admitted Tristan. "Parts of it, at least."

To the king's surprise, Zombia didn't look

incredulous; she looked enthralled.

"I know I sound crazy, but it's true. Look here." He placed the Grimoire gently into Zombia's lap. "It says one in every generation of wizards is born with clairvoyance."

"No, I don't think you're crazy at all," she said, placing a calm hand on her friend's shoulder. "I think this is fascinating. Do you realize how much this will help us? And other people?"

The king relaxed. *Good, we're on the same page.*

"How much of the future can you see?"

"It's snippets, not whole events. I'm apparently half-clairvoyant." Tristan looked to the Grimoire. "Most wizards are. Blanchett is the only one with full clairvoyance."

Zombia rubbed her chin. "Interesting. Now, we can be one step ahead of Malice."

Tristan released a breath and turned to Zombia. "Maybe. I have to warn Faye and Shadowstalker."

Zombia nodded, brushing strands of brown hair from her face. "And talk to Cerys about clairvoyance. See what she has to say."

As if on cue, the mage stirred and stretched, yawning. Rising from her spot, Cerys reached into her satchel and withdrew some bread, cheese, and dried meat from the night before. The smell of food brought Faye immediately into the group. Shadowstalker stirred, smelling the remains of last night's dinner. Rolling over, he stretched like a cat, his wings creaking as he did so. Tristan didn't feel hungry, not after the nightmare, but energy was vital for the long journey to the White-Talon Range. He forced down some goat cheese and dried beef, though it was flavorless.

Faye grabbed some of the dried meat and threw it to Shadowstalker, who gobbled it up heartily. Once done, Shadowstalker vaulted into the air, embarking on another hunting trip. He returned a few minutes later with two whole stags, which he happily tore into.

Halfway through breakfast, Tristan said, "Will someone please wake Tibia up?" He gestured to her sleeping form curled within her cloak.

"I'll wake her," Zombia offered. Reaching into her satchel, she withdrew a piece of parchment, crumpled it, and threw it at Tibia. The parchment ball bounced off her head, drawing stifled laughs from Cerys, Faye, and Tristan. Even Shadowstalker laughed, a deep guttural laugh. When Tibia didn't stir, Zombia crumpled another piece of parchment and threw it.

"Knock it off!" Tibia growled, pulling her cloak over her head.

"Finally, you're up," the king said, unable to maintain a straight face.

Tibia grumbled and blew some of her disheveled bangs out of her eyes. She stomped over and plopped down between her brother and best friend. Snatching a piece of bread from her bag, she glowered at Tristan the whole time she ate.

When nothing remained of the stag save for bones, Shadowstalker turned to Tristan, wisdom and concern beaming in those golden eyes.

*Did you have a bad dream?*

Tristan's eyebrows rose. *Yes...how'd you know?*

*Dragon intuition. It looks like you didn't sleep well,* responded Shadowstalker. *Want to talk about it?*

"Yes, but I have to tell Faye too. The nightmare I had involves you and her," Tristan said out loud.

The dragon's thick brow furrowed, but his eyes darkened with concern. *It does?*

"What involves Shadowstalker and me?" asked Faye, swallowing the last piece of dried beef.

Tristan swallowed. "I've been having nightmares where Malice controls your dragons, Shadowstalker included. I had another last night where Malice possessed you and forced you to do her bidding."

Faye's lilac eyes widened in shock; her brows furrowed in disbelief. "Those are...oddly specific nightmares, why have you been having them?"

Heat rushed to Tristan's cheeks, abashed. "It sounds weird, I know. But I'm telling you because these nightmares are premonitions. These are Malice's intentions when she's released from the Otherworld. I'm half-clairvoyant. I can see snippets of the future." Tristan locked eyes with Cerys, whose eyes widened but didn't appear as surprised as he expected her to be.

"Makes sense, a few wizards in Blanchett's court possessed clairvoyance," said Cerys. "In fact, in the first Apocalypse War, Blanchett used her own full clairvoyance to map out battles, keep track of the enemy, and even plan for her future generation of wizards." Cerys turned to Faye, her gaze hardening, jaw setting. She rested a hand on the elf's shoulder.

"He speaks the truth, Faye. Those aren't nightmares, they're warnings. If Malice isn't stopped, she'll bring the war to your queendom and people."

Faye's long, pointed ears drooped, her cool-gray skin blanching. "So when Malice is free, I'm her next target?"

"Yes."

"Once we save Emerson, I have to return to the Dragon Isles immediately." Faye shot to her feet and grabbed her dragon-eye staff. Sunlight made the teal eye glow, casting an eerie bluish sheen across Faye's face. She gathered her lilac tresses into a bun before climbing Shadowstalker's shoulders and placing her goggles over her eyes. "I must strike a treaty with the Icebloods and Moonbloods; I have no doubt Malice will target them too."

"We won't let that happen," said Tristan, casting his friend a hopeful smile. Though he said these words, manifesting them was a whole other story. Since he had no power in the Dragon Isles, he couldn't convince the Icebloods and Moonbloods to accede.  All he could do was give advice if needed—advice from one monarch to another.

After quickly donning their armor, Tristan pulled out the map from Blanchett's journal while the rest of his friends gathered their belongings. Tibia stood proudly with Karneleth's staff, the crystal glowing neon green in the morning light. The group was in the Zombie Forest, close to the Scale

Mountains. By flight, the wizards would reach the White-Talon Range by the next day. As Tristan pressed his foot onto Shadowstalker's arm, ready to climb, a snap of a twig drew his attention.

Several shapes marched through the leaves like wraiths in the night—cloaked and mysterious. Tristan and his friends drew their weapons, magic crackling in their fingers. A low growl rattled within Shadowstalker; his sharp teeth bared, tail lashing at the threat.

Tristan sniffed the air, but it didn't smell of decomposing flesh or unwashed clothing. He smelled sea salt, and they weren't near the Draconic Ocean. Tristan's heart thudded against his ribs as though it yearned to escape as panic set in.

The Cadre was nearby.

# Chapter Eleven

Pine needles crunched under boots, followed by many voices—one of which belonged to Kieran.

"Can we use an invisibility spell?" asked Faye. She was perched on Shadowstalker's back, her gaze darting everywhere. "We can't fly out of here; they'll see us."

"The Cadre has magic-detecting devices," Tristan hissed at her. His muscles tensed. Faye cocked her head, pointed ears twitching.

"Of course they do," Tibia said with exasperation. Her gaze locked on the towering pines. "Hide in the trees then?"

Tristan looked up. Thick branches were straight and sturdy, jutting out from their trunks. He nodded. "Good idea."

Shadowstalker leaned his head into one of the trees, allowing Faye to sprint across his flat skull onto a high branch, and into the curtain of green needles. A second later, the dragon hunched low to the ground and wriggled into the trees, shaking a few needles from the branches.

One by one, the group chose a tree and began scaling. Initially, Tristan considered levitating himself, but thought better of it, knowing the Cadre would sense his magic. Grabbing a low-hanging branch, Tristan made his way up. His feet slipped a few times, but his upper-body strength saved him. By the time he reached a high enough branch, his hands smelled of sap and bark. Looking down, Tristan saw he was ten feet off the ground; his stomach did a small flip as nausea set in. He clutched the branches, allowing them to cradle him like a child. Tristan wasn't a tree climber; that title belonged to his sister.

The king and Tibia played around in the castle's apple orchards as children. Tristan would sit against the trunk with a book and snack on the fruit while Tibia climbed. He wished she wouldn't have done that while he was beneath it since she shook the branches. Apples rained down on Tristan, who just wanted to read a book about the Haunted Lands' history. But instead, his peaceful day ended with several bumps forming on his head.

Zombia followed Tristan into the same tree. She

stood on the branch below him, clutching the trunk. Tristan offered his hand. After hoisting Zombia onto the branch, he let go, but he hated letting her calming touch go.

Blowing out a breath, Tristan searched for his friends. Tibia stood in the tree just adjacent to his. She didn't sit; she planted her feet firmly on the bulky branch. Cerys stood on the branch below her. Faye stood above Tristan on the branch Shadowstalker deposited her on. Tristan scanned the trees for Shadowstalker. If he squinted, he could make out the dragon's black scales between the green needles. *Hope he's safe there.*

Tristan sighed. *Better to lay low.* He knew Shadowstalker could wipe out Kieran and his troops with his fire if he wanted. But that would cause more damage than good. There were thousands of Cadre members alive, stationed all over the Haunted Lands. And what if Kieran survived Shadowstalker's attack? Tristan and his friends would be tied to stakes, left to burn in front of a jeering crowd of the same people who currently praised him.

Something dropped to the ground, landing on a blanket of needles.

"Oh, for the love of the gods," Cerys hissed,

smacking her forehead with her palm. She glowered down at the ground.

"What happened?" asked Tristan in a hushed voice.

"One of my potions came loose," Cerys replied with a frown.

Tristan's chest tightened, his palms went clammy and slippery against the tree's rough bark. Frustration simmered inside him, but not at Cerys—rather at the Cadre for their laws. If Kieran found the mage's potion, they'd have more evidence of magic's resurfacing. They might even trace the potion back to Cerys. They'd find the wizards with her, and their whole plan to save the Haunted Lands would go up in flames. Nothing would get saved, and Malice would rule the world. The voices drew closer and closer until they were directly beneath the wizards' hiding place. Each Cadre member sat atop a black mare and wore silver-trimmed robes. The smell of sea salt grew stronger than ever.

"Are you sure you're not overreacting, sir?" came a timid voice.

"You call opened portals and magic trails coincidences?" This voice unmistakably belonged to Kieran.

Intimidating and coarse enough to send chills through Tristan. *The Fortress of Portals; Kieran was there.* That wasn't something he had paid much thought, but now he wished he had. Tristan closed his eyes and gave a frustrated grunt. *Why weren't we more careful?*

The Cadre leader surveyed his surroundings and scowled. "Blanchett's wizards have returned; I'm sure of it. Once we find them, we'll confiscate the Apocalypse Grimoire and bring it to him."

Ice shot down Tristan's spine, his heart sinking like a rock sinking to the bottom of a lake. *Who is Kieran referring to? Is there someone in the Cadre of higher position than him?* His gaze fell on the zombies in the group. Evident green skin peeked from beneath their sleeves, revealing what they were. *They can't be working with Zokar, could they? Marcus maybe? That would explain why the Cadre has zombie members. But there are still discrepancies.*

*One: Zokar has dark magic, and that's not something Kieran would approve of.*

*Two: The Cadre stands against the Apocalypse. Ending the Apocalypse was their whole reason for eradicating magic—to lessen the chances of the zombies getting a hold of it.*

Tristan narrowed his eyes when he looked at the Cadre members mere feet below them. Would Kieran bend his own rules? Would he work with Zokar and cover up the fact he collaborated with a dark magic-wielding zombie? Or working with the zombies in general? *What are you up to, Kieran?*

"With the Grimoire, he'll have all the power he needs. Then he can reimburse us," Kieran said, his voice like oil.

"What about the public?" asked the same hesitant voice from before. "People can never know we possess a book on magic."

Kieran grabbed the smaller person's cloak. "We tell the public what we want them to hear. They won't question us if they know what's good for them. It's amusing what you can get a person to do with a little fear."

The Cadre leader released his grip on the person's cloak. "Once those magic-wielders are gone, we can proceed to our next step for complete magic extinction."

Tristan's mind reeled, his brain shuffling through the endless possibilities but coming out empty. Kieran was duplicitous; learning his true intentions wouldn't be easy. Tristan just hoped he'd discover them before it was too late.

Kieran dismounted from his horse and headed for the base of the tree that held Cerys, his black robes sweeping behind him like a wave of ink. Tristan's heart skipped a beat, his fingers digging into the rough bark.

*No, please don't find the potion bottle.*

Bending at the waist, Kieran retrieved Cerys's bottle. Tristan let out a defeated breath; his hands slackened against the rigid wood. *We have to get out of here as soon as possible.*

"What is it, sir?" one of the members asked.

Kieran didn't answer right away. He turned the bottle in his fingers, watching the bright-green liquid slosh against the glass. Bringing it closer to his face, he sniffed it. The Cadre leader wrinkled his nose as though he smelled a rotting corpse.

"Magic." He said the word with such disdain that it made Tristan quake where he stood. He didn't dare breathe.

Kieran withdrew a parchment and quill from his robe, and pressing the parchment against a slate, he began writing. When finished, Kieran showed the document to the other Cadre members. Tristan craned his neck to see its contents.

"Double the patrols. I want the towns searched twice a month." Kieran folded the warrant and placed it and the quill and slate back into his robes. He rolled the potion bottle between his fingers. "He'll be pleased to see that we've procured some kind of evidence. Even the smartest of wizards error eventually."

Kieran mounted his mare and gripped the reins. "Let's ride; we have lots to do. Magic has resurfaced and we must quell it once and for all."

Kieran's words sent goose flesh racing down Tristan's arms.

The Cadre disappeared down the path in a chorus of hoof beats. Tristan watched them intently. He didn't realize how tight he'd been gripping the tree trunk until he saw his white knuckles. Sure they were gone, the king turned to his friends. Zombia's face was pale green. Cerys looked defeated and guilty, and Tibia looked ready to kick something, as always.

"I think it's clear," said Tristan. Gently, he descended the pine, careful of the lighter branches that might snap under his weight. At the same time, he helped Zombia down. Her smile made Tristan's problems momentarily disappear. Even if it was transitory, the king was grateful for it. *I should tell her how much she means to me before it's too late.*

Leaves rustled and Shadowstalker's head poked through the green curtain. Tristan was amazed the dragon had stayed quiet that long.

"Are they gone?" asked Faye, sitting atop

Shadowstalker's head.

The king nodded. More leaves rustled as the dragon emerged from the trees. Pine needles and cones rolled down his massive form, pelting Tristan. Shadowstalker shuffled his talons and blushed, which was barely visible against his midnight-black scales.

*Sorry about that, little one,* said Shadowstalker telepathically. He took a talon and attempted to brush the needles from Tristan's hair, but at the last minute, Shadowstalker retracted his claw, grinning sheepishly.

Tristan grinned at the dragon. *Thanks anyway.*

"Just great, those idiots have one of Cerys's potions," grumbled Tibia as she climbed down. Once at the bottom, she brushed needles off her crimson cloak. "We have to get out of here now."

"Agreed," said Cerys. She kept her shoulders slumped, the guilty look still on her face.

Sighing, Tristan clutched the dragon-claw dagger's pommel and looked ahead into the forest, then to Shadowstalker. "I hate to say this, but I think we should travel on foot for a while. The Cadre is just down the path, and I think they'd hear Shadowstalker's wingbeats. We can't take that chance."

Tibia clenched her fingers. "Walking will take

longer though. And the longer we take, the more likely we are to cross paths with the Cadre again. We need to get to the White-Talon Range quickly."

"They'll see and hear Shadowstalker," replied Zombia. "We're better off walking quickly until we're away from the Cadre, then flying to the range."

Tristan had to admit Tibia had a point. The Cadre had Cerys's potion bottle. It was a matter of time before the Cadre traced it back to the wizards. If they were caught, they'd get burnt and Emerson would turn.

But if Shadowstalker took flight now, the Cadre would hear him, revealing the wizards now. Though the Cadre couldn't fight Shadowstalker at the moment, it didn't mean they wouldn't discover Tristan and his friends.

Tibia blew out a vexed breath and ran her hand through her short, tangled hair. "All right."

"Hopefully, they're gone soon and we can fly again," said Tristan. Knots formed in his stomach. A zombified Emerson flashed through his mind. "Time is not on our side."

So, the wizards walked. Tristan's legs ached from climbing; soreness sang in his fingers and arms from clutching the tree so tight. Shadowstalker tread softly, careful not to shake the ground, but his massive form knocked trees down, bringing needles and a few small branches down waves on Tristan and his friends. Birds fled in droves as the dragon's wings interloped in their nests.

"Quiet." Tristan glowered at the dragon.

Shadowstalker frowned. *I'm trying. Flying over the trees is what dragons usually do.*

"Tuck your wings in more," suggested Faye who sat on his shoulder.

The dragon nodded and curled his leathery wings close to his sides, which helped a little, but not by much. At least Tristan found fewer pine needles in his hair and clothes. The sun hovered overhead just before its apex, yet the late-autumn air nipped at Tristan's skin. Reaching into his satchel, he withdrew Blanchett's journal, focusing on that, hoping to quiet the questions and nervousness rising in his mind for a little while.

The trees around Tristan grew thinner and spread out into small copses. Shadowstalker stretched out his wings, a huge smile spreading across his scaly face.

"I'm sorry."

Tristan turned to see Cerys beside him, her shoulders hunched, her hands in her pockets.

"What for?" asked Tristan.

"Dropping my potion bottle. I didn't mean to." The mage looked away, unable to maintain eye contact with her friend. "Thanks to me, the Cadre has evidence."

"That's not your fault," the king replied, offering his friend a small smile. "Kieran was already onto magic's trail when he found out the Fortress of Portals had been used."

Zombia wrapped an arm around Cerys. "Don't be hard on yourself. It was an accident."

"And it's not like the Cadre will trace the vial back to us immediately," said Tibia. She adjusted the shoulder strap holding her crossbow. "We have some time before then."

Cerys frowned. "Not much, which is why we need to get to the White-Talon Range. We'll travel until dark. We need to at least get out of the Zombie Forest."

There was a brief pause where the silence was filled only by boots crunching against a bed of pine needles and dirt.

"Who do you think Kieran was referring to?" Tristan asked the entire group.

Zombia pursed her lips. "Zokar?"

Tristan shook his head. "Can't be. Zokar has black

magic. He'd be the last person Kieran would collaborate with. However, working with Zokar would explain why the Cadre had zombie members."

"It's possible there's someone in the Cadre with a higher position than Kieran," offered Zombia. She ran her fingers through her brunette hair.

"I feel that's more likely, but I don't know." Tristan rubbed the back of his neck nervously.

"Let's focus on getting to the White-Talon Range before we cross paths with Kieran again," said Cerys.

Tristan nodded and continued walking, locking eyes with the path ahead, but his mind eventually wandered, lost in a sea of trepidation. He understood how Cerys felt; it mirrored how he felt about Emerson.

A soft hand brushed against Tristan's shoulder. He turned to find Zombia casting him a small smile. While her eyes were wide with uncertainty, her smile was reassuring.

"Are you okay?" Zombia asked. Her hand now enveloped Tristan's hand, their fingers intertwined.

Tristan shook his head. "No. The Cadre knows magic's resurfaced, they have Cerys's potion bottle, and Emerson is dying because of me. I should've known Zokar bit him. If I knew, we might have had a chance to save him. A better chance." Tristan's voice was flat and dejected.

Zombia squeezed his hand, her gaze hardening. "It's not your fault he got bitten."

"It's Emerson's," said Tibia, walking at her brother's left-hand side. "He should have told us sooner. I knew his dare-devilish personality would end badly. And I thought I was brazen."

Zombia shook her head. "No, it's not his fault, either. It's Zokar's fault. He wants nothing more than to destroy those in his way and gain power." She turned back to Tristan. "You're not responsible for what that maniac does."

"But I let him fight Zokar, even after I offered to do it." Tristan's eyes burnt; his vision blurred. He couldn't shake the image of Emerson's wound from his head. The ring of toothmarks, the green tint crawling over his skin, driving away the vestiges of his humanity. A tear trailed down Tristan's cheek; he brushed it away. "I can't help feeling that it should have been me."

Zombia stopped in her tracks, gripped Tristan's shoulders, and threw him a glare that he normally never saw on her face. "Stop. Saying. *That.*" Her pinched lips and set jaw told Tristan he'd better be careful or she might end up slapping him. "Just because you're king doesn't mean you're responsible for what others do. You can't control others' actions, especially not the zombies' or Malice's actions. So please, quit blaming yourself, Tristan." A sigh escaped her lips; she released her grip on her friend's shoulders. "It hurts me when you do."

Tristan scratched his cheek, unsure of what to say next. Deep down, he knew Zombia was right. Blaming himself would get him nowhere. Certainly not closer to saving Emerson or topping Malice. He had two choices before him: gripe about an atrocity Zokar caused or work on said atrocity and terminate the chances of more. The zombies and Cadre weren't wasting time; why should he?

Since his coronation, Tristan saw it as his duty to protect his people. He'd told himself that if he'd failed, he was to blame. But it was Zokar who bit Emerson, not Tristan.

Taking a deep breath, the king nodded and smiled. "What would I do without you?"

Tristan looked overhead at the noon sun. Further north, dark clouds gathered, a warning of inclement weather.

X Zombie

Zombia giggled and picked up her pace. "Let's go. We have a High Wizard to find."

# Chapter Twelve

Marcus sat in his guest quarters, pulling his boots on as he huffed out an irritated and dejected breath.

Gray sunlight spilled through the windows of the guest room. Its layout was simple: a small bed, night stand, an armor stand, a chest for clothes, and several unlit torches. After pulling on his boots, Marcus stood from the bed and made his way to the armor stand where his iron epaulets and bandolier rested. He crossed the room to get them, not wanting to look into the mirror. Not wanting to see the face of a failure. After pulling them on, Marcus rubbed at his sleepy eye.

Sleep the previous night didn't come easy. The entire ride back to the outpost, Zokar didn't speak to anyone, not even to Marcus. What transpired the night before was close. Too close to blowing his and Wren's cover. Zokar already distrusted Marcus. Getting Zokar to trust him was already difficult enough. Marcus constantly treaded on thin ice with Zokar, but Malice often alleviated that.

It was easier with the Shadowblood around; she would be the target of Zokar's animosity. Now, in her absence, Zokar was free to do what he pleased—unhinged and violent.

The other zombies kept themselves and their horses far from the zombie king for the rest of the night, even after returning to the outpost. No one wanted to be on the receiving end of the zombie king's wrath. There was no erasing the image of a doomed zombie bursting into enchanted flames from Marcus's memory. Guilt gnawed at the back of his mind. If the assassination attempt had worked, no lives would've been lost. Bringing more harm was the last thing Marcus wanted. The plan was so clear: kill Zokar, cover it up, then become zombie king.

But this wasn't the ending Marcus envisioned. He was not zombie king, Zokar still drew breath, and one of Wren's soldiers was dead.

*I should have planned this better. Zokar has dark magic, of course he's more powerful than us. If I had considered it more, Wren's soldier would still be alive. If I'm going to be a better zombie king, I can't get people killed.* Marcus shuddered, picturing the zombie's charred remains once more, regret winding its way through him.

Marcus sighed, threw his quiver over his shoulder, grabbed his bow, and made his way to the mess hall for breakfast. Upon arrival, nothing seemed out of the ordinary. Zombies mingled and ambled. Some sat in groups at the elongated tables, eating a breakfast of what looked like porridge. The smell of burnt human flesh wafted into Marcus's nostrils, making him swallow back bile. *I guess some of the zombies went out and caught their breakfast.*

Marcus scanned the green crowd for a few moments. Zokar was nowhere to be seen. Though the zombie king was a massive coward, it seemed too suspicious that he'd disappear after a failed assassination attempt. *He must be deep in paranoia's clutches.* For a normal zombie, without dark powers, paranoia would've driven them to hiding. But Zokar was a zombie with dark powers. There was no telling what he'd do, and that was what set Marcus on edge. *What are you up to, Zokar?*

The second-in-command did spot Wren sitting among five soldiers—her best soldiers, he guessed. Marcus approached them and sat beside Wren. Her expression was crestfallen, yet determination danced in her copper eyes. Each of them nursed a bowl of honey porridge, topped with raisins, and a ceramic mug of coffee.

*Thank the gods,* thought Marcus. *I'll need coffee after the night I've had.*

A plate piled with meat sat between the zombies. Wren shoved the plate of human meat toward Marcus, causing him to recoil. However, when she passed him porridge and coffee, he obliged. Dipping the spoon in, he ate, barely tasting the food.

"We need a new plan," said Wren through a mouthful of porridge.

"Like what?" asked Marcus, defeated. He didn't even face Wren; instead, he stared into his coffee cup before taking a sip. He hissed when the hot liquid burnt his tongue. "Zokar has black magic; we don't. That was our first mistake."

"That's a mistake we have to override," said Wren. She clenched muscular fingers, a composed look on her face—far too composed given yesterday's events.

"How?" asked one of the zombies. "You saw what happened. Last night was our only chance; now Zokar will be even more cautious."

Marcus leaned in. "Then we have to play his game."

Unsure glances burrowed into Marcus. He stared across the green, scared faces—hopeful, expecting faces. *They hate Zokar. They want a new zombie king. I have to deliver.* He sipped more coffee, which had cooled, sparing him from more burns.

"His game?" Wren cocked her head.

"Go along with what his commands and proceed like normal, let Zokar think he's survived and won. Let him feed off power-lust; his ego will sooner or later suffocate his mind, causing his guard to drop." *When we free Malice, Zokar will be so busy dealing with her, he'll be less privy to what I do.*

There was a scream, then a crash, followed by more screams. Panic arose from the courtyard's direction. Marcus and Wren shot to their feet. They sprinted to the courtyard to find several zombies lying motionless on the ground. Blood seeped from stab wounds in their foreheads, their eyes frozen open in sheer terror.

A shiver worked its way up Marcus's back. "What in the Underworld—"

The color drained from Wren's visage. "Who—"

"Who was in on it? Tell me!" came Zokar's

The Hidden Wizard

belligerent voice.

Marcus found the zombie king standing toe to toe with another one of Wren's soldiers. Zokar's lone knife was gripped in his white-knuckled fist, his crimson eyes bulging out of his skull. The soldier was a head shorter than Zokar, only meeting his chest.

The little monster cowered in the zombie king's shadow. "I-I-I didn't know there was an assassination attempt."

Zokar grabbed the front of the smaller zombie's breastplate. "Don't lie to me. You had to have been in on it; there are only so many zombies at this outpost."

The monster shook in the zombie king's grip. He squirmed, all to no avail. "I swear, I know nothing of the assassination attempt. Please believe me."

"I don't tolerate liars." In a swift motion, Zokar plunged his dagger into the zombie's forehead, then let the limp body crumple to the ground, joining the other zombies sprawled out across the courtyard.

Terror seized Marcus. *That brute. He's been killing Wren's soldiers to get a confession. I have to stop this.*

Before Marcus could say anything, Wren sprinted past him and faced the zombie king, her muscular shoulders squared.

"Just because you're king doesn't give you the right to kill my soldiers," said Wren. Her brows were turned down with anger.

Zokar whirled on her, magic crackling in his fists; dark red blood dripped from his dagger, leaving splotches against the gray stones. "It's my right when one of your soldiers attempted to assassinate me. All those involved are to be charged of high treason and are deserving of a public execution."

"Sire..." Wren started. "We—"

"I order a public execution," said Zokar. "Ready the guillotine." Zokar faced Marcus. "All the accused, round them up and bring them to me." Veins popped through his green skin, his nostrils flaring like a bull ready to charge. "We aren't leaving this outpost until the perpetrator is dead."

Marcus swallowed hard, contemplating a response. *He's serious. He'll murder every zombie in sight until Wren and I come clean. I can't let more zombies die. But I need to protect Wren, too. Think of something, Marcus. Think of something.*

In his peripheral vision, Marcus watched Zokar step toward another soldier, murder in his eyes. The monster shrank and turned to run before Zokar clutched his cloak, stopping his escape. An idea formed in Marcus's head. *Malice.*

"Sire, this is a huge waste of energy and time," said Marcus. He tried to strike a balance with his voice. Level and calm but firm.

Zokar spun around to face his right-hand man. He still clutched the smaller zombie's cloak. "Finding the culprit who tried to kill the king of the zombies is *not* a waste of time. It's the only sane procedure to protect my reign and bring justice to the crown."

"Did you forget we have to free Malice?"

Zokar's face fell, shoulders slumped. His grip on the zombie loosened. Marcus grinned. *Now he's listening.*

"If we don't free her, the Haunted Lands will never be ours."

"My life is in danger, Marcus," Zokar said, fists clenched. "Malice can wait."

Marcus pressed his lips together. *Fuel Zokar's ego. That's the only way to get through to him.*

"But your victory can't wait. Don't you want Malice to return and help the zombies conquer Skeletonia? Besides, you'll want revenge on those wizards. Did you stop to think this assassination attempt could have been one of them?" Marcus bit his lip, hoping he said the right thing. He didn't feel right blaming Tristan and his friends for something he and Wren planned. He even admired the gallantry Tristan had in battle and the way he led his people in comparison to Zokar who forced his people onto the front lines, callous to whether they lived or died.

If he got Zokar to believe Tristan had something to do with this assassination, then that would buy

Marcus some time to formulate a new plan and stop Zokar from *actually* bringing harm to Tristan and his companions. *I hope to the gods this works.*

Zokar's face softened.

Marcus continued without a second thought. "Finding the Silver Flame Tribe and releasing Malice is how we exact revenge. Then, your perpetrator will be defeated. You can live in safety forever."

The tightness of the zombie king's body released, shoulders relaxing. The murder in his eyes faded. "Fine." Zokar sheathed his blade. "But if another attempt happens, I won't hesitate to kill those in my path until a confession is uttered, you included. Got it?"

Marcus blew out a breath and bowed his head reverently. "Understood, sire."

"Ready the horses," Zokar said to Wren. She scowled as she nodded and sprinted in the direction of the outpost stables. The zombie king slapped Marcus's armored shoulder. "Move out. We're finding those sorceresses."

Thunder rumbled in the distance as thick, dark clouds rolled in, completely swallowing the sun. Wind howled, whipping through Marcus's hair and clothing. Relief washed through him. He had convinced Zokar not to murder everyone in the outpost. He saved himself and Wren. And, if he planned his next attempt strategically, he'd become zombie king, help the zombies, and stop Zokar from harming the wizards.

A confident smile split Marcus's face. *Maybe I'm not a failure after all.*

# Chapter Thirteen

Tristan, Tibia, and Zombia stood in a line, shoulder to shoulder, across from Cerys. The mage clutched her wand tightly, her determined grin stretching wide. The late afternoon sun beat against Tristan's back, a welcome sensation after a frigid morning.

"Remember the chapter you read last night about cloning and illusion?" asked Cerys. "We're going to practice that now."

Waving her wand, the mage whispered *Multiplicare*. Within seconds, another Cerys materialized before the king and his friends. Save for the transparency, her clone resembled the mage entirely. Next, Cerys launched a bolt of white lightning at her clone. Upon impact, the clone vanished in a puff of smoke. The wizards and Faye clapped. Even Shadowstalker clapped. Sitting on his back legs, the dragon smashed his scaly talons together. The sound resonated through the forest and shook the trees, sending a flock of birds to the skies. Tristan didn't know dragons could clap. He imagined their claws were too long to clap, but somehow, Shadowstalker managed without slicing into his own skin.

"Cloning buys the user time when in combat." Cerys turned to Tristan. "Now, you try."

Tristan nodded. Magic crackled through his body like a static shock, except ten times stronger. Breathing deeply, he drew all his power in. The king spoke the rune to life, drew it then imagined the magic pulling another of himself into existence. When he looked up, Tristan nearly gasped.

There, across from him, stood another Tristan. Other than slight transparency, the clone, like Cerys's, resembled the king perfectly. Same armor, same hair, same crown.

Cerys nodded with a growing smile on her face. "Well done."

Slowly, Tristan approached his clone. It didn't speak or move. It just stood there like a sentinel awaiting their officer's command. The king poked his clone and his finger passed through as though he was dipping his finger in water. When he poked it again, the clone vanished in a puff of smoke, causing the king to jump back. "Is it supposed to do that?" he asked, glancing over his shoulder to Cerys.

"Clones are temporary, Tristan. They're only meant to fake out your opponents, which buys the wielder valuable time. That's why you can conjure multiple." The mage held up her index finger. "However, the more you conjure, the more energy it takes. I wouldn't recommend fledgling wizards going above five."

A mischievous grin formed on Tibia's face. Tristan didn't want to imagine all the trouble she'd cause with her clones. Hide-and-seek just got harder.

"Can you clone yourself, Faye?" Zombia asked.

Faye gave a nonchalant shrug. "We can, but elves don't do it often. Our expertise lies with dragon magic. Sorry."

Shadowstalker gave an affirmative nod. Tristan couldn't place it, but for some reason, when he looked at the dragon, he felt reassured. Though he felt that way with Cerys, it was sort of refreshing having someone as powerful as a dragon giving him encouragement.

"It's still a vital skill to have, though." Faye leaned against Shadowstalker and gave Zombia a reassuring grin.

"Now, all of you try," said Cerys, pointing her wand at her apprentices.

They did. The chilly night was filled with laughter. Tibia managed to make three clones of herself, each one as cold and stoic as she. Before Tristan knew it, a trio of Tibia's clones ran around at her will, showing themselves off to Faye and Shadowstalker like a child showing off their new toy. Tibia directed them as though they were puppets obeying her every command. After a few minutes, they vanished.

Zombia only managed to conjure one clone of herself. When she tried again, only half a clone appeared: just legs and half a torso. Tristan put a hand over his mouth to stifle a laugh. Grumbling, Zombia conjured as much magic as possible, putting her whole heart and soul into it before, finally, a fully intact clone appeared. When she cast Cerys an embarrassed look, the mage reassured her with a gentle touch on the shoulder.

"It's okay; one clone is better than none," Cerys said.

Zombia's eyes beamed as she guided her clone around the campsite. The clone followed her commands, weaving around every rock and dip in the ground as if it had a mind of its own. Then it vanished.

Tristan conjured two clones of himself. Slight nausea shrouded him, followed by a nagging pounding in his head like a blacksmith's hammer repeatedly pounding on his temples. One clone, he placed near

Shadowstalker and Faye. They glanced at it with a smirk. Tristan made the clone pat Shadowstalker on the head, which Tristan assumed the dragon wouldn't feel as the clone was nothing but an illusion. The other, he placed behind Cerys. When she turned around, she reached out to touch the clone's shoulder, thinking it was the real Tristan, it disappeared. The king doubled over in laughter at the look on baffled Cerys's face.

"See how well they work?" she said, her cheeks reddening. "Even fooled me."

Soon, the entire group bent over in a fit of giggles. Little spurts of fire flickered out of Shadowstalker's nose as he laughed. When the laughter faded, all three wizards made their clones vanish, filling the forest clearing with enchanted smoke.

Cerys stood proudly with her hands clasped behind her back. "Seems like you learned to clone yourselves quickly. Well done. Now, do you remember crafting weapons from pure magic?" the mage asked.

The three apprentices nodded enthusiastically. Having the Cadre on their tail didn't dampen Tristan's eagerness much.

Cerys wrote *Hagalaz*, then waved her hand and

watched as a shimmering blue sword materialized in front of her. After grabbing the sword, the mage picked up what remained of a loaf of bread the group had for dinner and sliced her magic sword through it. The bread fell away in two perfect halves. The mage turned to Shadowstalker. The dragon reached to the side and found a large, fallen branch, and tossed it to Cerys.

*Slice!* The branch thudded in the grass, cleanly split in two.

Tristan's eyes widened with wonderment. The wizards clapped, Faye clapped, even Shadowstalker's golden eyes rounded.

"That's so impressive," said Tristan.

Now, it was their turn.

They continued to summon more magic weapons. Tristan molded his energy like a smithy forged a sword. Bright gold light took the shape of a battle-ax, then he summoned daggers, maces, any weapon he could think of. The magic was like clay, and he was the sculptor. It was that simple until a burning sensation began. What started as a light heat progressed until Tristan felt as though he'd been standing in a desert for days. Sweat poured down his forehead and arms; he realized he wasn't in skeleton form anymore. He barely heard his surroundings and his vision began to fade.

These side effects made Tristan realize his error—the error Cerys specifically told him wizards should never make. He was burning himself out.

*Sever the magic ties! Sever them now!* Shadowstalker screamed into Tristan's mind. He imagined himself taking a dagger and slicing the bonds of energy overpowering his body, but they didn't waver. More heat rushed through his face, blurring his vision even more as dizziness clutched him like a dragon's claws. The weapons around him began to spark and warp into amorphous shapes.

His friends' voices reached his ears, but Tristan could barely decipher what they were saying. Their voices melded together, all shouting his name, which increased the pounding in his head. Next, he felt the ground collide with him; the soft grass cushioned his fall. His vision flickered again, and the last thing he saw was Cerys sprinting towards him, Shadowstalker clambering behind her.

Darkness enveloped Tristan.

# Chapter Fourteen

Fire coursed through every portion of Tristan's body. Cold water splashed on his face quelling the liquid fire burning through his blood. Another sensation, like soothing ice, tore through the pain. This one was not in his body but in his mind. It was refreshing, restoring like aloe on a sunburn. After another icy splash to the brain, Tristan opened his eyes and blinked, sunlight seeping into his vision in slivers.

He heard the soft gurgle of water. The weight on his body had been lifted; one of his friends removed his armor, making it easier for Tristan to breathe. His white linen shirt was soaked around the collar, and his hair was pasted to his forehead.

He rubbed his head and tried to sit up, but a hand gently pushed him back down.

Tristan blinked a few more times, and his vision cleared enough so he could observe his surroundings. He was lying on the bank of a stream. Setting sunlight

The Hidden Wizard

peeked through the leaves, glinting off the water as
it scrambled through the trees. The puffy clouds
glowed gold then pastel pink. Zombia, Cerys, and Faye
stared at him, their foreheads crinkled with worry.
Shadowstalker looked at him with confidence.

*What happened?* Tristan asked.

*You overexerted your powers, young wizard,*
Shadowstalker said telepathically.

Tristan's heart beat faster. *Oh gods, this is what I feared would happen. I didn't think it would be me, and I can't ever do that again.*

Tibia appeared, holding a bucket.

Cerys put up a hand. "That will be enough, Tibia. He's fine."

Tibia drenched him anyhow. "Don't *ever* scare me like that again! Got it?" she shouted—every inch a Skeleteria warrior. Then, her voice drew unusually soft. "Thank the moon goddess," she whispered.

He'd never seen this sort of affection from Tibia. Of course, Tristan knew his sister loved him, but her reticent nature never pushed her beyond a shoulder punch or a slap on the back. Now, she fully embraced her brother, which caused a smile, not only because Tibia cared but because Tristan liked that it actually showed her sensitive side.

After a few moments, Tibia released Tristan. Then she punched him in the shoulder.

"Don't do that!" shouted Zombia. "Although, it wasn't entirely undeserved."

Zombia wrapped her arms around him. Her embrace felt like being wrapped in a cozy blanket on a freezing winter's night.

"Tristan, what were you thinking? You overexerted your powers!" Cerys blurted. Tristan flinched. This outburst from the mage startled him. Cerys was always so calm and composed.

The mage folded her arms and shook her head. "Even after I told you *not* to. Clearly, you haven't been listening to anything I've said." Cerys pinched the bridge of her nose. "Gods, that was reckless."

Tristan slowly rose to his feet. He anticipated dizziness and fatigue, but they never came. In fact, he didn't feel ill at all. Tristan flexed his fingers and felt brand new. His magic even felt different, as though he received more magic. It felt as though the water had washed away dirt that had long been stuck to him.

Tristan wrung his hands. "I didn't mean to. I was summoning different weapons, and it sort of... happened." The king glanced to the ground sheepishly.

"Do you realize that each weapon you created required a portion of your energy?" Cerys said, her voice stilted. "With each weapon, you deplete your magic content, and you weren't counting. Too many weapons mean more magic and overexerting your powers and body."

Heat rose to Tristan's cheeks. "I didn't mean to,

all right. I'll remember that next time."

The king's apology did nothing to stop Cerys's chiding. "Next time? If Shadowstalker hadn't saved you, there wouldn't be a next time. Magic isn't a game, Tristan." Cerys's face was red now, her emerald eyes alight with fury. She pressed her finger to his chest like Tibia or Zombia would do. "You are a wizard, one of the most powerful magic-wielders in the Haunted Lands. You can't use your magic haphazardly. You need to plan your magic, conserve it, think, then fight. What you did was use your powers without thinking. Wizards also learn discipline. Without discipline, there is arrant chaos."

Tristan winced, then froze. While most would be shocked that anyone would speak to a king in such a manner, Tristan didn't care. He was equal; they all were. Behind Cerys, Faye's brows were pulled together—a face of disappointment and worry. Elves were taught magic at a young age; Faye knew how dangerous it was to overexert your magic.

"You're right. I'm sorry." Tristan's words were solemn.

Cerys rubbed her forehead with the palm of her hand. "Don't be sorry for me. You almost died,

Tristan. If Shadowstalker hadn't saved you, you would have perished. If we have any chance of defeating Malice, we need you to *not* die, okay?"

The king touched his face, feeling his skin cool. Tristan felt not only normal; he felt better than that. All the muscle aches from sparring disappeared too. His magic felt like it had been filtered of impurities and restored. Tristan felt like a new person. Shadowstalker smiled, showing his pointed teeth.

*What did you do? How'd you save me?*

*I gave you some of my energy. By feeding you some of my energy, I revived you, giving you enough strength until I was sure you'd survive on your own.*

Shadowstalker saved him by severing some of his energy and gifting it to Tristan. Gratitude fully enveloped the king's heart as he locked eyes with Shadowstalker.

*Thank you.*

The dragon didn't reply. He just bowed with a huge grin.

Tristan glanced down at his fingers, flexing them, feeling as though they might morph into sharp talons any moment. "So...do I have dragon powers now?"

Faye rubbed her angular chin. "In a way, yes.

But you can't fly and are not immune to fire. Dragons can share their powers. Elves and dragons can share powers due to our special bond. Only in rare cases have dragons shared bonds with wizards." Faye's lilac eyes focused on Tristan as though he'd sprouted a second head. "You're the first wizard-dragon bond performed in decades."

No words formed on Tristan's tongue; astonishment had gobbled them up like a ravenous lion. None of his friends responded either. Zombia and Tibia exchanged glances while Cerys looked to the Dragonblood elf and nodded, probably knowing the same information.

After the abrupt halt, training was complete for the night. Tristan and his friends built a campfire.

Tristan rolled a chopped log next to the fire and sat when he asked, "How can I be bonded to Shadowstalker if he already shares a bond with Faye?"

Faye took a seat in the grass beside Shadowstalker and patted the dragon's snout. "You're not bonded to Shadowstalker the same way I am. You share his magic, but you aren't connected bodily."

Tristan furrowed his brow.

"Elves can lock themselves into their dragons' minds. When I do this, I can see what Shadowstalker sees, which is helpful when we aren't together. If he's scoping out a battlefield and I'm not there, I can lock my mind with his and see the field for myself. Same goes for pain and suffering. When Shadowstalker's in pain, I can feel it. You wouldn't because you don't share the elf-dragon bond."

*Still so much to learn,* thought Tristan. *Mom and Dad never talked to Tibia and me in depth about dragons. This is good to know. Strange and fascinating too.*

"I think that would be a fun power," said Tibia. She stoked the fire with a twig. "Send your dragon out to set zombies on fire then watch their stupid, horrified faces through the dragon's eyes." A smirk formed on her face.

Laughter erupted from everyone in the group, save Zombia and Tristan. *War isn't funny. Zombies may be the enemy, but they still deserve respect and second chances like anyone else.*

"No one should enjoy war," Zombia said, nudging her friend with her elbow. The healer in her couldn't abide by war.

Faye snorted, which drew a louder snort from Shadowstalker. Then, everybody laughed.

Tristan's near-death experience dashed their appetites, leaving a majority of the food uneaten. A small dinner meant an early night. Tibia fell asleep almost immediately. She curled up in her cloak on a soft patch of grass. Her crossbow rested beneath her hand. Zombia did the same, curled up in her cloak with her hand resting on her glaive.

Shadowstalker coiled himself into a spiky ball. Tristan smirked, knowing by morning, the dragon would be sprawled out again and drooling. Faye rested against his side, sheltered under his leathery wing.

Despite the events that occurred, Tristan felt no fatigue. His mind was wide awake. He stared off into the scene ahead. A star-spangled sky with sporadic clouds. Beyond the treetops, he saw white mountains jutting up from the ground. *Is that where Blanchett lives?*

"I owe you an apology, Tristan."

The king turned to find Cerys standing behind him. The mage cast him a chastened smile before sitting in the grass beside him.

"Years ago, when I was a fledgling mage,

Wizards of the Apocolypse

Blanchett had told us about magic-wielders combusting by overusing their magic. She ingrained it into our heads; in fact, there wasn't a day that passed when she *didn't* remind us about the dangers. However, not everyone listened."

Cerys paused and took a deep breath. Time seemed to slow.

"One of our fellow mages accidentally went too far. His name was Gavin, and he was one of the most ambitious mages in Blanchett's court. He'd devour every book he was given and even spend late nights in the Citadel Library, reading. He'd excel in all the spells he tried; Gavin was one of Blanchett's star pupils. However, he got too confident, and he tried to summon a dragon entirely composed of magic energy. It worked."

"He shouldn't have tried that," said Faye. She shook her head. "Only elves and wizards can summon animals out of magic, let alone an entire dragon."

Tristan's breath caught. Summoning something as large as a dragon would require an amount of energy he couldn't even imagine.

Cerys continued, her voice cracking. "Every part of Gavin burnt. We threw water on him, yet he still burnt. He burnt and screamed until there was nothing left of him save for a pile of soot. I wasn't close to him, but we were friends. And watching him burn left a mark. His terrified face, the face of someone who will never laugh or love again, and his screams are still branded into my mind. Not only did I lose a friend, but it reminded me how lethal magic is. If handled trivially, magic kills. If handled with respect and knowledge, magic saves." Cerys sniffled and wiped away tears.

Tristan's heart ached, his throat dry. Now, he understood why Cerys had been so furious with him. Why she acted as though he had murdered someone.

"I see," Tristan repeated, wrapping his arms around Cerys. She shuddered in his grasp.

"Now, you understand. Gavin didn't have discipline, and that killed him. One must have control, especially a wizard. That's how he failed, and we can't afford failure, not if we want to defeat Malice."

Cerys locked her eyes with Tristan. It felt like her gaze was slicing through muscle and bone, cutting right to his soul.

"Don't make the same mistake, Tristan Skeleton."

# Chapter Fifteen

What started as a few dark gray clouds an hour ago turned into the zombies getting blasted by a roaring downpour. Zokar frowned as the freezing droplets soaked through his cloak, causing it to cling to his shivering body. He and Marcus no longer rode through the Zombie Forest. They were in the Gravestone Woods, clustered at White-Talon Range's base.

A regiment of zombies from Wren's outpost followed closely behind on war horses, creating a subtle crunch of dirt and pine needles. The leaves should have protected the zombies from the torrents, but they didn't. Water filled the leaves, causing them to tip and douse everything beneath them. Zokar growled. At the same moment, thunder rumbled, drowning out his display of discontent. Fear bolted through the zombie king. The horses neighed, startled by a sudden clap.

*I can't let anyone, especially Marcus, know my fear of thunder and lightning.* For as long as he could remember, Zokar had feared thunderstorms. He hated the loud noise. It reminded him of heavy stones being catapulted at the castle walls, tearing down Zokar's fortifications. More thunder rumbled, making him shrink inside his cloak, pulling it farther over his head. Marcus and his horse were a few paces ahead, but Zokar didn't doubt there was a smug smile on the second-in-command's face.

*I strongly believe Marcus was in on my assassination attempt.* The zombie king glowered at Marcus's back. He listened to the zombies behind him, the same zombies from Wren's outpost.

*Possibly ones that planned my assassination. But of course, Marcus suggested we need them, as did Wren. I suppose they were right; I don't want to face Blanchett's wizards alone. Once Malice is free, I'll decide what to do with Marcus. Force him to admit he was in on the assassination attempt. It's too suspicious that he opposed me seeking out the culprit.*

"How close are we?" Zokar shouted over the torrential rain.

Marcus pulled on the reins, bringing his steed to a halt. From under his cloak, he produced the Haunted Lands map. He shielded it with his cloak, but the sodden fabric did little to keep the parchment dry.

"It's just through those trees," responded Marcus. He groaned at the almost-soaked map and shoved it back into his doublet. "The Silver Flame Tribe lives in a fortress wedged into the mountain's cliff side."

Lightning flashed, casting ominous shadows over Marcus's angular face as he said the words. The zombie king gripped his horse's reins, fear rolling through him, but he quickly dashed it.

*Malice's waiting,* thought Zokar. *My victory is waiting.*

The greenery around them blurred until they skidded to a halt at the base of the mountains. Their peaks jutted high into the sky, entangling themselves in the dark clouds. The whitewashed crags reminded Zokar of why they earned the name White-Talon Range. And there, wedged into their side, were the towering walls of Silver Flame Tribe's fortress. Spires of what looked like gray granite soared. While most cities were encapsulated by walls, these sorceresses apparently had a different idea. High up and out of reach of the zombies.

"We need a plan," said Marcus. Water dripped from the hood of his cloak onto his nose, and he shivered. "These are powerful sorceresses. We need to approach them in a composed and polite manner."

Zokar's eyes darkened, his face flushing. "No, we need to show them how powerful *we* are. Force them to submit to the undead."

"That's incredibly foolish, sire." Hooves slapped the wet dirt as Marcus brought his horse closer to the zombie king. "We're the ones who need their help. Angering them won't give us what we need. We'll need to reciprocate too."

Zokar's pointed ears twitched with fury. "What's happened to you? You've lost your brutality! Gods, you're beginning to sound more like a human than a zombie. Show too much kindness, and suddenly the serfs become trained soldiers, ready to steal the throne. Striking fear into your subjects ensures a successful reign. Kindness is why Skeleton is such a failure."

"Unity is how we'll win this war," said Marcus. "Not division." After glowering at Zokar, the second-in-command nudged his horse in the side and urged him forward a few paces before breaking into a gallop. Many hoof beats echoed behind them as the army pushed to keep up.

Rain continued to pour; thunder pealed in the distance. Droplets pattered against Zokar's armor hypnotically; his rage boiled. The two galloped through the clearing until they reached a path leading to the ominous fortress. Marcus's brows turned downward in anger, but his eyes were calculating. Zokar narrowed his gaze. *What is he thinking? Marcus has been so confrontational lately like he doesn't want the zombies to be successful. Has he forgotten what the zombie motto is: kill or be killed? In a world that needs conquering, there's no space for generosity.*

Zokar scowled at the narrow path winding up the mountain's side, leading to the fortress. Seeing no doors, passages, or gatehouse, he guessed this path was the sole entrance. Lightning split the sky, highlighting the mountains' pearly crags. Thunder boomed in the distance, startling the horses. Zokar's horse bucked and neighed in fear before the zombie king tugged on the reins and patted the horse on the head.

Marcus started up the jagged path but stopped short when Zokar waited. Fear gripped the zombie king like a vice as he listened to the thunder paired with the looming fortress. The magic surrounding the mountains was palpable, and it made Zokar's stomach coil. Shoving down his fear, Zokar nudged his horse into a trot and headed for the winding path to the fortress.

More lightning cracked across the cool gray-blue sky.

"We'll be stronger with allies," said Marcus in a firm tone. "Not enemies. If they have the ability to free Malice, who knows what other powers they have."

Neither zombie spoke the whole way up. The only sounds filling the silence was the rumbling thunder and the slow trot of the horses' hooves. Zokar swallowed, trying not to peer over the cliff side. Tiny pebbles tumbled down the mountain, sending a jolt of fear through the zombie king. The path grew more narrow as they ascended; at one point, Marcus forced his horse past Zokar, pushing him closer to the precarious edge. He sighed with relief when they reached the white-bricked fortress. Its pointed towers soared high, touching the deep-gray clouds. Instead of gargoyles, the entrance was guarded by stone ravens. Real ravens flitted around the battlements, cawing, sending shivers down Zokar's spine. There were no sentinels present on the ramparts or parapets, which he found odd—and stupid. Zokar scoffed. Every diligent king knew soldiers and guards were how he protected his home from invaders.

"Are you coming or not?" called Marcus. He sat atop his horse, gripping the reins tightly with a too-gallant posture. Zokar wanted to slap that haughty grin off the second-in-command's face.

"You go first. See what lies ahead." The zombie king's tone was firm and laced with a threat. He bit back the anger rising in his chest.

Marcus blew some of the sopping hair off his forehead in an irked manner. "Stay close." The zombies passed a stockade and into the gatehouse. Orange flickered in the towers, but there were no guards. Zokar's lips broke into a sinister grin. *They're hiding most likely—not very admirable of a magic-wielder.*

In the courtyard, the zombies dismounted and tied their horses to one of the pillars, deciding to continue on foot. Sets of stairs led up to innumerable rooms. A balcony wound around the courtyard's perimeter, connecting all the rooms together. Rain had gathered in little pools between the stones and in unlit braziers. Ancient magic was evident, making Zokar draw his last dagger.

*Where are the sorceresses?* The zombie king thought to himself. *There must be thousands of them.*

Marcus's lips parted, but Zokar glowered at him. The second-in-command kept his mouth shut.

Zokar wrung out his cloak and looked back to his army. "Wait here. If any sorcerers attack, kill them without hesitation, got it?"

The rotting monsters nodded. Instead of entering a massive throne room or great hall, Zokar and Marcus stepped into the warmth of a grand library. It was a labyrinth of bookshelves enclosed by a colonnade of decorative stone pillars. The floors were lustrous black marble, so polished that Zokar could see his reflection and the reflection of the over packed shelves. Long, vertical windows on each wall provided a perfect view of the fleeing storm. Desks were stationed in the center of the library. Each was strewn with books, loose parchment scrolls, and inkwells.

Ravens were carved into the top of the pillars, their wings fanned out, ready to vault into the sky. Oil lamps hung from the ceiling, suspended by chains. Zokar noted the eerie yet sophisticated scene was tied together with white banners dangling between each pillar. The sorcerer's crest, featuring a raven perched on a branch, wearing a floppy wizard hat was drawn with ink, the black professionally contrasting with the white canvas.

Inhaling the scent of old paper, Zokar began weaving between the bookshelves, scanning for any members of the Silver Flame Tribe. He never found them; no one seemed to be there. Zokar shivered as the magic ebbing through the fortress thrummed through his veins—slow and cadenced. He guessed this was what a heartbeat was like, considering zombies' hearts didn't beat at all.

"This place is incredible," said Marcus. His eye flitted around the room, taking in the unique, arcane structure. "This place hasn't seemed to age at all."

"Don't get distracted," hissed Zokar. "Find the Silver Flame members."

As if on cue, footfall sounded—footfall from multiple people. Drawing his dagger, the zombie king spun, turning his attention to the doorway. Three people emerged—three women—one elf with wavy ginger hair and another with a short blond bob. The woman in the middle was tall and well-muscled.

Her silver hair was tied into a braid, offset by her olive skin. A black witch hat sat on her head, complemented by a single rose quartz in the center, like a third eye. Zokar assumed this was Maeve Argent.

All three wore white robes trimmed with a silver filigree pattern. Unlike most robes, these only reached their knees, revealing leather boots with gray heels. Black cloaks cascaded down their backs. They each wielded staffs that resembled the one Karneleth held, except they were crafted from a red and dark turquoise stone. Zokar learned it was called a bloodstone, the crystal used for strength and vigor. A necklace bearing the same stone hung around the leader's neck.

Power radiated off her in a way that made Zokar want to break for the exit. But he wouldn't dare show such cowardice in the presence of others. The trio had their staffs drawn; lavender-purple magic danced in the violet orbs, poised to strike like a viper. Zokar planted his feet firmly on the shiny tile. It was all he could do to keep from retreating.

To the zombie king's surprise, the sorcerers didn't attack. Not yet.

Maeve looked Zokar and Marcus up and down with piercing pale-blue eyes. "I never thought I'd see you stinking creatures crawling around the White-Talon Range." She stepped forward, closing the space between her and Zokar. "What do you mangy monsters want?"

Marcus dropped to one knee, bowing his head before the sorceresses. "We beseech your aid. Malice Sanguine has been entombed in the Otherworld and we read that only the Silver Flame Tribe can free her."

Maeve's toned face and shoulders fell. The sorceresses beside her also slumped, their eyes rounded with shock.

"She's...gone?"

The terror on her face made Zokar smile. *Got her now.* He hated admitting Marcus had a way with words.

Maeve tucked her arms into her white sleeves, looking down the bridge of her nose at the zombies. "Shadowbloods are stronger than any demon in the Underworld. There's never been one in the Otherworld unless by their own volition. Who's responsible for putting her there?"

Zokar inched closer to Maeve. "This group of wizards who work for Ashley Blanchett."

Maeve's face paled, as did her sorcerer friends behind her.

"And if you help us free her, we can ensure she

helps you maintain your control of the triumvirate," offered Marcus.

Maeve's lip curled as she shot Zokar a daggered gaze. "Why should we trust you? Haven't you zombies done enough?"

Her insolent tone made Zokar bristle with rage; he brought his dagger up, angled toward Maeve. "How dare you—"

Gold light erupted from the obsidian blade. The sorceress's eyes lit up as they stepped back and Zokar advanced. The second-in-command grabbed Zokar's knife hand, keeping the blade from plunging into Maeve's neck.

Grinding his teeth, Zokar yanked out of Marcus's grip. "Do that again, and I'll take your last eye." His voice dropped an octave.

"You want Malice to return?" Marcus hissed. "Then don't create enemies out of possible allies." He turned from the zombie king back to Maeve.

"Zombies with magic," Maeve breathed.

"Great upgrade, isn't it?" asked Zokar. "It's a gift from Malice, actually." A smile curled on the zombie king's face. "Yes, we know her personally."

Maeve couldn't stop blinking. "Typically, the

undead are too simple-minded for such an arcane practice."

"We also read that the Silver Flame Tribe wants to end the triumvirate and rule absolutely, is that correct?" Marcus extended his empty palms, his face guileless.

Zokar scowled. *Pathetic.*

Slowly, the sorceresses nodded.

"It's worse now," said the redheaded sorceress. "The Solar Flare Tribe and Blue Moon Tribe combined forces and defeated the Silver Flame Tribe when our prowess in dark magic was still weak. We've remained discreet since."

Maeve kept her lips turned down, but the ire in her eyes dimmed subtly as she turned from Zokar and faced Marcus. Rage heated up the zombie king's core; his magic elevated to a boil.

"Malice promised my mother, Meredith, that she'd return after defeating Blanchett," explained Maeve. "But she never did. I held disdain for her for many years, until now. You really know her?"

"She granted the zombies dark magic recently," Marcus responded. "That's why we've come, seeking your help. We're in the same predicament: both the zombies and sorceresses are weak without Malice. If you help us free her, she'll grant your tribe all the black magic you could want. With her, you'll end the triumvirate and establish yourselves as rulers over the entire Sorcerer Territory." By the end of his explanation, the corners of Marcus's mouth were turned up subtly, confident in his words and their delivery. No pride fluttered in Zokar's chest, just envy.

Maeve pursed her lips, a pensive expression falling over her face. Turning around, she addressed the other sorceresses, discussing and mulling over the offer.

Zokar's fingers tightened around his dagger, tension gripping his shoulders and jaw. Though he hated admitting it, the zombies needed Malice back as much as the sorceresses did.

As much as Maeve already vexed him, Zokar truly hoped the sorceresses would agree. Through helping free Malice, Maeve and her tribe would be in debt to the Shadowblood. She'd have leverage over the tribe. And through that leverage, Zokar could wage his own power over them. Force the sorceresses to submit to zombie rule after he overthrew Malice. Then, he'd kill Maeve and scare the rest of the tribe into submission. *And I'll add an army of sorcerers to a crew of zombie dragons when we cross that bridge. The zombies and sorceresses created a formidable alliance that Blanchett wouldn't dare confront. I'll make Tristan Skeleton fear me. I'll make the entire Haunted Lands fear me.*

Zokar's muscles tightened as seconds ticked by, and his fingers balled into fists.

"We'll do it," Maeve finally said. The tightness in Zokar's arms and shoulders abated. Maeve tapped his chest with the glowing purple orb.

Heat flushed the zombie king's face. *How dare she show such disrespect to a monarch?*

"However, I hope you zombies understand you're at our mercy. Don't allow your inane mistakes to cost us, got it?" Maeve was face to face with Zokar, their noses practically touching. He inhaled the sweet scent of cinnamon and citrus. It made him sick; he couldn't abide nice things.

"Go to the Underworld!" The zombie king raised his dagger; an incantation was already on his lips when a pair of hands grabbed his cloak, yanking him back.

"Zokar, stop it!" Marcus hissed, his eye beaming with irritation. His knuckles were white as they clutched the zombie king's torn cloak. "We need their help just as much as they need ours." The second-in-command severed the path between magic-wielders and the zombie king.

Zokar had been clenching his jaw so tightly that it hurt. He mentally collected himself and took a long breath through his nose. "My sincerest apologies," Zokar said through gritted teeth. The words tasted bitter on his tongue.

"So, where do we start?" asked Marcus.

Maeve spun around and gestured to one of the doors leading out of the library. "Through there is the war room. We will plan our next moves there."

She began heading for the open door, her apprentices following in her tracks. Their black cloaks sailed behind them, boasting the Triple Goddess woven out of gold stitching.

Upon reaching the door, Maeve glanced over her shoulder; her pale-blue eyes glinted in the light, making Zokar quake where he stood. "Be warned, if either of you cross me, I'll have both of your heads on a pike before dawn."

# Chapter Sixteen

When Tristan woke, the sun's rays barely grazed the treetops. Birds tweeted in the distance, filling the atmosphere with their morning melodies. His friends' sleeping forms dotted the campsite. Shadowstalker, sure enough, had his feet in the air and a runnel of drool flowing from his mouth. Tristan smirked, but it quickly died as unease and memories of the previous night crept in.

The king grabbed his satchel, pulling out the Apocalypse Grimoire. As he did so, Zombia yawned and approached Tristan, with her cloak still wrapped around her, and sat in the grass beside him.

He grinned at her, his face warming up. "Morning, Zombia."

"Morning, what are you going to read about?"

Tristan chewed his lip in thought. He couldn't stop contemplating the dragon bond Faye discussed. It was like a constant itch at the back of his mind he couldn't scratch. "I'd like to know more about this dragon bond Faye discussed and check to see if Blanchett had any notes on her experimentation for a cure." He flipped to a page titled: "History of Dragon Magic."

It read: *Dragon magic is the oldest magic in the world. Dragon magic, like the tribes, is divided into three major classifications:*

*Fire: Dragonblood elves*
*Ice: Iceblood elves*

*Lunar: Moonblood elves*

*While each dragon and elf species has its own individual magic, only one can have all three abilities, and those are the three-headed dragons. But they're extremely rare. Before the Apocalypse, the world and dragons thrived; all species lived together in harmony. No wars, only peace. Magic was practiced freely.*

*When the Ice dragons' queen died without an heir, the Moon dragons wanted to place their own heir on the throne to rule over the Ice Queendom, Fire Queendom, and Moon Queendom. This sparked the war between the dragon tribes. Conflict over land tore the once-peaceful tribes apart. It was not long after that the first zombie outbreak began. With the undead posing a greater threat, the Elf Wars ceased, and a treaty was issued.*

Tristan's jaw hung slightly open as he exchanged glances with his friend, her expression mirrored his.

"Keep reading," Zombia said, turning the page. The weathered parchment crinkled before revealing new, riveting information.

*Elves and dragons from each tribe share an unbreakable bond. If the rider is wounded in a battle, the dragon can grant them a portion of their magic to heal them. During the Great Apocalypse War, Blanchett became allies with the dragons and elves. Because of their strong alliance, the dragons began healing and forming bonds with other magic-wielders.*

*Once the Cadre took power, Blanchett and her people were forced to flee. Dragons were still allowed into Blanchett's new home of Aramore; however, they had to remain inconspicuous. Very few dragons, save for a species called demi-dragons, reside in Blanchett's location. With the Cadre's ban on magic, Blanchett's resources for discovering a cure for zombification became few and far apart. Unable to travel, Blanchett was forced to stay in her underground home of Aramore, supposedly never to return to the public.*

Tristan exchanged an awe-struck gaze with Zombia.

"I can't believe our whole lives, we were taught the Cadre were the heroes. That they were fighting for the Haunted Lands and working to end the Apocalypse." Tristan's fingers tightened around the book's worn edges. "It was all a lie. The Cadre were the ones obstructing the outlets for a cure." Tristan pressed his lips together. *I wonder what else Kieran has lied about. What are his true intentions for the Haunted Lands?*

Zombia got a wistful look in her eyes. "I'm

hoping when we find Blanchett and save Emerson, we can bring the truth and undermine Kieran and his syndicate before they cause more damage."

Tristan nodded. "I agree." He flipped to the Grimoire's index in hopes Blanchett had a section detailing her quest for a cure. He grumbled when he found nothing of that sort.

Zombia tugged at her sleeve. "Cerys was right. Blanchett hasn't written a cure in here."

Tristan almost closed the Grimoire when he found a few extra pages behind the index. Looking through them, he found a bunch of Blanchett's notes. His heart sank deeper when he discovered a note. A letter from the High Wizard written to Tristan's father and mother.

*Dear Archibald and Ulna,*

*As I finish this Grimoire, I am disheartened to say I have yet to find a cure for the zombie virus. The Cadre is close to invading the Crimson Citadel, so I am forced to gather my apprentices and go into hiding. Though I must remain inconspicuous, I can assure you, I won't rest until I find a cure. Please stay in contact with me and prepare my next generation of wizards. If anything happens to me, please continue my research and use the notes in my journal and this Grimoire as guides.*

*Hope is light in the darkness,*

*Ashley Blanchett*

At the end of Blanchett's missive, Tristan looked to Zombia, his mind reeling. *My parents were told to continue the search?*

"Luckily, Blanchett is still alive," Zombia said with a small, confident smile. "And she has an elixir according to Cerys. Once we cure Emerson, we can cure the world."

"Doing so would be easier without the Cadre around," said Tristan. He closed the Grimoire and shook his head. "Kieran will do anything to impede the elixir's distribution. With him and his crew around, magic is as good as extinct."

Tristan rose to his feet and shoved the Grimoire in his satchel. It was sort of funny that this lexicon had access to every spell and potion in the Haunted Lands but no cure for the zombie virus. No one else in the world had a cure either. He read history books in the library about the Cadre "developing" a cure. After witnessing Kieran having zombies in his employ, Tristan knew the history book was a fabrication. The Cadre wasn't looking for a cure.

Not only that, but the Cadre banning magic had impacted the Apocalypse for the worse. Even if Blanchett found a cure, allocation was a whole other story.

Magic was how Blanchett protected herself and her people during the First Apocalypse War.

Magic was how Tristan and his friends defeated Malice.

Magic may perhaps be the only way to save Emerson.

Without magic, the zombie population would only increase.

Tristan whispered a prayer of gratitude to the gods when he and his friends could finally ride on dragonback again. The fresh air blew through his hair, and thanks to the goggles, no bugs splattered into his eyes. Green pines, which Tristan learned made up the Gravestone Woods, flew by beneath them in a green blur.

For a portion of the ride, Tristan had been immersed in a conversation with Shadowstalker. In fact, he'd been so immersed Tristan lost track of time and his surroundings. He listened as Shadowstalker relayed tales of historic dragons and an insight into life in the Dragon Isles.

Though Shadowstalker wasn't looking at him, the dragon spoke to him.

*What's on your mind, Tristan?*

*I want answers, Shadowstalker,* Tristan responded. *I want to know if Blanchett truly has a cure to the zombie infection. Why the Cadre has zombies and who Kieran is working for. What the Cadre's true intentions are for the Haunted Lands and their motives behind them. When is Malice returning? I want to understand what's going on and how we can end the Apocalypse.*

The dragon nodded. *I know how you feel. Though the Cadre has never invaded the Dragon Isles, that doesn't stop me from wondering why they want to eradicate magic. What good would that do? Why can't we return to the time where all tribes lived in harmony?*

*I can understand the fear of evil magic. Look at the damage dark magic has done. Evil magic was how Malice nearly won the First War. The only way to stop evil magic is to ban it all together. But would that actually work? And what about beneficial magic? Kieran refuses to acknowledge its existence. Magic that can heal people, save people. I feel magic is the only cure to the zombie virus.*

A sigh left Tristan as he stared wistfully into the trees ahead. *Banning magic can only go so far. If someone's desperate enough, they'll find a way to practice dark magic.*

*Think about it this way: people get in horse and chariot crashes all the time, yet they're necessary for travel,* Shadowstalker offered. *Fire can kill, but other than the sun, it's our only source of light. Everything in the world has positives and negatives, including magic. When used properly, magic saves; when used improperly, it kills.* The dragon flew through a cloud, cold moisture clung to Tristan's cloak. *We shouldn't stop using helpful things because of the consequences they hold when used improperly. The world needs a cure. The world needs healing and other forms of light magic to end the Apocalypse and return to good rapport and peace once more.*

Tristan nodded. *I hate to say this, but I don't think the Cadre wants peace. I think they want power. Eradicating magic isn't about safety. They want to eliminate their competition.*

Shadowstalker's large head bobbed up and down. *I believe that, too. Blanchett should have the answers you're looking for. She's described as a wise, competent leader in the elven archives. After Emerson's cured, we'll work on ending the Cadre's reign.*

Tristan's brows rose, eyes lighting up. *You're going to help us?*

Part of him hadn't expected the dragon to help him beyond saving Emerson. He understood Shadowstalker and Faye had political dilemmas of their own.

*That's what friends do. They support each other, lift each other up, fight through ordeals together.*

Friends were rays of joy in this new dismal world.

The trees began thinning out as crisp, white rock peeked through them. Soon, Shadowstalker hovered over the White-Talon Range. Clouds encircled towering peaks as thunder rumbled in the distance, heralding a storm. A chilly breeze caressed Tristan's cheeks.

Tristan smiled at the dragon; his heart felt lighter. A voice that wasn't Shadowstalker's pierced his thoughts.

"Blanchett lives beneath the peaks," Cerys shouted over the howling wind, pointing her small finger toward the snow-capped mountains. "Perfect hiding place, isn't it?"

Tristan broke from his conversation and stared

at the mountains, eyes wide and mouth slack. When they were at the Crimson Citadel, he thought the ancient wizards did a fantastic job, marking them as expert craftsmen. But these mountains were crafted by nature's hand. Tristan didn't even notice Shadowstalker bank; he was too dazzled by the blinding, white peaks.

The dragon perched himself on a flat ledge overlooking the forest below. Faye hopped off Shadowstalker's back with ease. One by one, she helped the rest of her friends down. Tristan was grateful when his feet hit the ground. No matter how many dragons he flew on, he would always prefer a chariot, horseback, or walking. The king was built for land; elves and dragons were built for the sky.

"So Blanchett lives behind these mountains?" asked Faye as she rubbed Shadowstalker's scales.

The mage tucked a loose strand of brown hair behind her ear. "No. She lives beneath these mountains. With the Cadre and people turning their backs on her, the only safe place left for Blanchett was underground."

"Do they still get sunlight?" asked Zombia; she recoiled slightly. "I'd hate to be deprived of sunshine. Zombie would have nowhere to grow his flowers."

"Luckily, the Cadre doesn't venture through

the mountains very often. Blanchett can even practice outside sometimes. But she doesn't risk it often."

Tristan glanced at his feet. He couldn't imagine being sequestered underground, shielded from the world outside, all due to a magic-hating faction. He balled his hands into fists, shaking with anger and disgruntlement.

Cerys looked up from her map. "Let's go this way."

The mage led Tristan and his friends along the

mountainside; her hand traced the stony wall as though she was feeling for something. The rock was entirely smooth, and so was the ground; no markings were willing to divulge Blanchett's whereabouts.

*A secret door, perhaps?*

Cerys breathed in and whispered another incantation. When the rune materialized over the mage's wand. Tristan tilted his head quizzically. It was a rune he'd never seen before, and it was overly complex—so complex, surely it was known by few.

"That's a cool rune!" said Tibia. She peered over Tristan's broad shoulders. "I don't think you've taught us that one."

"I didn't," Cerys responded. The rune hovered over Tristan's head. Sadness washed over her face. "Since the war and Malice betraying her, Blanchett reserved this rune for her closest mages so only they could enter her new location." Even if Tristan wanted to break into the High Wizard's home, the rune was so complex that he didn't think he'd remember it to do so.

Excitement suffused Tristan. Since the beginning of this journey, well before that, he wondered what type of person Blanchett was. The books he and Tibia's tutors read all defamed the High Wizard, claiming she was a power fiend. But, for some reason, he never agreed with that. He felt there was more to her story. Yes, he did know some magic-wielders were driven by their powers, which made Tristan weary sometimes, but his curiosity was stronger than his fear.

Cerys paused in front of the smooth cliff face, holding the rune up with her wand. "Once I place this rune on the stone, a portal will open up."

"Um...none of the zombies know that rune, right?" asked Tibia. Her enchanted crossbow was already in her hands, locked and loaded. Tristan reached for his bow, his chest tightened. It wasn't fresh mountain air Tristan smelled; he smelled filthy clothing, rotting flesh, and blood.

Cerys's face blanched. "Why do you ask?"

"We've got company."

# Chapter Seventeen

The sight of Zokar and his undead army embedded ice into Tristan's spine. They emerged from a slightly higher cliff across from the wizards. A rocky bridge connected both cliffs, creating a pathway for Tristan's enemies. *Terrific. Just terrific,* thought Tristan.

He saw Faye remount Shadowstalker while Tibia had pulled Karneleth's staff from her back. *Good, we'll be needing it.*

He recognized Zokar and Marcus immediately, but didn't recognize the three white-robed women within the cluster of green. Not at first. Suddenly, a memory surfaced in his head. His eyes fell on the sorceresses' hats. *We're in sorcerer territory.* Tristan's knees locked, and a freezing sensation rolled over him, much colder than the climate warranted. *Zokar and Marcus are trying to bring Malice back. Dear gods, we have less time than I thought.* The zombie king peered down at Tristan from the cliff. Tristan pulled his bow from his back and nocked an arrow, stopping on the path mere feet from his adversaries.

"You've made my job easy; I get to kill you without invading Skeletonia." Zokar stuck his index finger through the pommel in his knife and twirled it confidently. "It seems as if fate has sided with the zombies." Zokar stared at his foe with eager eyes—eager to bite Tristan and turn him into one of the walking dead.

Tristan stood his ground. He fired an arrow at Zokar's forehead, but it never touched its target. The sorceress with the fanciest hat whispered a spell that touched the arrow and set it ablaze. Ashes fell harmlessly on Zokar's boots. The three sorceresses eyed Tristan, not so much with hatred but with interest. Like they could use a wizard like him and his friends. Drain their magic and use it for their own nefarious purposes.

"I'm tired of your petty games," said the zombie king. "When will you learn black magic always prevails?"

"We defeated you once," said Tibia. She brought her crossbow level with Zokar's head. "We'll do it again."

"Don't waste your breath, little wizard," said Zokar. "With the Silver Flame Tribe on our side, you'll be lucky to see tomorrow's dawn."

A plan didn't even form in Tristan's mind. Footsteps and crunching gravel resonated off every rocky wall. Green shapes wrapped in metal approached. Tristan's heart sank. At least a hundred zombies, clad in armor and wielding various weapons, rounded the cliffside corner.

The zombies leaped off the peak toward the king and his friends, landing clumsily but on their feet—while some did miscalculate their steps and tumbled over the edge, it did little to diminish their numbers. Tibia and Zombia fought back to back. The sharp blade of Zombia's glaive sliced through zombies with ease. A fire rune lit the blade, burning those who got too close. Tibia used Karneleth's staff to trick the monsters into tossing themselves over the cliff's edge. Their panicked screams echoed through the air.

Shadowstalker leaped over Tristan's head, his massive form momentarily eclipsing the sun, and landed with a jarring thud. Rearing back, he breathed. Hot orange flames burst from his mouth, sending a good portion of the zombies running. He whacked another handful of zombies off the ledge with his massive tail. Pivoting on his hind legs, he swatted another handful with his massive talons. More fire spewed from his mouth, lighting zombies up like little green torches. The scent of burnt flesh wafted in the air, making Tristan want to gag, but there was no time. Spinning on his heels, Shadowstalker whacked another group of zombies over the cliffside with his mighty tail.

A rune flitted from Zokar's palm, and a golden shield formed in his hand. Effortlessly, he blocked Shadowstalker's attacks. Marcus wasn't so fortunate. While Zokar deflected Shadowstalker's flames with his magic shield, the second-in-command had to rely on ducking and dodging. Disgust rolled through Tristan when he saw Zokar shove Marcus in the flame's trajectory to save himself. The zombie captain was quick on his feet but not quick enough. Fire grazed Marcus's leg, burning through his armor and clothes, leaving nasty charred and blistered skin. A pained cry tore out of him, to which Zokar paid no attention.

Tristan couldn't help but feel bad for the second-in-command. He always felt sorry for his enemies, but Tristan especially felt sorry for Marcus. *I don't know why he saved Zombia at the Hall of Black Mirrors, but I hope it was out of genuine goodness.*

Pivoting, Marcus fled from Shadowstalker's path. Shadowstalker continued sending volleys of flames at Marcus for good measure, beating his wings as he homed in on his adversary at breakneck speed. Marcus winced as he limped. He managed a few steps before collapsing; his bow clattered against stone, inches out of reach. Seeing his enemy was immobile, Shadowstalker redirected his anger at the offending sorceresses and zombies.

Tristan's heart wrenched watching Marcus attempt to stand. Learning about dragon fire opened Tristan's eyes to how deadly it was. Zombies stormed past Marcus to attack Shadowstalker and Faye. Not a single one offered to aid him; Tristan's blood boiled, appalled. *Zombies are so selfish.*

Looking left and right, Tristan began making his way over to the injured captain but halted when he saw Zombia was already there. She didn't smile as she placed a gentle hand on Marcus's wound. Tristan watched in awe as a golden ribbon of magic swathed Marcus's lower leg, healing the damaged skin and repairing charred nerves. The light vanished as quickly as it appeared.

Next, Zombia whispered something into Marcus's ear; the captain nodded and fled with his injuries healed.

*That was a dangerous move, Zombia,* thought Tristan. *We still don't know Marcus's motives, and she risked her life to help him? It's fortuitous that he didn't kill her. What did she whisper to him?* A moment later and the king's emotions softened. *The sooner this war could end, the better.*

Tristan pulled himself from his thoughts and turned to Cerys, who was holding off the sorceresses with a shimmering gold barrier. "How quickly can you open the doorway?"

"Pretty quickly. I already have the rune; I just need to place it and complete the incantation." The mage didn't face her friend as the lead sorceress, the one with rose quartz on her hat, blasted Cerys with crimson fire. The flames pounded on the magic barrier, luckily to no avail.

"We'll hold them off. You open the portal."

Tristan didn't wait to hear Cerys's response. Zokar stood across the cliffside, his deep red eyes filled with unfathomable hatred—hatred not just for the king but for anything that dared to draw breath.

"Let's finish what we've started, shall we?" Zokar

called. "Speaking of, how do you like the gift I gave your friend?"

Tristan's rage simmered; his fists ached to punch through Zokar's skull. Usually, violence turned Tristan's stomach, but this was the zombie king. That heartless monster doomed his friend to an eternity of being a zombie. He didn't respond. What would he say? A harsh name formed in Tristan's mind, but he didn't utter it. It wouldn't change the ramifications of the zombie king's actions.

"Thanks to my black magic, your knight will turn in no time!" Zokar charged for Tristan, but the king jumped out of the way in time. Midair, Tristan shifted to his skeleton form. His pale flesh melted away, leaving crisp white bone behind. This caused Zokar to roll his eyes.

"Still a foolish wizard you are," he said. "When are you going to learn shifting won't save you?"

The zombie king charged with supernatural speed. It was a pace that Tristan had never seen a zombie accomplish without tripping over their own feet. His blade narrowly missed the king's face. In close combat, Tristan switched his bow into a sword and brought it up in time to parry and clash against Zokar's. A loud clang bounced off rigid cliff faces.

Tristan glanced from Zokar to Cerys, who was preoccupied with opening the gateway. *We just have to hold them off, jump through the gateway, and close it.*

One of the sorceresses—a redheaded girl—emerged from the crowd of zombies, her eyes presumably searching for the king. Her staff was raised. The bloodstone on top glowed an angry purple; bolts of violet crackled over the sphere, pulsing with lethal power. Tristan whispered *Multiplicare*, then pointed behind the sorceress. A clone appeared behind her, bow in hand. An exact Tristan duplicate. Tristan's muscles relaxed when he saw the sorceress pivot and pursue his clone rather than him. He could focus on Zokar.

Then he remembered in his lessons, back in Skeletonia, with Cerys, she had taught Tristan the same paralysis spell Malice had used. Initially, he thought Cerys was teaching him black magic, but she reassured him it wasn't. It was self-defense magic. He whispered the incantation and threw it at the zombie king. It touched him, coating him in the same sickly orange sheen it had for him. Zokar froze in his tracks, his arms and legs stopping mid-stride. The zombie king was frozen in place as though he had been encased in ice.

Tristan breathed a sigh of relief; the spell had worked.

Tristan sprinted to Cerys's side. The complex rune lay at her feet, glowing and vibrating the ground. Seconds later, a crack formed between her feet and snaked ahead of her and up the cliff face. The rock split open, revealing a secret passage. Golden light spilled from it, lighting up its surroundings.

"Go through, now!" shouted Cerys. Then, a wave of blue light enveloped the mage, dragging her to her feet. Her wand flew from her grasp as a hard, jagged stone rushed up to meet her. Blood trickled from her nose after smashing face-first into the ground. Tristan whipped his head around to see one of the sorceresses— the one with the ostentatious wizard hat—controlling the magic bound to Cerys.

Acting quickly, Tristan switched his sword into a bow and fired. The glistening projectile sliced through the air and struck the sorceress in the stomach. Crying out, she collapsed and loosened her enchanted bonds. Tristan offered the mage his hand. After grabbing her wand, both she and the king darted for the glowing portal.

Shadowstalker swatted at a trio of unfortunate zombies, then, together, both rider and dragon charged for the portal and slipped through.

Zombia slashed a zombie's throat, spun on her heels, and darted for the opening. Behind her, Tibia was cornered by three tall and robust zombies wielding hatchets. Before Tristan could fire an arrow, Zombia gripped her glaive in one hand, wrote the rune for earth, and flung the rune to the ground.

Large, sharp pieces of earth jutted up between Tibia and the zombies, each rock embedding itself in the monsters' chests. The zombies sat in the air, impaled on jagged pieces of mountain. Still holding her magic, Zombia shouted, "RUN!"

Tibia darted toward the portal, and at the same time, the monsters pried themselves off the rocks, charging at her with gaping wounds. They ran as though the wounds weren't present at all. A wall of fire blasted the zombies, courtesy of Shadowstalker. Screams cut through the air like a sharpened blade, slicing through Tristan's soul. *I hate this violence.*

The king briefly locked eyes with Zombia; her baffled expression matched his. *I think her magic is improving faster than she knows.*

Zombia and Tibia sprinted past Tristan.

"Let's go!" Zombia said, gripping his wrist. Tristan barely got a foot in the portal when something wrapped around his waist, yanking him to the ground and toward his assailant; his sword clattered to the ground.

"Tristan!" shouted Tibia.

Over his shoulder, he saw an elf sorceress gripping an incandescent blue chain, pulling him farther from his destination. Dirt scraped his armor and bones, making a dull screech. A second later, a flash of purple washed over Tristan as his skeleton form faded, and he returned to his human form. *Stupid reverse spell. If I'm going to maintain my skeleton form, I need to get better at blocking these reverse spells.*

"Get away from my brother, magic menace!" A bolt leaped from her crossbow and struck the sorceress in the stomach. She cried out as red blossomed over her white robe. The chains loosened and vanished as being wounded severed the sorceress's magic. At the same time, a blade whizzed through the air and embedded itself into Tristan's bicep. He sucked in a breath as pain raced down his arm and out his fingers. Hot tears threatened to fall, but Tristan gritted his teeth through the agony. A second later, the blade, as though it had a mind of its own, wrenched itself free and returned to its sender: Zokar.

To his horror, the king realized the blade was meant for his heart. *Thank the gods for the zombie's poor aim.* Even with magic, zombies' movements were still cumbersome and imprecise. Wincing again, Tristan shot a dagger of magic at the zombie king. He didn't wait to see if the blade hit its target.

Tristan wrote a cyan rune in the sky. Within seconds, his surroundings became shrouded in a thick fog. It was so thick that Tristan could barely make out the shapes of the zombies and sorceresses. That was all he needed. As long as his enemies couldn't see through it, they couldn't see them escape.

"Let's go!" Tibia shouted. Lifting her brother under one arm, Tibia helped Tristan to his feet, retrieved his sword, and together, they entered the gateway. Safe from danger...for now.

# Chapter Eighteen

Granite doors slammed shut, enclosing the king and his friends safely. The entire place was dark. The passage was cool, damp, and the air smelled of mineral springs with a touch of sulfur. But the amount of magic Tristan had used made him feel like he had sprinted through the desert. All he heard was a faint drip-drop of water in the distance and their echoing footsteps.

There was a sudden whoosh, and a flame burst to life, hovering in front of Shadowstalker's mouth. A tiny torch in a vast ocean of blackness. Judging by the downward slope of the floor, Tristan could tell the passage took them deeper into the earth. A distant growling echoed in his ears. He heard Zokar's faint cursing in the background, which too, slowly faded.

*We must be actually under the White-Talon Range,* Tristan thought in awe.

With low light, Tristan assessed his wounds. A short but slender knife wound stared back at him, making him hiss at how grotesque it was. Each step sent a sharp pain through Tristan's shoulder and arm. Warm blood trickled with every step. He sacrificed some of his kilt's hem to stop the bleeding; luckily they where shrouded in semi-darkness. He didn't want his friends to make a big deal of his wound. Emerson was the top priority.

"Just down this tunnel will lead us to Aramore," said Cerys. Her skin had a pale complexion; sweat coated her forehead and stained her collar.

Tristan placed a hand on her shoulder. "Are you okay? That was a lot of magic you used back there."

The mage huffed out a breath and nodded. "Nothing a good night's sleep can't fix. Those sorceresses know how to put up a fight."

Zombia glanced over her shoulder as though she were expecting the zombies to pop out of the foreboding darkness. Her consternation matched Tristan's in every way. "Who were those women back there?"

"The Silver Flame Tribe," answered Cerys. How the shadows fell over her face made her statement all the more ominous. A wicked bruise formed on her nose, but at least the bleeding stopped, thanks to Zombia.

"Why do the zombies need the Silver Flame

Tribe?" Tristan echoed, his voice imbued with an inquiry. The king had only heard about the sorcerer tribes once it was during one of the nights when his parents would tell him and Tibia a little magic-wielder history before bed. They kept the information sparse, likely not wanting to give away too much information with so many ears in the castle. Beyond learning of each tribe's unique powers, Tristan's knowledge on them was next to nil.

"Like the elves, all the sorcerer tribes were at war over who'd rule over all three tribes," Faye explained. "Except, they didn't cease fire to stop the zombies. The tribes lived in harmony in a triumvirate for years. After Cressida Moonwatcher died, turmoil followed. Meredith Argent, head of the Silver Flame Tribe, wished to destroy the triumvirate in exchange for her own authoritarian rule. Now, all three tribes are locked in a civil war." Faye shook her head. "How do people not realize the zombies are the ultimate threat?" She rode on Shadowstalker's back. The dragon's wings scraped against the ceiling, knocking some of the formations loose. He quickly pulled his wings in at his sides as he ducked his head down. Shadowstalker's discontented face said it all. Dragons don't belong in cramped spaces, he telepathically told Tristan. And he had to agree.

Tibia huffed and shot Faye a sarcastic grin. "Great, so now we have sorceresses, demons, the Cadre, and zombies hunting us. This just gets better and better. Let me guess, three headed gryffins are next?"

*Harmony is elusive these days,* Shadowstalker said to Tristan. *Too bad. While learning magic and spells helps, it's through harmony that those aspects will actually manifest and be successful.*

The king nodded though the darkness wouldn't allow his friends to see he did. Tristan thought about all the wars between tribes. All the wasted resources and casualties. People seemed more interested in warring over land and valuables rather than the growing number of the undead. At this rate, the Apocalypse would never end.

Cerys rubbed her head. "Blanchett taught me that the Silver Flame Tribe sought dark powers to win the land—the powers of the Shadowbloods. They can reach dimensions wizards can't and are the most powerful out of the three sorceress tribes. They can free Malice."

"And that's why the zombies were with them." Tibia finished Cerys's sentence. The mage nodded and frowned.

Tristan had only read about the sorcerer tribes once, and it was during his tutoring. It wasn't much, and his parents never discussed it, likely not wanting to give away too much information with so many ears in the castle.

Tibia was more fascinated by them, though. He never was, not as much as his sister. He knew the Silver Flame Tribe tried claiming the Blue Moon throne, but other than that, he wasn't aware of the Silver Flame's macabre abilities. Tristan caught his foot on a rock, knocking him off-kilter. Pain flashed down his arm once more, drawing out an agonized grunt.

"Were you wounded?" Zombia asked. Light from Shadowstalker's flame showed Zombia's brows were pulled together, her lips turned down in a concerned frown.

"It's nothing," Tristan said, sucking in a sharp breath. Gods above, it hurt. "Let's find Blanchett, okay?"

Zombia's lips thinned. "I don't believe you; I'm taking a look when we're in proper lighting."

Tristan just nodded. Not only was his skin on fire right now, but the idea of Zokar enlisting help from other magic-wielders was also enough to send his nerves into a frenzy. *But I don't need to worry my friends with my mild injuries.*

*What other magic-wielding societies are out there? I barely knew about the Silver Flame, and Zokar and his army are already persuading them to free Malice.*

Tristan suppressed a shudder. Zombies gaining access to magic was the worst thing to happen to the Haunted Lands. They were already dangerous. With magic, the undead were indomitable.

"I didn't think they'd simply join Zokar's forces. No one likes working with zombies," Zombia said. "Why would they?"

"The sorceresses must have something to gain from the collaboration," Tibia said, materializing behind Tristan. Her black leather armor allowed her to melt with the shadows. With her hair equally as dark, only her pale face showed. It looked as though her face was floating in midair, completely disconnected from her body.

Tristan pined over Zombia's question. Until gaining magic, the zombies were pretty inferior to those with magic. In those moments of thought, Tristan listened to his footsteps echo off the cavern walls. Then, a possibility dawned on him, sending terror through him like taking a dip in a frigid lake. "With Malice being trapped in the Otherworld places the zombies and the sorceresses in the same predicament. Though collaborating with the undead would be less than fun, the sorceresses might endure their antics long enough to set Malice free and use her dark powers to finish what they started."

"I'm sure Zokar has his own plans as well; he'll use the sorceresses' magic for himself," Zombia said. She made a face, which Shadowstalker's flame caught. "He'd turn the Silver Flame Tribe into pawns in his own game."

Tibia huffed out a sigh. "As much as I hate admitting it, I gotta give the zombies some credit. They don't know when to quit. Personally, that's a trait I admire."

"Tenacity can be both a curse and blessing," Tristan said with a snort. "It can build an empire or destroy a nation; it depends on how you use it." He said the last part more seriously. "I know the zombies aren't using it for good."

The tunnel widened as the ground began to level out. Light spilled from ahead. *Is that the sun?* Tristan asked himself. *How can that be? Isn't Blanchett's new home underground?* The tunnel's end drew closer until the wizard apprentices entered an enormous cavern—large enough for a castle and a city. The dragon extinguished his flame. Shadowstalker shook out his wings and smiled, his scaly cheeks dimpling.

Those lights Tristan thought were the sun turned out to be issuing from the thousands of oil lamps erected through the bustling streets. The city had a simple, organized grid layout with buildings stacked elaborately on top of each other. This place looked like the Crimson Citadel's motte and bailey, except everything was composed of flowstone and limestone. Surrounding the city was a large forest and river.

Tristan raised an eyebrow. *How can trees survive down here? Magic maybe?*

Stalactites hung from the ceiling, glimmering like an earth-crafted chandelier. The flowers reminded Tristan of his best friend, Zombie.

*I feel bad I can't tell him about our magic. I wonder if Zombia feels the same.*

"Welcome to Aramore, Blanchett's relocated city of magic," Cerys said proudly, puffing her chest and smiling.

The opening spilled into a wide flagstone street leading to the heart of the city. Despite being a subterranean dwelling, the place was abuzz with life and luminosity.

"I knew you were wounded." Zombia's voice was sharp with concern, so sharp it startled Tristan a little.

Tristan held up his arm for his friend to see. Horror fell across their faces. A makeshift bandage, made from his kilt, encircled his bicep, decorated with a splotch of dried blood. Tristan heard Zombia suck in a breath.

"Zokar got me with his dagger," said Tristan. He unraveled the bandage, unveiling a two-inch slit. "The blade went clean through."

Zombia placed her hands around the wound. "I'll heal it."

"No, your magic is already low," said Tristan. He hissed in pain again. "I just need some kind of poultice." Sweat clung to Zombia's hair and clothes, and though she appeared fatigued, she was willing to sacrifice her energy to heal him. Tristan's face heated as he grinned. *What would I do without a friend like her? Honestly, the world would be a better place if there were more altruistic people like Zombia.*

"Let's get to Blanchett, then deal with my wound." The king sucked in another breath and continued down the city streets.

Tristan and his friends merged into a sea of garish robes and armor. Tristan looked left and right, mouth agape at the throng of magic-wielders. The streets and marketplace were an array of multicolored tents where people bartered and conversed. Staffs, potions, wands, and tomes containing cryptic spells were set on display, each one catching Tristan's curious eye. These stands carried everything necessary for a witch, warlock, mage, or wizard. People furiously scribbled away in their ledger books as brass scales overflowed with diamonds. Successful business.

The aftermath of spells and enchantments pulsed through the air. He listened to the jangling of potions and keys hanging from belts, satchels, and hats. The flagstone roads teemed with magic-wielders of every kind—a few zombies, skeletons, and people. But as Tristan expected, a majority of them were elves. With the elves were their corresponding dragons. The place was packed with white, black, and blue scales. Tristan noticed there weren't any Firebournes or wyverns; that made sense. They dwelt in the Underworld.

Shadowstalker walked proudly, chest out, with Faye mounted on his back. A few of the elves and dragons greeted the duo with toothy smiles.

However, an odd group passed by drawing the king's attention. They resembled Shadowstalker, except they were smaller and walked upright. A dragon's spiked tail swished behind them, complemented with wings protruding from their backs beneath vibrant cloaks. Tristan stared at their clawed feet, and he quickly turned his gaze down when he thought the creatures sensed his presence.

Through all his years of tutoring, Tristan learned about all the fascinating creatures living in the Haunted Lands—of course, elves were painted as evil due to their intrinsic powers. As he was jostled around by magic-wielders, he sifted through his mind to recall what these anthropomorphic dragon creatures were.

A low grumble drew Tristan's attention to a grumpy dragon-elf. His scales were a dark forest green, peppered with flecks of gold. His eyes narrowed on Tristan before he turned and continued his slouched gait, his spiked tail flitting back and forth.

The king spun around and continued on the path to Blanchett's fortress.

"Come on, Tristan, it's not polite to stare," said Tibia playfully. Tibia smirked at her brother. "And you call me the rude one."

"Sorry, but I've never seen an...elf like them before," replied Tristan. His cheeks heated. He turned to find Zombia, who gave the dragon-elf a glance and then looked back at her friend, sharing the same inquisitive glance.

"Who are they?" asked Zombia.

"Demi-dragons. They're a subspecies of dragons," Cerys explained, pushing through the magic-wielders. "I'll explain more later; we need to get to Blanchett."

Tristan itched to ask more, but their mentor was already ahead of the group, walking as fast as her legs could carry her. He frowned, thinking about Emerson. Cerys was right; the longer they dithered, the further Emerson slipped away, further into zombieism. Zombia must have sensed the king's unrest because she grabbed Tristan's hand and squeezed gently. Instantly, his heart felt lighter as they made it to Blanchett's fortress. *Maybe we will save Emerson.* New hope blossomed in the hollow space in the king's chest.

In a way, Tristan felt foreign, but at the same time, it felt like home. It felt like he belonged. Pulses magically charged through Tristan's limbs; it was as though he felt each of these individuals' magic. Children played on the sidewalks, pointing their wands at random objects. A pile of apples exploded in a shower of croaking frogs, while another wizard's brown hound morphed into a hound covered in black and white stripes.

Tristan couldn't help the jittery feeling bubbling inside as he attempted not to stare. These kids ran around using their magic without a care in the world. *What was it like using magic freely? What was it like living in a place where you didn't have to worry about zombies or the Cadre?* If he'd been born here, in Aramore, Tristan would be as skilled with magic as he was with a bow. He and Tibia would have been able to speak freely about magic.

By the time they were halfway through the city, Tristan had immersed himself so deeply in his thoughts that he crashed into Zombia. He followed his friend's gob-smacked gaze and found himself standing before a large portcullis. Through the gatehouse loomed a white marble fortress.

# Chapter Nineteen

Breath fled Tristan's lungs as he beheld the most beautiful structure he'd ever seen. He couldn't tear his eyes from the fortress until he made it through the stockade. Soldiers in decorative bronze and steel armor marched along the ramparts and inside the gates. Even the guards looked like they had a touch of magic. They didn't carry swords or spears; they carried staffs. Tristan felt the weight of his enchanted bow on his back and pondered if the soldier's staff could transform into weapons like his.

Cerys stepped forward, her chin held high. The guards, having recognized her face, opened the portcullis a few moments later, revealing a courtyard packed with guards and courtiers. It was nearly unfathomable to see so many magic-wielders in a single area. Tristan saw the obelisk Cerys mentioned on their last adventure. From what he remembered, this obelisk boasted a litany of the wizards who perished in the First Apocalypse War.

It was a large white marble structure, prominent against a black-tiled floor. A lump formed in his throat as he approached it. Sure enough, he found what he expected. The inscription on the base said:

*Here's to our fallen wizards. Thank you for fighting valiantly.*

Fresh tears welled in Tristan's eyes. He found his parents' names.

## *ARCHIBALD & ULNA SKELETON*

Tristan bowed his head, stealing himself a moment of silence for his parents and those murdered by Malice's hand. *The Haunted Lands will be saved.* When the king opened his eyes, he realized his fists were clenched. Wiping his eyes, Tristan found Tibia and Zombia behind him. Their heads were bowed—well, Tibia looked ready to throttle someone.

"Malice will pay for this," Tibia grumbled. She locked eyes with her brother, and they softened. She grabbed his hand, squeezing briefly. More tears tumbled down his cheeks while he tried to swallow the ache in his throat. Tibia was the only family he had left. And family and friends were what one needed in these dire times.

A hand rested on the king's shoulder.

"I'm sorry for your loss," said Faye. Tristan faced her. The Dragonblood's amethyst eyes beamed with sympathy. "We've all lost too many good people in the Apocalypse. But you can change that; the Apocalypse can end."

Tristan inclined his head. He appreciated the sentiment but wasn't sure he could form a reply.

"Are you here to see the High Wizard?"

The wizards turned. One of the guards—an Iceblood elf boy—approached and greeted Cerys.

Tristan nodded. "We are; we need an elixir."

The elf boy gestured toward the fortress's entrance. "Please, come inside."

His ice-blue eyes fell on Tristan, traveled to Zombia, and landed on Tibia. The elf stared, not in ire or distaste but rather curiosity and disbelief.

Tristan had been to the Dragon Isles for solstice parties and witnessed diplomatic meetings, but of course, Faye never took him outside of Castle Elandorr. But these meetings allowed Tristan to see both Iceblood and Moonblood elves. No matter how many times he'd seen them, these pale-blue elves with frosty hair would forever fascinate him. The king and his companions offered the elf genuine smiles.

Casually, the elf led the group through the limestone pillared courtyard, up the stone stairs, and into a massive throne room. A balcony wrapped around the room, with two staircases leading to the second story. Rooms lined the walls, wrapping around like the balcony. A chandelier made of gold hung from the vaulted ceiling, diamonds and rubies sparkling. Doorways lead to deeper parts of the castle, most of them cordoned off by guards wearing burgundy robes underneath crystalline armor. Hanging from the balcony, were crimson banners bearing the High Wizard's crest: a garnet flanked by two inward-facing dragon heads.

The court swarmed with conversation as more magic-wielders, all very young, milled about. Some cast spells with their wands, others carried long staffs, pointing them into the air and shouting in the ancient language to vault runes across the room. Surprisingly, the magic-wielders in Aramore included a few zombies. So far, Zombia and Zokar were the only magic zombies he'd met. The tenseness in his shoulders abated, and he was glad there weren't too many undead who possessed lethal powers.

Runes of all colors flitted about, catching Tristan's

eye. Demi-dragons—as Cerys had called them—and elves from all three clans darted around the room, making the air shimmer with magic. It was unusual to see so many magic-wielders roaming freely casting spells. But this was possible in a sequestered area that the Cadre had no idea existed.

A great eagerness swelled in his chest. *So this is where magic-wielders go to train? Never thought for a second that I'd witness it.*

"Wow," said Zombia, craning her neck and looking around. "This is phenomenal! I can't believe this is where we'll get to train!" She paused. "After we get Emerson a cure."

"Well, you can train anywhere, but here, in Blanchett's new home, is ideal," said Cerys. "It's good to be home."

The mage breathed a deep sigh, an unrestrained smile forming on her face. His friend's glee brought a smile to Tristan's own face.

*I don't think I've ever seen Cerys this happy. Though I've traveled far from home, I've always had my friends with me, or I returned home within a short period of time. But Cerys; this is her first time being home in months. In addition to the new territory, she's been away from Blanchett, the only motherly figure in her life since her real mother's death. Her sister must be here as well.*

A passel of magic-wielders ambled from one room to the next, each clutching heavy tomes and wearing large, floppy hats. Potions of multicolored liquids dangled from their belts and satchels, like Cerys had. Tristan waved at them. To his surprise, they returned the gesture, acting as though Tristan was a regular in Aramore.

*Cerys grew up free to practice magic. She could wake up in the morning and cast a rune summoning water from the river to wash her face. If she injured herself, she could find a healer within record time. She could devour all the magical tomes at her heart's desire without the impending fear of being caught. It was hard enough hiding Tibia's and my magic. But Cerys never had to hide hers until she left Aramore and met us. The outside world surely caused her much distress and homesickness.*

A sudden tightness formed in Tristan's shoulders and chest as a daunting thought struck him: *After retrieving Blanchett's elixir, will Cerys return to Skeletonia?*

*I can understand if she wants to stay here.* He watched the magic-wielders wandering joyfully through the courtyard. *They're her people. This is the life Cerys knows best and feels comfortable with. We'll miss her dearly, but if she chooses to stay here in Aramore, who am I to discourage her?*

Pulling himself from his thoughts, Tristan and his companions continued through the courtyard, magic thrumming through his veins like the metrical beat of military drums.

The looks Faye and Shadowstalker received were of reverence. Many young wizards and mages went up to pet the dragon, perhaps sharing a telepathic conversation. Tristan had expected to see more of Faye's tribe here. However, Dragonbloods learned their magic in the Dragon Isles, close to their reptilian familiars.

"Shadowstalker loves this place already," said Faye. Her tone was peppy, as usual, with an undercurrent of confidence.

A young girl emerged from a corridor on the left wall of the throne room. She wore a cerulean tabard with a belt of red and blue potions. The whole ensemble was offset with a black wide-brimmed hat with a band of the same color wrapped around it. Beside her was an Ice dragon, complete with pastel blue, almost white, scales. The girl held a lead attached to a leather harness wrapped around the dragon's body. When a group of children passed in front, the dragon stopped, forcing the girl to stop too, only resuming when the path was clear. When and wherever the dragon moved, the girl followed like a shadow.

"Hey, sis!" Cerys said.

*Sis?* thought Tristan. *This must be Ingrid.*

A huge grin covered the girl's face. She looked ready to bounce off the walls at any minute.

Tristan stifled a laugh. *Wow, she's got as much energy as Cameron.* What was odd was the fact Ingrid didn't look directly at the king or Cerys. She looked in their general direction, but not directly at them. The Ice dragon led Ingrid the several paces until she stood inches from the mage. That was when Tristan noticed she had the same shade of startling emerald-green eyes as Cerys, except Ingrid's eyes were milky and glazed over.

Cerys and Ingrid shared an embrace.

"It's so wonderful to have you back!" Ingrid said, nearly shouting. Ingrid's skin and hair were a few shades darker than her sister's; her hair was also straighter than Cerys's, cascading down her back like an obsidian waterfall. What captivated Tristan's eye the most was the numerous vials on her belt, each containing a different-colored liquid. Tiny bubbles floated around like little magic particles.

"It's wonderful to finally meet you, Ingrid," said Tristan.

Ingrid tilted her head. "Who'd you bring with you?"

The mage released her sister and turned to her apprentices. "These are the wizards I'm training."

"The Wizards of the Apocalypse, as we've decided to call ourselves," Tibia added with a smirk. Tristan had to admit, the name grew on him.

She turned back to the king. "And this is my sister and her guide dragon, Snowflake."

Zombia lifted a brow. "Guide dragon?"

"I was born blind," Ingrid said. "Luckily, Blanchett managed to adopt a dragon for me. I formed a bond with Snowflake, and now we do everything together." The girl reached up and patted Snowflake's snout, which Tristan imagined was tantamount to touching a frozen lake. "I've wanted to be a potion master since I was a child and she's been helping me."

*Another non-elven dragon bond,* thought Tristan with wonder. It was for a good cause. *Just like Shadowstalker healing me. With Snowflake's help, Ingrid's an even more powerful sorceress.*

One by one, Tristan, Zombia, Faye, and Tibia

reached out and shook Ingrid's hand. Snowflake looked at Tristan with pale-blue eyes. Shadowstalker turned to Snowflake, prominent brows raised in curiosity. Both dragons inclined their heads, and smelled, inhaling each other's scent like village hounds. They circled each other and locked eyes, their tails lashing and wings flaring. Shadowstalker was a whole two heads larger than Snowflake; the small Ice dragon only met his shoulders. Though they didn't speak outwardly, their facial expressions showed a telepathic conversation took place. At the end of it, both dragons concluded their greeting with smiles that flashed rows of sharp teeth.

Snowflake turned from Shadowstalker to Tristan. *It's an honor to finally meet Blanchett's new generation of wizards.* Her telepathic words swept against his mind.

"It's great meeting you too," responded Tristan.

"It's an honor to meet you, Ingrid," said Zombia. There was an undeniable eagerness in her voice. "Cerys has told us wonderful things about you."

"Do you really research and brew your own potions?" Faye asked eagerly.

Ingrid nodded, presenting a proud smile. "Indeed! Well, I research and write while Snowflake here does the pouring and mixing." The Ice dragon grinned.

"Blanchett also brought in wooden tablets with raised lettering so I could do potion and herb research! How generous!"

"Now if only you'd spend as much time studying for your tests as you do playing around with potions," Cerys said, nudging her sister in the side.

"Just like someone else I know," Tristan said, smirking at his sister. Tibia stuck her tongue at him, causing her brother to laugh. "It took forever for you to finish the assignments for our tutor."

"Hmph. I considered training for battle more important."

Ingrid made a face and said to Cerys, "I *do* my homework before the due date. Also Blanchett is still super proud of me keeping Aramore stocked with potions and elixirs."

Cerys just laughed. "Is Blanchett available?"

"Yes, she is! I'll take you to her quarters," shouted Ingrid. "Oh, you're just going to *love* this place!" She had a lot of pep in her voice, more than Cerys. Tristan could immediately guess Cerys was the student who stayed up late studying, and Ingrid was the one who'd rather dive headfirst into new assignments and visit with friends.

Ingrid led the group up the staircase to the right.

Shadowstalker's footsteps shook the stairs and the sconces rattled. He tucked his wings closer to stop himself from knocking any over. Once they spilled onto the balcony, the sorceress took a sharp left turn; Tristan listened to the muffled voices behind closed doors—magical students congregating for various classes. The balcony narrowed into twisting hallways. Arches supported by stone wyverns soared over Tristan's head. There were oak doors on each side of the corridor. Presumably, they had entered the dorm rooms where all the magic-wielders slept. The walls were adorned with murals of the war. Wizards battled zombies with volleys of vibrant magic. Dragons took to the skies, flecks of orange and red spewed from their mouths onto the undead masses. Tristan remembered seeing halls like this at the Crimson Citadel.

He wondered what the world was like before the war when magic thrived and the Cadre didn't exist—the times when people didn't fear magic. A tingle slithered down his spine.

Ingrid and Snowflake turned a sharp left and stopped outside a set of double oak doors. "Blanchett is in here. This is her study. I wonder if she cleaned up all the stray papers she leaves after every spell."

"I can for sure tell you it's nothing like your room, Ingrid," laughed Cerys.

The sorceress blushed and stamped her feet. "Hey, I have a lot to study for."

"You wouldn't have to study so much if you paid attention in class instead of folding parchment wyverns and passing notes."

Zombia, Faye, and Tristan laughed. He nudged Tibia in the ribs, meriting her irked look.

"I studied...for battle school. Oh, come on, that counts!" Tibia said in a heated tone.

The friends shared another laugh. Tristan had never once thought magic school would resemble a regular school in Skeletonia, and he always thought wizards would be more reserved and studious. Nope. Even magic-wielders could have a tendency for mischief, except with many more spells and grimoires to study.

"Well, I have a class to get to," said Ingrid, stroking her hair. "I'll meet you in the mess hall later, okay?"

"Sounds good," Cerys said, patting her sister on the shoulder. Ingrid tittered and, with Snowflake leading her, she vanished down the winding halls. The king turned to the High Wizard's door. Tristan adjusted his satchel's shoulder strap, feeling the Apocalypse

Grimoire's weight. Heavy with spells and responsibility. Sucking in a breath, Tristan rapped lightly on the door.

"Please, come in," called a soft. feminine voice. A chill laced through Tristan as he held his breath.

Shrugging, Tristan pushed the doors open, revealing a lowly lit room. A window provided a grand view of the wizard city. On the left side, books stacked the shelves; on the right side, shelves were stocked with scrolls, glass beakers, bottles, and vials. A desk sat in front of the window with parchment unfurled across it and an inkwell, feather inside. Tristan realized the dim orange glow emanated from the lone candelabra sitting on the desk's left corner.

And there, at the simple pine desk, sat the High Wizard.

# Chapter Twenty

Tristan's skin tingled, his posture stiffening as he decided whether to bow or not. Seeing the High Wizard made his knees weak. The legendary Ashley Blanchett was sitting before the king and his friends.

A sheet of parchment lay unfurled before the High Wizard. She held a quill, which stopped scratching when she looked up from her work. She appeared the same as she did when she first visited him in his dreams: blond hair dangling over one shoulder and youthful electric-blue eyes. Low torchlight glinted off the red garnets inlaid on a crown of gold. She wore blue crystal epaulets over flowing scarlet robes.

He never thought he'd meet the High Wizard in person. In a dream, it was wild enough, but in real life? He couldn't stop blinking.

"It's rude to stare," Tibia said, jabbing her brother in the shoulder, sending more pain from his wound lacing down his arm and out his fingers.

"It's an honor to meet you, your highness," Zombia said, dropping to one knee. Faye and Cerys followed suit.

Blushing, Tristan sank to one knee in deference. Tibia did so as well. Shadowstalker inclined his massive head, leaning down on his front legs. His wings brushed against the bookshelves; glass bottles clanked against one another. Luckily, none of them fell. Tristan swallowed back a snort.

There was a rustle of robes before Blanchett said, "Rise, my apprentices. I view everyone as equals. Titles are frivolous."

Her voice soothed Tristan's nerves like a warm summer breeze. He brought his gaze to Blanchett. Warmth spread through his chest. *She's a just and humble ruler. She's exactly the leader the Haunted Lands need.*

In unison, Tristan and his friends stood.

Blanchett grinned and bowed her head slightly, her platinum-blond tresses spilling over her shoulders. "It's an honor to finally meet you, my apprentices." The High Wizard turned to Cerys. She grabbed the mage's hand, like a loving mother. "Thank you for guiding them here."

A red tint blossomed on the mage's cheeks. "My pleasure."

Squeezing Cerys's hand one more time, Blanchett returned her gaze to her three wizards. The relationship between Cerys and Blanchett reminded Tristan of his rapport with his people. It was comforting to know the High Wizard wasn't an iron-fisted ruler.

Blanchett's face went soft when she faced Tibia and Tristan. "Your father and mother were two of my best wizards. I know you'll take up after them."

Blanchett turned to Zombia, who wrung her hands looking mortified. "And your mother was a powerful wizard, dear. In fact, it was her magic and leadership that brought so many demi-zombies into my army."

Red crept through Zombia's cheeks, her fingers now fiddling with her glaive's bandolier. "Thanks. But my magic isn't nearly as powerful as my mother's. In fact, I think I'm...weaker than Tristan and Tibia. But I try. I really do."

Blanchett squeezed Zombia's hands gently. "Every wizard has potential. Everyone has their own pace, and magic manifests in various ways and unique times. Don't compare yourself, young wizard."

Zombia lifted her chin, her hazel eyes shining. "Thank you for your confidence in me."

"We need your help," said Tristan. He shifted his feet, mortification flooding him like a river. He didn't mean to blurt that. But all the pent-up worry and fear concerning Emerson forced the words out in a less-than-eloquent way. "Our friend was bitten, and he needs a potion."

A pallid complexion settled over the High Wizard's face. Without another word, she reached behind her desk, grabbed her golden staff, and threw open her study door. Tristan and his friends followed her.

They followed Blanchett through a maze of hallways and archways, hastening to match her quick strides. Young magic-wielders wandered the halls. Each wore lavish robes with potions and vials belted to their waists. Books that Tristan knew the Cadre wouldn't approve of were clutched to the students' chests while they talked and laughed on their way to class. Everything about Aramore screamed magic. The people, the buildings, even the stone ravens bearing torches radiated mystery. Fire lit their intricately carved eyes. Tristan cringed when he thought one of the statues winked at him.

Tristan wondered what it would have been like to grow up here. If the Cadre wasn't around, would his parents have sent him and Tibia here? Though he wouldn't trade his childhood for anything, Tristan couldn't curb his curiosity. *Once we save Emerson and kill Malice, we'll overthrow the Cadre. We'll give the next generation the freedom to practice magic.*

Blanchett stopped outside a massive iron door, flanked by two guards. Their javelins were crossed in front. Tristan's mouth dropped slightly when he saw the guards' armor. It was crystal, like Emerson's, except black.

*Are they wearing...onyx?*

The guards bowed their heads. "High Wizard."

Blanchett smiled before drawing a complex rune on a pressure plate on the door. It resembled the rune Cerys drew to open the secret door to Aramore.

Once drawn, Blanchett pushed the plate and the iron doors gave way.

They emerged onto a balcony overlooking a vast rectangular room with vaulted ceilings.

Shelves were arranged in neat rows, holding more books than Tristan could read in his lifetime. Every tome was placed with purpose. Torchlight glinted off glass vials and bottles, filled with various potions. Across the room was a fireplace with a cast-iron cauldron sitting inside, hovering over logs that had yet to be kindled. A table sat before the maze of bookshelves, laden with unfurled parchment, inkwells, quills, and open tomes.

The sight of Blanchett's brewing room only sent waves of dizziness through Tristan's vision.

After descending the stairs, he approached a shelf stocked with potions. A pale-purple potion read: *Healing*. Another read: *Fire Resistance*. But the one that ensnared Tristan's attention the most was *Magic Regeneration*. Only once did his mother discuss the various types of potions magic-wielders could make; however, only the most powerful wizards could brew magic regeneration potions. It was the only potion that could replenish one's magic capacity for a period of time.

Tristan remembered hearing his parents discuss potions, but never showed him or Tibia the art of brewing such concoctions.

Zombia tapped the healing potion with her finger and smiled at Tristan. "I wish we could bring some of these back home."

When Tristan reached up to grab a potion, pain shot through his arm, causing him to clutch his bicep.

Zombia placed her hands on the king's shoulders. "That's it. You're getting that wound fixed." She turned to Blanchett. "My magic's low. Do you have a poultice for his wound?"

The High Wizard gently took Tristan's hand and examined his bicep. She gasped. He noticed the bleeding had resumed as more red blossomed through the makeshift bandage.

Concern pulled Blanchett's thin brows together. "What happened to you, child?"

"Zokar got me with his dagger," said Tristan. He unraveled the bandage, unveiling a two-inch slit. "The blade went in deep."

Zombia frowned. "If my magic wasn't weak, I'd

heal you. I'm so sorry, Tristan."

The king shook his head. "I just need some kind of poultice."

"I'll get a poultice for that," said Blanchett. "And a healing potion." The High Wizard bound around the room the next minute, grabbing the necessary herbs, and mortar, and pestle. After, she approached the shelf Tristan had been inspecting moments earlier and swiped the healing potion from the top. Blanchett turned to Cerys. "Brew some willow bark tea please. He can drink it while I bandage his wounds."

The mage nodded before striding to the shelves, selecting a jar of willow bark, and heading to the cauldron.

Tristan mostly drank cinnamon or chamomile tea, but he remembered the apothecary back home would brew willow bark tea whenever he or Tibia injured themselves. It was odd how such a simple thing made Tristan so nostalgic.

"Sit here," Zombia said, pulling out one of the chairs for Tristan.

Sitting, he smiled as he watched Blanchett hurry around the room. Once she had her necessary items, she poured them into the mortar and began grinding its contents.

Cerys returned with the warm tea. Blanchett pulled the stopper from the healing potion and tapped the bottle with her finger. Two drops of purple plopped into the mug, turning the tea a slight periwinkle hue. He wrapped his fingers around the mug and sipped.

Zombia cast Tristan a stern look, grasping his left hand; her skin was soft in his and fit so…perfectly. "Why didn't you say you were hurt?"

Tristan blushed and shrugged, focusing on her words rather than her closeness. She smelled of rose, the smell of home. "I…didn't want you to worry. We need to continue focusing on Emerson."

"Well, he won't get cured if you're dead," Faye said calmly.

Zombia nodded. "That's what friends are for; we worry about each other."

Tristan melted a little. *If we weren't in Blanchett's brewing room with our friends, I could hug her and tell her what she means to me.*

Blanchett placed the mortar, lavender, and aloe, in front of Tristan. In her other hand, she held fig leaves and fresh linen bandages, and she had a jar of fresh honey. Tristan hissed in pain as Blanchett spread the poultice over the wound, followed by honey. After wrapping it in clean linen, the High Wizard said, "There, that should heal, but you'll have a scar."

"Thank you," he finally said. Tristan flexed his fingers and rolled his shoulder. It stung, but other than that, it felt brand new.

"Now, I'll brew my potion for your friend."

The High Wizard rolled up her sleeves, and got to work. Tristan noticed the burn scar covering Blanchett's arm—the same one he saw in his dream at their first meeting. His heart broke as he thought about Malice, once a girl named Astrid, turning against her mentor and delving deeper into the realm of dark magic. *I hope that never happens to any of us,* thought Tristan. *I don't want to turn against the people who have given me everything.*

Shaking off the nightmarish thoughts, Tristan and his friends watched the High Wizard dart around the brewing room, swipe herbs off the shelves, and lay them out on the table. Cinnamon sticks, chamomile, and hibiscus created a sweet aroma. Using her magic, Blanchett lit the fire after pouring fresh water into the cauldron. After tossing in the herbs, she produced something from one of the many pouches on her belt.

Tristan looked closer. The object was a sleek black oval, nearly the size of her whole hand.

Tibia squinted. "Is that a—?"

"A dragon scale," Faye finished for her.

Blanchett nodded, walked over to the cauldron, and dropped the scale with a delicate plop. Tristan peered over Blanchett's shoulder to see the potion shift from a dazzling pink to a deep crimson.

"So, is it true?" asked Tristan. "Could dragons cure the zombie virus?"

Blanchett continued stirring the brew and sighed. "I don't know. I never got a chance to test it. When the Cadre threatened my home, my focus shifted to protecting my apprentices. However, I have experimented with the qualities of dragon magic."

Tristan's face must have looked horrified because Blanchett quickly followed up with, "Their claws and scales, which dragons shed. I use those."

"That's good," said Zombia, her face relaxing. "I doubt I could bring myself to harm another living creature."

Blanchett smiled at her. "You have a noble heart, and that's a trait I wish more magic-wielders possessed."

She turned back to the now boiling cauldron. "After I created this elixir, I began planning how it would be distributed. The main dilemma came in the fact that zombies multiply too fast—faster than it took to make a small vat of this elixir." The High Wizard stopped stirring and allowed the potion to simmer. Tristan stared into the now-pale liquid, listening to its rhythmic gurgling. "I'm still searching for a stronger, more permanent cure." A wistful gaze appeared in Blanchett's eyes. "I believe if dragons were as profuse as they were before the war, the zombie virus could be cured. But for now"—Blanchett took a ladle, scooped the potion out, and poured it into a round bottle—"this will have to suffice."

After placing the stopper on the top, Blanchett handed the potion to Tristan. He held it up in the lantern light; pallid liquid sloshed inside, unknowing its cryptic powers. *I hope this saves Emerson. I don't know what I'd do without my head knight.*

Tristan placed the bottle in his satchel and turned to Blanchett. "Thank you for everything. We best be returning to Skeletonia."

Cerys stepped in front of her friend. "Is that a good idea? We all just used great quantities of magic.

We need to recuperate."

"But Emerson is losing his humanity with each passing minute," Tristan protested; a heaviness settled in his stomach. "We need to fly back now."

"Not when our energy is low." The mage slowly shook her head. "Need I remind you of what occurred the other day? Who knows what dangers we'll encounter if we ride back at night. With low energy, we won't be able to defend ourselves."

Faye patted Shadowstalker's nose. He sat down, tail wrapped around his talons. The dragon yawned, his forked tongue unfurling.

"Rest isn't a bad idea," Faye said. She rubbed her eyes.

"Who knows if Zokar and his army are waiting outside the entrance," said Tibia with a low tone. "With our magic so low, there's no fighting them."

Tristan's mouth went dry as the thought struck him. He hadn't thought of that. *What if the zombies try to find a way in? Would they be smart enough? Zokar, not at all. But the sorceresses might. As much as I want to rush home and help Emerson, Cerys is right. We need rest if*

*we're going to be ready to battle anything in our way.*

"Is it all right if we stay the night?" asked Tristan.

"Please do," the High Wizard said with a smile. "I'll show you to your rooms after dinner."

As if on cue, a loud rumble resonated through the room. Heads turned to Shadowstalker, who hunched his shoulders, wings pinned to his sides. The faintest red tint crept up the dragon's cheeks. The rumble sounded again. Tristan stifled a laugh, realizing the source of the rumble was Shadowstalker's growling stomach.

Blanchett smiled. "Good thing dinner is nigh."

# Chapter Twenty-One

Blanchett took her wizards to the mess hall. It was empty, but soon enough, this place would be teeming with magic-wielding students.

The layout was simple but fancy at the same time. A brass chandelier lit up the place, and trestle tables were arranged in neat rows. Windows allowed for a direct view of Aramore, bathed in the fiery glow of the lanterns. Even the goblets were engraved. Some with dragons and others with phoenixes.

After making it through the maze of tables, Blanchett gestured for her wizards to sit beside her at a table close to the windows. Tristan took a seat beside Blanchett, with Zombia to his left. Tibia seated herself at the High Wizard's right-hand side. Faye and Cerys sat across from them. Shadowstalker's massive shadow blotted out the light from the chandelier. He pinned his wings close to his sides to keep from knocking over any tables as he sidled his way and plopped down beside

Faye. A few benches did squeak as the dragon's wings brushed against them, pushing them further into the tables.

"So, how does it feel to be back home?" Zombia asked Cerys.

"Wonderful," the mage answered, leaning forward and resting her chin on her hands. "It feels good not worrying about concealing my powers. I don't have to worry about being caught and burnt. Magic is a part of me and I'm glad I don't have to stifle it here." Then, Cerys's shoulders slumped. "I wish we didn't have to leave so soon."

"If you prefer to stay longer, go ahead," Tristan said, swallowing a lump in his throat. "If it makes you happier, please stay; we have the elixir, and we can heal Emerson." *We'll miss you greatly, though.*

The mage blew out a breath and shook her head. "Though this is my home, my duty is to help you three hone your powers and defeat Malice. So, no, I'll be returning home with you."

Warmth spread through the king's chest. "You'd do that for us?"

Cerys giggled. "Of course. Who else would train the Wizards of the Apocalypse?"

Blanchett raised a brow, the corner of her lip curling up in jest. "I see you've given yourselves a new moniker."

Heat rushed to Tristan's face. "It was sort of Tibia's idea."

"It suits you. Wish I had thought of it myself."

The doors to the dining hall burst open, drawing Tristan's attention.

Magic-wielders poured in and took their seats, laughing and discussing their day's accomplishments. Each one wore unique, colorful robes. Potion bottles jangled like wind chimes. Servers poured what looked like cider into the goblets, filling them to the brim. Some students raised their cups in toasts of success. Other students griped about upcoming exams or potion brewing mishaps.

Snowflake entered the room with Ingrid on her back. When the Ice dragon made eye contact with Blanchett, she made her way through the sea of trestle tables and students before depositing Ingrid on the bench so she sat across from Tristan.

"How was class, Ingrid?" Tristan asked.

Ingrid turned in his direction. "Wonderful. I managed to learn a few new brewing recipes. Here are my notes." They weren't parchment; they were wooden slates with raised letters on them. She ran her fingers across them and read about her latest project. "Snowflake brews the potions for me while I read them to her."

Zombia smiled and leaned in. "Fascinating."

Soon after, chefs carted in plate after plate of delicious dishes. Roasted quail on a bed of basil and parsley, fresh bread and goat cheese, homemade potage, and fresh-picked seasonal fruit.

Faye threw a whole quail to Shadowstalker, which he lapped up quickly, followed by another. Though he was a dragon, his begging for food reminded Tristan of the village puppies that hung around the bakeries and taverns on the cobblestone streets. Likewise, Ingrid cut off a piece of quail and held it up for Snowflake to eat. Gently, the Ice dragon picked up the roasted bird with her talons and let it drop into her mouth.

The quail was the best thing Tristan had ever tasted, better than anything the castle cooks prepared in Skeletonia.

*Was magic used? Or are they just talented with spices?* Tristan wondered as the flavors burst across his tongue.

Throughout the meal, Ingrid regaled her newcomers about her job brewing potions, but mostly she discussed what life was like in Blanchett's new base of operations.

Tristan listened, intrigued by this new life in Aramore. Ingrid was a lot like Cameron. She joked and teased Cerys at times. Snowflake seemed to enjoy Shadowstalker's company. Though Tristan couldn't hear what they were saying, judging by the grins on their faces, he concluded both were discussing light-hearted topics.

"So, your Highness, your Wizardness, I'm not sure what title to use here," Zombia said sheepishly. She fiddled with the ends of her brown hair. "Have there been any wizards with partial clairvoyance?"

Blanchett took a sip from her goblet. "Yes. But it's very rare." Her gaze fell on Tristan. "Clairvoyance is an advantageous ability. You got lucky."

Tristan dropped his fork. "Y-you know of my clairvoyance?"

Blanchett nodded, giving the king a knowing smile. "I can visit your dreams, Tristan, remember?"

The king grabbed his fork and nodded. "Oh, right. Wait, so you've seen my dreams where the dragons are under Malice's power?"

The High Wizard sipped some of her cider and nodded, frowning. "I have, and things aren't looking good. Malice will do anything for power."

Tristan blinked a few times, his brain reeling; he took another bite of quail but barely tasted it. *So all those dreams with Malice controlling the dragons are contingencies. We have the power to stop them.*

Tristan took in a deep breath and rubbed his forehead. "Were our parents partially clairvoyant?"

Blanchett tapped her chin with her finger. "No. They weren't. But someone in your lineage possessed partial clairvoyance."

"Who?" asked Tibia.

"I didn't know them. But clairvoyance is a recessive gene; every other generation will possess this power."

Tristan tilted his head. *Could it be one of our grandparents? Great grandparents? Guess we'll never know.*

The following moments were filled with silence. Tristan barely made it through another bite of quail when Ingrid spoke.

"Is it true your friend was bitten?" she asked, her

voice filled with sympathy. She reached toward a bowl of red, plump grapes. Snowflake noticed and pushed the bowl to her. She plucked off the juiciest one and popped it into her mouth.

Tristan paused and set down the chunk of quail he'd been eating, his hunger evaporating. "Yes. He was."

Ingrid chewed slowly on the grape and frowned. "I'm so sorry to hear that." She reached out to touch Tristan's shoulder. Seeing this, Snowflake nudged her rider's hand in the right direction. The sorceress's compassion warmed him, chasing away the coldness of fear and dread.

The king nodded and frowned, staring into his goblet. "That's why we came to Aramore."

"He was bitten by the king of the zombies, Zokar," Tibia said through a mouthful of quail.

When the color from Blanchett's face drained, Tristan wondered if she knew something about the zombie king he and his friends had yet to learn.

"It's a good thing you came when you did." Blanchett pressed her fingers to her forehead, blinking in disbelief. "I knew Malice would leave her mark in some way."

Tristan stopped short and swallowed nervously.

"Malice and Zokar must've been allies forever," said Zombia, folding her hands in her lap, locking eyes with the High Wizard.

Blanchett's voice dropped a couple of octaves, her vibrant eyes darkening. "*Allies* is putting it lightly, Zombia." The High Wizard straightened her back, her eyes bearing deep grimness. "Malice spawned the zombie king. Zokar is Malice's son."

A sinister silence bled around the table. The chatter around Tristan was drowned out, nothing more than low, garbled voices.

"Tell me this is a joke," Tibia ground out. The Skeleteria queen remained stationary. She blinked rapidly as though that would change the truth. It wouldn't.

Tristan's bones went cold as terror seeped through him. "He's...her son?" *No, it can't be. Was Zokar raised by Malice?* Skeletonia and Zombieshire were always at war, but that didn't stop Tristan from wondering about the zombie king's origins. When the first zombie king, Brian, abdicated—or disappeared. Then, poof, Zokar became the new zombie king.

Tristan felt the walls were closing in, ready to crush him.

"Well, he's not her biological son," said Blanchett, maintaining eye contact with her wizards. "Zokar is Malice's spawn."

"Spawn?" Zombia asked, tilting her head.

"Yes. Wielders of black magic can spawn evil beings into existence with their incantations," Blanchett explained.

Tristan rubbed his forehead, his crown suddenly feeling heavier. "I thought demons possessed people. They can create entire new beings?"

Blanchett nodded, taking another spoonful of potage. "They prefer to possess people, but there's always a chance of someone breaking their hold on their victim's soul. If they create a new being from scratch, there's no separating their soul from the magic. Zokar will forever be bound to dark magic."

"Guess there's no forming an alliance with the zombies," Zombia said with a somber tone. "But they can still be saved. We just need Zokar off the throne."

Tristan shuddered, his mind still reeling. *So this entire time, one of Malice's spawns has beset Skeletonia? And I thought holding the title of zombie king was bad enough.* What followed was a sudden wave of sadness; breathing became hard. *I hoped to form an alliance with Zokar some day. Convert him, find an agreement, and end the war. Now there's no hope. There's no negotiating with black magic.*

Tristan didn't bother eating the rest of his food. Hunger fled him, and now he was positive sleep would too.

"Is this where the students sleep?" Zombia asked.

After dinner and a dessert of caraway cake, Blanchett led her wizards to the second story of her fortress. Shadowstalker was led to the dragon dorms, which Tristan assumed were like regular dorms except much larger. Cerys and Ingrid retired to their rooms after bidding Tristan and his friends a goodnight.

The wrap-around balcony provided a good aerial view of the throne room. There was no activity save for the guards changing shifts. Before dinner, the oil lanterns burnt bright; now, they were dimmed, indicating it was time for rest. Tristan wondered if someone had come to dim the lanterns or magic was at work here.

"Yes. The upper floor of my fortress is a dormitory. Each room has enough space and beds for three people. Perfect for the three of you." Blanchett turned to Faye and cast her a sad smile. "I'm afraid someone is going to have to sleep on the floor."

Faye shrugged. "That's fine with me."

Nodding, Blanchett rounded a corner to the right, emerging into another lavish corridor displaying more oil lanterns and vibrant dragon murals.

Pulling his gaze from the ornate scenery, Tristan swallowed before saying to Blanchett, "Do you believe magic will ever return to the Haunted Lands?"

Blanchett kept her brisk gait, but a few moments of silence arrived before an answer.

"I do." Blanchett clicked her tongue. "But it's going to take a colossal amount of work. When I moved to Aramore, I built the place expecting the worst."

"Worse than Malice and her zombies?" Tibia asked, the corner of her mouth curled up in a smirk, which quickly died when Tristan jabbed her in the ribs with her elbow.

"I constructed an entire city where I could teach

and house magic-wielders in the case magic never sees the light of day again. Aramore is a haven where wizards, witches, and mages of all kinds can hone their crafts without the Cadre ever knowing." Blanchett stopped outside the dorm and rested her hand on the curved, brass handle before sighing. It was a sigh Tristan recognized as the one he often huffed out when he reached an impasse. When a situation seemed too bleak, Tristan felt there was no way out. The impulse to touch Blanchett's shoulder was overwhelming, but he opted against it. She was the High Wizard. A formidable, revered being.

"If Lucian is as shrewd as I remember him to be, magic being free will be as easy as hiking up a mountain side covered in sharp brambles."

"Who's Lucian?" asked Zombia.

"The Cadre leader. At least he was when I still lived at the Crimson Citadel," Blanchett said as she opened the door revealing a large dorm room.

Three beds, larger than cots but smaller than most castle beds, were laid in a neat row by the window overlooking Aramore, awash with a pale orange aura. Two oak desks rested in the left corner and the third in the right, each bearing a stack of parchment, an unlit rushlight, quill, and an inkwell. An armor stand sat at the foot of each bed like wooden sentinels.

Tristan tossed his satchel on one of the beds and turned back to Blanchett. "The Cadre has a new leader, actually. Kieran Bennett. He visited Skeletonia a few days ago. He found the Fortress of Portals used and the trails of black magic. He knows magic is still alive and he's hunting for us."

Color drained from the High Wizard's face. "Bennett? Lucian Bennett had a son?"

Tristan exchanged glances with his friends.

"I guess so," Tibia said curtly. She clenched and unclenched her fists, her shoulders tense at Blanchett's revelation.

"After we save Emerson, we are formulating a plan to end the Cadre," said Faye, slamming a fist into her palm.

The smallest smile materialized on Blanchett's face. "That's a valiant decision, but like I said, it's going to take lots of work. The Cadre's reputation among society is highly positive. People praise them for ridding the Haunted Lands of dark magic, so their downfall won't come easy. I hope I'm around to see magic thrive in the world once more."

A burning lump rose in Tristan's throat as though the air to his lungs was abruptly cut off. "What do you mean?" He knew the answer to the question, but he felt he should ask anyway.

"Magic can prolong someone's life, but it doesn't make them immortal," said Blanchett. She rested against her golden dragon staff. "I won't be around forever, but I've hoped for years to see magic thrive again. But that won't happen with the Cadre in power."

"We need to remove them from power," said Zombia, taking a seat on one of the beds. "That's going to take a revolution."

"A revolution of wizards," added Tibia.

"Indeed," Blanchett said, rubbing her pointed chin. "I'd spent so many years in Aramore searching for a cure to the zombie infection, but now that I've found one, I can focus on dethroning the Cadre."

A lightness poured through Tristan's chest. "You're going to help us?"

The High Wizard nodded. "I'll do what I can. Unfortunately, I can't leave Aramore, but we'll keep in contact." A wistful look entered Blanchett's eyes.

After a long pause, Tristan asked, "Do you believe Kieran is banning magic because he wants what's best for the Haunted Lands?"

Blanchett shook her head. "I don't. Though I never learned his true motives, I grew suspicious of Lucian fairly quickly. I understand the fear surrounding dark magic and not wanting it to rise, but the heartless murder of innocent magic-wielders and totalitarian attitude steers toward more narcissistic. If my scouts hadn't learned of Lucian's trek to the Crimson Citadel, he would have imprisoned everyone and made a huge show of burning us to threaten the public. I bet his offspring is hardly different."

The tension in Tristan's shoulders released. *At least we're on the same page. Kieran is up to no good and we're going to find out his true intentions for the Haunted Lands.*

Blanchett clutched her staff and headed for the door. "Get some rest, my wizards." The door shut softly, snuffing out the light from the hallway.

Tristan sank on the bed closest to the window. The pillows and blankets were soft. Dull aches rolled through his body as Tristan removed his armor, making him glad he took up Cerys's offer to stay the night. He stretched his shoulders and arms. Pain laced through his bicep; he gritted his teeth before quickly letting his arm drop.

"I'll take the floor," said Faye. She sat on the decorative sapphire-blue rug. Gold stitching wove flying dragons and birds around its edges. She turned to the three wizards. "Someone hand me a pillow, please?"

"Here," Tibia said, chucking one of the extra pillows at Faye, who caught it in midair. Tibia snickered.

"Thanks, Tib." Taking her cloak, Faye threw it over herself for a blanket.

"Are you sure you're okay on the floor, Faye?" asked Zombia. She pulled off her boots and placed them by the armor stand.

The Dragonblood nodded. "I'm too tall for these beds. My feet will hang uncomfortably over the end. I'm better on the floor. Thanks."

Zombia smiled. "If you say so." She pulled the white blankets over herself. "These beds are so comfortable."

"Agreed," Tristan responded. Sleep pulled at his eyes despite having learned hours ago that Zokar was Malice's son.

"Do you really think Blanchett can help us defeat the Cadre?" Tristan asked.

"She's the High Wizard," said Zombia with a firm smile. "I'm sure she has a plan."

"I just worry for her safety. Society hates her. Would it be in her best interest to help us?"

"Working together is the only way we're going to accomplish these feats," Tibia said from over Tristan's shoulder. "We are the Wizards of the Apocalypse after all."

Tristan smirked. *Leave it to my sister to pick out the silliest monikers.* "Let's get some sleep."

Though Tristan said these words, finding sleep's welcoming embrace took some time. Eventually, the whirlwind of thoughts in his head ceased, and he could close his eyes and drift into a fairly decent sleep.

# Chapter Twenty-Two

Zokar didn't know where the sorceresses were leading the zombies. All he knew was they were headed southeast, presumably to the place where they were to perform the releasing ritual for Malice.

A sea of green surrounded them again, complemented with the scent of pine and wet soil. The downpour had thankfully ended, but dark-gray clouds clotted the sky, and chilly autumn air knocked small branches from pine trees. A bed of pine needles crunched under boots and horses' hooves.

Maeve and her two tribe members walked at the head of the formation; Zokar and Marcus rode behind them on horseback. Blood splotches decorated the front of the sorceresses' robes, but Maeve appeared the worst. She limped, her complexion pale. Bloodstains streaked from her stomach down the front of her once-pristine white garment showing a significant amount of blood loss that would have weakened or killed anyone else.

"Do you need something for those wounds, ladies?" Marcus asked. A low growl wound up inside Zokar's throat, slipping past his gritted teeth. *They're here to help us free Malice; they're no friends of ours.*

Maeve didn't bother turning around. "Magic has its benefits. We'll be fine." Though she was a woman of few words, Zokar groaned upon hearing her monotone voice.

Zokar glowered at his right-hand man, who shrugged and returned his gaze to the path ahead. His horse whinnied as if agreeing to stay clear of the zombie king.

The remaining undead brought up the rear. The zombie king turned around in his saddle, glowering at his heavily diminished numbers. He'd lost over half the zombies he brought because of that infernal dragon.

Energy pulsated through Zokar's body as his rage mounted. By the time they reached the Gravestone Wood's edge, his teeth hurt from grinding them. *Whatever plan Malice gives us, it better overpower the dragons. Otherwise, this whole rescue endeavor will be useless.* Zokar's fists tightened around the reins, so hard his knuckles whitened. The truth was, he didn't want to bring Malice back. He despised her leadership. He despised the way she recruited his zombies. Though she was his mother, he didn't care. He wanted to be the one who defeated Blanchett's wizards and rule alone.

Zokar stared at the damp path ahead of him. *If she keeps at it, my subjects will adore her more than me. Can't have that.* As much as he hated to admit it, the undead were hapless without the Shadowblood's magic. Before Malice, the zombies knew nothing of forging durable weapons or armor. Malice granted Zokar's people advanced military and combat knowledge and black magic. *After Malice's victory over the Haunted Lands, I'll take the reins and rule. I'll return her to the Otherworld forever!*

"Where are we headed?" asked Zokar in a gruff tone.

"To the Moonlit Mountains," Maeve responded without turning around. The sorceress leader grunted as her foot got caught on a stray, gnarled root. She shook it free and continued walking, her face grimacing with each step. Zokar knew magic could heal wounds, but not the pain. That lingered. After Skeleton's knight stabbed him, he felt the pain for days after. The zombie king smoothed out his cloak. *As long as Maeve and her sorceresses can free Malice, the severity of their injuries don't matter to me.*

Zokar's throat tightened. "The Moonlit Mountains? You mean in the Dragon Isles?"

Maeve scoffed. "Of course I mean in the Dragon Isles, you ignoramus."

The zombie king minutely shook his head. "Why are we heading there? Couldn't you perform the ritual in the White-Talon Mountains?"

Maeve spun around and tossed Zokar a glassy stare. "The Moonlit Mountains have one thing the White-Talon Range doesn't have: a portal platform."

"What's that?" asked Marcus.

"A platform we use to access the Otherworld," answered the elf sorceress. "The Fortress of Portals only grants one access to the upper levels of the Underworld. Not the deepest one." The sorceress glanced down at her boots, her lips turning downward into a somber frown. "We had other portal platforms but the Blue Moon Tribe destroyed them to keep us from accessing the demons' dark powers. Luckily, they never found the one in the Moonlit Mountains."

Zokar sank in the saddle, pulling his cloak over himself to hide his shaking body. He knew where they were headed—right into dragon territory. Those scaly beasts terrified Zokar. Talons so sharp they could slice through chain mail as though it were soft butter, teeth that could chew their prey to pieces, and fire so hot it would devour anything it touched, leaving nothing save soot and ash. Marcus rode beside him, his chin held high, higher than someone should after getting burnt by a dragon. The zombie king's eyes traveled down to Marcus's leg. The dark-blue fabric of his pants and the leather of his boot were charred, but the skin was... *completely unscathed.* Zokar raised an eyebrow while an icy chill sliced through him.

*A shame the dragon-fire didn't kill him. I wouldn't have to worry about Marcus overthrowing me. Marcus can't be magic, can he? If he is, he's done an excellent job of hiding it. As if I needed another reason to watch him. I still suspect he knows more about my attempted assassination than he's letting on.*

The dimming light behind the clouds indicated the sun was setting, and they weren't even out of the Gravestone Woods. And when Zokar didn't think things could get any worse, Maeve said, "Let's rest here for the night; we'll leave at dawn."

"No, we need to keep moving," argued Zokar. "We need to free Malice as soon as we can."

The silver-haired sorceress spun on her heel, her messy braid revolving in an arc. "There's no success without rest."

Zokar ground his teeth, ears folding back as he cast a scowl at Marcus. *Why does he insist on allowing the sorceresses to lead? Does he understand that the greatest quality of zombies is that we don't hesitate? These magic-wielders lack ambition. Zombies don't. We act without thinking.*

Soon enough, Maeve and her crew had camp set up, logs encompassing a kindled fire, casting their shadows on the shrubs and tree trunks. Throughout the meal of bread and dried meat, the sorceresses didn't utter a word toward the zombies. Knowing the dried meat was the strongest form of sustenance, Zokar chewed it quickly, not wanting to taste the spices and salt used to preserve it. He hated the way the meat didn't squish and tear within his sharp teeth. It was too brittle and desiccated. After two small pieces of dried meat, Zokar stopped eating it and opted for some bread. At least the texture was closer to human flesh.

Maeve conversed with her two tribe members in an ancient tongue Zokar couldn't understand. He glowered at the women, knowing they purposefully wanted to exclude him and Marcus from the conversation.

Zokar couldn't take his eyes off the onyx-colored box Maeve carried with her, nor could he ignore the bloodstone around her neck, peeking out from the collar of her robes. Or the bloodstone from which their staffs were made.

Despite Malice claiming crystal magic wasn't for the "doltish" minds of zombies, Zokar had read about bloodstones. They were used for strength and reserving the user's magic, extending its capacity. Seeing the crystal gave the zombie king a brilliant idea—at least in his opinion. The only opinion that mattered.

Marcus finished off a piece of dried meat and said, "What needs to be done for the ritual?"

"You'll find out when we arrive," answered the elf sorceress. "I didn't know the undead asked so many questions." Her tone wasn't as harsh as Maeve's. In fact, it sounded genuinely curious. Not that Zokar cared about her personality, but at least she didn't appear to be challenging his authority. Suddenly, her pale, turquoise eyes glossed over. "Do you promise to restore the throne to the Silver Flame Tribe?"

Zokar wanted to laugh at her innocence. *Zombies don't do tasks for free. We aren't slaves. We'll help rebuild your queendom and take the throne back from the Blue Moon Tribe, but for a price.*

"Of course, we will," answered Marcus. He smiled at the redheaded girl. Zokar swiveled his gaze to him. "Malice will help you once you bring her back."

The redheaded girl beamed like a child who stumbled into a bakery and saw Summer Solstice honey cakes were on sale. The blond girl shared her expression; even Maeve seemed to perk up. Zokar's stomach rolled in pure disgust.

"Don't forget our stipulations, zombies," Maeve said, her voice deep and threatening. "You need us more than we need you; remember that."

Marcus bowed his head. "Understood, ladies."

Shooting up from his sitting position, Zokar grabbed the second-in-command's arm and yanked him into the woods, just out of earshot.

"What are you doing?" Zokar hissed. "Why in the gods' names are you being so friendly? We have to show them that zombies are running the show."

"Being cordial helps us make allies," explained

Marcus. He folded his arms, staring. "We don't need more enemies."

Zokar wanted to take Marcus and throttle him as rage crawled out. All this kindness was *not* the zombie way. "If we're too lenient, the sorceresses will get greedy and forget their place. They might even overpower us. Speaking of which, I have a plan."

Marcus's face paled.

"Once Malice is free, let's kill those three," Zokar said coldly. "Then we can annex the sorcerer territory. And I'll have Maeve's bloodstone, and whatever's in the onyx box."

The second-in-command blew damp, green hair out of his eye. "Greed and power-lust get us nowhere, sire. Do you want to strengthen our forces or not?"

"I *am* strengthening our forces!" boomed Zokar. His voice sent a colony of bats squeaking in a frenzy and fleeing from their nesting spots. Magic crackled under the zombie king's skin like unearthly veins.

"Getting rid of them will allow us complete access to their queendom, trades, and valuable magic resources!" Zokar turned his back on Marcus, staring off into the never-ending curtain of verdant trees. "You're beginning to seem more human than zombie.

It's decided. We're killing the sorceresses." At the last word, Zokar pivoted to face the second-in-command. "Whether you're in or not."

Marcus wanted to slam his head into one of the tree's trunks, vexed by Zokar's foolishness. The second-in-command couldn't believe what he heard. *Making enemies will lead to the zombies' downfall; how does he not realize that?* He ran his fingers through his tangled fern-green hair and sighed. *Malice should crown me the new zombie king promptly upon her return. Life would be better for the zombies.*

By the time they returned to camp, the sorceresses were asleep. It was complete silence save for the sputtering fire and their soft snores. Zokar looked over the slumbering women, probably considering a way to kill them now. Thankfully, he didn't. It took a while, but finally, Zokar wrapped himself in his cloak, rolled over, so his back faced Marcus, and supposedly closed his eyes. The truth was, Zokar hardly slept. That was normal for dictators: extreme paranoia.

Back in Zombieshire, Marcus was forced to stay up late at night to guard the zombie king. Standing outside his quarters at attention began wearing on the captain, depriving him of his own rest. However, if Zokar chose to rule with generosity rather than pure fear, he'd have no reason to be this anxious.

Removing his re-curve bow from his back, Marcus seated himself in the soft grass and ran his fingers over his leg where the dragon burnt him. The deep-blue fabric of his pants was charred, with the middle burnt away.

Marcus scowled at Zokar's sleeping form, nausea washing through his vision. *That brute tried to kill me. He wanted that dragon to set me ablaze. Zokar's probably stewing about the fact I'm still alive. Zombieshire doesn't need monsters like him.* After Zombia healed him, Marcus continued to fight, again, opting to wound rather than kill. Honestly, he was done with killing. The way Zokar killed with ease churned Marcus's stomach.

Gently, Marcus caressed the unscathed skin. Dragon fire would have left terrible blisters and third degree burns, eventually begetting infection.

*"Now, we're even"* were the words Zombia whispered into Marcus's ear as she healed him. He remembered the coolness of her magic trickling through his body, washing over his searing wound like a fresh,

cool waterfall. Within seconds, the burns vanished, and the skin and nerves pulled themselves back together.

Zombia was the enemy; enemies weren't supposed to help each other, yet she did.

Marcus had fought at Zokar's side for years; he didn't deserve kindness from Tristan or any of his friends. Their hate toward him was justified.

Even so, Zombia risked her life in the middle of a battle to heal Marcus. Saving Zombia in the Hall of Black Mirrors wasn't something the captain should have done. *But could I live knowing a barely adolescent girl got killed and I had the power to stop it?* Marcus swallowed hard, feeling like an apple was lodged in his throat. *No, I couldn't.*

Growing up in Zombieshire, Marcus never had any friends—maybe Zombia would have been if they'd crossed paths then. The agora was constantly packed with zombies buying and selling wares; even if he'd seen Zombia, he wouldn't have recognized her, considering she was a few years younger than him.

Besides, undead weren't the friendly type; they were cutthroats and seasoned hunters. From birth, violence and bloodshed were customary. As a child, he refused to bite people. On a hunting trip with his siblings, Marcus watched with repulsion as they bit and devoured people. This was deemed an act of weakness and his siblings teased him, even revealing to their parents Marcus's lack of the urge to kill. His whole family viewed him as a disgrace and threw him out.

Not long after, Marcus, like all preteen zombies, were conscripted into the zombie king's army. He saw this as an opportunity to prove his worth.

He became an adept archer, which earned him respect. He treated his fellow soldiers as equals. That was the way it should be, and Zokar couldn't accomplish that. In fact, his sadistic rule showed Marcus the *wrong* way to rule.

Tristan put his people first, cared for the wounded, and chose unity over avarice. That was something he had never seen before yet yearned for. Zombia healing him was the first act of true kindness Marcus ever received.

The Hidden Wizard

Leaning back, Marcus rested his head on his satchel, sparing a glance at the star-filled sky above, thoughtfully. The late-autumn chills drove crickets into hibernation, but owls hooted their nocturnal songs, letting them drift through the trees. Sleep was the last thing on his mind.

*When Malice crowns me the zombie king, life will improve for the undead nation. I'll make sure of it.*

# Chapter Twenty-Three

Emerson barely recognized himself. One hour, he was the honorable knight his friends knew. An hour later, he was a bloodthirsty, flesh-craving zombie. It had been on and off for hours—well, Emerson started counting the hours, but soon enough, they melded together.

It had been two days since Tristan left, and the knight couldn't stand to look at his reflection. Each time he looked in the mirror, he watched his skin transform; his personality slipped further away. His nightshirt was soaked in sweat and blood, completing the undead ensemble.

There was a knock at his door. More like three loud bangs. Emerson bolted upright, his vision swaying a bit in his feverish state. Rolling out of bed, the knight almost knocked over his mug of now-cold chamomile tea before ambling to the door. Opening it, he stepped back. Breath caught in his throat. He saw Radius, dressed in full chain mail beneath a cobalt surcoat. Cameron stood at his side, goggles in hand, fiddling nervously with the straps. Behind them were three skeleton guards holding sharp poleaxes. The guards' bony faces were set in grim expressions paired with underlying regret.

His best friend frowned. "This isn't personal, Em."

Before Emerson could process what was occurring, bony hands clamped around the knight's arms, dragging him from his room. One of the skeleton guards held her sharp poleax at the back of the knight's head. Tears slipped down Emerson's cheeks, his eyes burning. He knew it was the truth. When someone was bitten, they were escorted by the king's guard to the forest's perimeter to be exiled.

As Emerson was pulled down the hall, he glanced over his shoulder to see Cameron tugging frantically at Radius's arm.

"I-is this necessary?" stammered Cameron. His emerald eyes roved over the armored guards. "Tristan will return soon. Please, don't exile him. I'm begging you."

His friend's voice cracked at the end of his sentence.

"He's not being exiled, Cameron," said Radius,

pushing his glasses up his face. "He's being taken to the dungeon to reside until Tristan returns."

Emerson kept his gaze downcast, not wishing to show the guards his red eyes. He listened to Cameron's pleading as he followed the captain like a shadow. Windows boasting ominous rain clouds with flickers of lightning passed his peripheral vision. More armed guards were stationed outside the corridor leading to the dungeons. Reaching the end of the hall, Radius opened the door, revealing a foreboding spiral staircase, only lit by candles held by iron sconces. The deeper they went, the stronger the smell of wet stone and dank air grew.

Cold, damp air seeped through Emerson's nightshirt, sending goosebumps down his arms and back. Candles were placed between each cell, casting low light and barely illuminating the cells' occupants. Most of them weren't occupied due to Skeletonia's citizens obeying the laws. The few cells that held prisoners were at the end of the hall. One contained a scrappy-looking zombie. The other contained an Iceblood elf that Emerson and Radius caught a few weeks ago. He was a spy from the icy tundra—one who ignored the treaty between the elf tribes and wanted to subvert

Faye's allies.

The guards stopped outside a cell; Radius took another key and unlocked the bars before gently pushing Emerson inside. He listened to the jarring *clunk* of the door slamming shut and the key re-locking it.

Radius and Cameron emerged from the darkness. The guild leader rushed at the bars and wrapped his leather-gloved hands around them, tears falling freely from his green eyes. The captain dismissed the guards and faced Emerson. "I never thought I'd have to do this. My sincerest apologies. Tristan ordered for you to be placed here. When he returns, you'll get Blanchett's elixir."

Emerson shook his head. "No hard feelings. I understand."

The captain offered a small smile. "The guards will be around, and you'll be fed regularly. Believe me, Tristan didn't want to do this to you."

"I know. Skeletonia can't be overrun. We can't let the sanctuaries fall." Emerson bowed his head, his fingers wrapped loosely around the rusty bars.

"I'll check on you soon," said Radius. He turned and exited the dungeon, leaving Emerson and Cameron.

The two friends stared at each other for a long

while. Cameron wiped his eyes. Emerson only saw his friend cry once, and that was when he injured himself in a blacksmithing accident. But that didn't mean Cameron didn't care. Under his jovial personality, he cared for his companions.

Emerson sat dejectedly on the dirty pile of hay. "You don't have to wait here for me. It's cold, and I don't want you getting sick."

Cameron snorted. "You were bitten by a freaking zombie, and you're worried about me falling ill?"

Emerson smirked. "Though I'm doomed, I still care about you."

A second skipped before Cameron's face went stoic, and he stood very still, making direct eye contact with Emerson. "Why didn't you say anything? We're best friends, did you forget?"

The knight's heart dropped as though it was being yanked underwater, to the bottom of the ocean. He knew this question would come sooner or later. He had already received it from Tristan; Cameron was sure to ensue. He couldn't tear his eyes from his friend's expression. His head was lowered; his chin trembled slightly.

Emerson sifted through his words carefully. "I

didn't want you to worry. I'm meant to serve the king, not the other way around. You know how he is."

Cameron's fingers curled around the bars. "But if you said something sooner, we could have done... something." Emerson heard the pause in his friend's voice. As far as he knew, there was no cure. "Also, why didn't you at least tell me? Do you not trust me anymore?"

A lump formed in the knight's throat. He did trust Cameron. They grew up fishing, swimming, and hunting together. They supported each other's careers and cheered one another on. And they told each other everything. Guilt gnawed at the back of Emerson's conscience.

"I do trust you. Again, I didn't want to worry you. I wanted to spend as much uninterrupted time with you. If I told you, that's all that would have been on your mind." Emerson's gaze hardened. "Also, there's no cure."

Cameron's face softened as he clutched the metal bars. "I know, but...we could have tried. Maybe even had a temporary cure. Anything to keep you around longer."

Emerson wiped his cheeks and sniffled. "I

appreciate it. Really. But my fate is sealed.”

The two friends stood in silence, listening to the footfall of dungeon guards, chains rattling, and the scurrying of rats.

“Hey, Cameron,” said Emerson, looking up from the floor.

“Yeah?”

“Want to stay and chat for a while? If I’m going to spend my last few hours with someone, I’m glad it’s you.”

# Chapter Twenty-Four

*Knock, knock, knock.*

Tristan sat up, rubbed the sleep from his eyes, and blinked a few times before throwing off the down covers and making his way to the door. Opening it, he found Cerys.

"Morning," she said with a grin. She practically glowed. Her emerald eyes sparkled, and her hair was retied into a neat braid, not a single loose strand.

A smile tugged at the corner of Tristan's mouth. *She's so happy to be home. I feel horrible taking her away from this.*

"Morning?" Tristan ran both palms down his face and turned toward the window. The city glowed, but not in sunlight, but rather the lanterns burnt at their brightest. "How do you tell when it's morning or night, being underground and all?"

"There are guards outside the mountain; not near the entrance, but hidden in alcoves and under precipices," Cerys explained. "They're mostly to watch for any signs of the Cadre, but they also give us the time of day."

*Interesting,* thought Tristan, rubbing the back of his neck. *I can't imagine living underground, deprived of sunlight and the aroma of flowers and pine trees.* "I'll wake the others."

Cerys nodded. "I'll meet you in the courtyard."

Her footsteps faded down the hall. Tristan turned around to see Zombia rubbing her eyes.

"How'd you sleep, Tristan?" Zombia asked.

He considered this. Though Aramore was not Skeletonia, Tristan slept better than he had in weeks. No nightmares of Malice or possessed dragons plagued him. Perhaps it was the magic in the air, or it could've been the fact they were underground where zombies weren't a constant threat. Whatever the case, Tristan was grateful for it. "Great, actually. No nightmares."

"Good." Zombia rose from the bed and approached the armor stand. She donned her epaulets, yawning. "I slept...okay."

Tristan raised an eyebrow. "What happened? Don't tell me you're getting bad dreams, too."

His friend shook her head. "It's not that. I don't

know if you saw during the battle yesterday, but I healed Marcus. I can't stop thinking about it."

A sudden chill settled over Tristan like a sheet of ice. "I saw. Why'd you do it? That was a risk, Zombia." After he asked why, he considered his own question for a moment. *I'd be lying if I denied my own urge to help Marcus, though. Zokar cruelly shoved him in the line of Shadowstalker's fire.*

Zombia tugged on her boots. "I know, but he needed help, and none of his brethren were stopping to do so. I felt I should return the favor since he saved me in the Hall of Black Mirrors." Shoulders slumping, Zombia sighed. "He may be the enemy, but watching Marcus struggle after a nasty dragon-fire burn felt... wrong." Zombia grimaced at the end of her sentence. "The healer in me couldn't abide by it."

Tristan nodded, the tension in his shoulders and chest abating a little. "What did you say to him?"

"I told him we're even," responded Zombia. "He saved me, so I saved him. I'm hoping that teaches him that kindness knows no bounds. Maybe he'll take that into consideration." Zombia grabbed her glaive from beside the window and stepped closer to Tristan. Her gaze met his, hope swirling in those hazel irises. "Maybe he'll...change."

Tristan bit his lip and stared at the cold, marble floor. *Could Marcus really change? Part of me says no. He fought by Zokar's side for many years, torturing and hurting people. Pillaging and killing. But another part of me says he can change. It wouldn't be a quick, easy change, but I feel he could if he wants to.* The king offered his friend a small smile. "Maybe."

"Thank you for having us," said Zombia, bowing her head to Blanchett and Ingrid.

"Why do you keep bowing?" Blanchett asked with a laugh. "We're equal here."

Tristan's heart soared. *Just like Skeletonia. All equal.* His fingers gripped his satchel's shoulder strap as he hefted it over his shoulder gently, knowing it contained the life-saving elixir. For breakfast, they ate a delicious potage topped with blueberries and raspberries. Shadowstalker scarfed down three bowls of it, which made Tristan repress a snort. Now, they stood before the fortress door, ready to depart for Skeletonia.

"I do hope you return soon!" Ingrid said merrily, following Zombia's voice. "I can't wait to show you our classes. Maybe you'll enroll?"

Tristan smiled. "Hopefully. We'd take a grand tour if we weren't in a hurry."

Ingrid stretched out a hand, indicating for a handshake. "Oh, I do wish you the best of luck."

Tristan clasped the sorceress's hand and gave it a cordial squeeze. Ingrid then took Zombia aside and handed her a round bottle of a vibrant magenta potion. Tristan cocked his head as his mind enumerated endless possibilities of what the potion could be.

"What potion did she give you?" asked Tristan.

"She said it was one she and Snowflake have been working on for a while," Zombia answered before gently placing the bottle in her satchel. "She says it's a type of regeneration potion." A smile tugged at the corner of her mouth as her brows rose. "She's working on finding a cure as well."

Tristan turned to Ingrid. "It never hurts to have more potions."

The potion master's smile stretched from ear to

ear.

"Are you returning to Skeletonia with us?" Faye asked Blanchett.

The High Wizard frowned. "It's too risky. With all the hate my visage garners, it wouldn't be safe." Blanchett's lips pressed together as she observed the great hall. "Besides, my place is here. Aramore needs me."

Students bustled to their morning classes, and teachers pushed carts of potion bottles, inkwells, and parchment after them, most likely for the day's lesson. They teased each other, erupting in fits of laughter as they raced their friends to class. *Just like regular school.* Tristan tried not to gape—there was no getting over this small snippet of what the Haunted Lands were like decades ago.

The High Wizard's fingers tapped her staff, her nails making a soft *clink* against solid gold. "But you're not leaving empty-handed." She handed a cloth bag to Tristan. The clinking of glass revealed the bag's contents.

"In case you needed more potions," said Ingrid with a hopeful smile. "It's great to be prepared."

"Thank you! It's much appreciated!" said Zombia, embracing Ingrid. Tristan saw Zombia move to hug the High Wizard, but presumably, she thought better of it, considering she was the most powerful being in the Haunted Lands. Tristan's shoulders slumped. He looked over to Tibia, who frowned. "So, you're never going to visit Skeletonia?" she said.

Blanchett placed a hand on her shoulder; her electric blue eyes filled with sadness. Tristan understood. "I'll visit when the war's over and society accepts magic once more. However, I haven't forgotten about the Cadre. Once you've saved your friend, we can collaborate on allocating the cure and deposing Kieran."

Tristan could see the longing to return to the surface, show her face, and use magic freely. To banish the Cadre and end the Apocalypse. Looking down at his golden cuff, Tristan ran his fingers across it, knowing good and well his wizard's marking lay underneath—a marking that could cost him and his companions their lives.

Cerys said to her mentor, "See you soon."

Blanchett enveloped the girl in an embrace. Releasing the hug, the High Wizard allowed her gaze to roll over Tristan, Zombia, and Tibia. Pride flashed in them as she took in the dragon-claw dagger at the king's hip. "I know you'll make the right decision. Stop Malice before she destroys what's left of the world."

Tristan clapped a fist to his chest and bowed. He felt like Emerson—a knight pledging loyalty to their king. Though he was royalty, he felt like a serf in Blanchett's presence. But like him, she made those around her feel like equals.

"Stay safe, sis." Ingrid pulled Cerys in for a hug. "Please write. I enjoy it when Blanchett reads your letters to me. Your writing and her voice send me over the moon. Your adventures are the best!" The girl tittered.

"Absolutely. I'll come back when I can," Cerys answered and released her sister's embrace. Watching the sibling love made Tristan's heart feel full. He remembered when Tibia went away for a few years to train as a warrior when they were children. Those were the longest years of the king's life. Yes, he and Tibia bickered over who got the last honey cake or who had to clean up after the castle hounds, but they cared for each other at the end of the day. Being separated for so long made Tristan feel like he was missing a piece of himself.

"Ready to go?" asked Tristan, turning to his friends.

"Just a minute, I need to locate Shadowstalker,"

answered Faye. The Dragonblood queen swirled around, her lilac locks flowing around her in a wave. "He was at breakfast." Putting her fingers to her mouth, she whistled. A rush of heavy footsteps later, Shadowstalker came bounding into the great hall, ducking in time to not smash his head or horns on the door frame.

Snowflake, who sat beside Ingrid, cocked her head and rolled her frosty-blue eyes. *Big lummox.*

Tristan heard her words in his head, loud and clear, and he held back a laugh. Shadowstalker shrugged his massive shoulders. *Whoops.*

Shadowstalker, Tristan had learned, deviated from how he perceived dragons. While he had wisdom and diligence like Blanchett, he was kind of quirky, like Emerson.

"Looks like Shadowstalker has been visiting everywhere," Blanchett said with a smile. "Perfect for our various classes."

Tristan smirked as he became lost in his thoughts once more. *What would it have been like to grow up in Aramore? I would have taken classes on magical creatures, the elf tribes' history, and magic.*

"We better head out," said Cerys, breaking Tristan from his thoughts.

He and his friends nodded. Looking back to Blanchett, Tristan nodded at her. "Hope we meet again soon. Thank you for everything."

While on the way to the White-Talon Range, the wizards had stopped for lessons. On the return home, they wasted no time. Shadowstalker beat his wings hard, not stopping. Tristan's only thought was curing Emerson. He knew the flight back would take two to three days. Hopefully, he and his friends wouldn't be too late. Hopefully, Emerson hadn't turned yet. *Come on, Shadowstalker. Fly faster.*

Shadowstalker looked back at him with brows furrowed. *I'm going as fast as I can, Tristan.*

Tristan smacked his forehead. He hadn't intended the thought to be directed as Shadowstalker. *Sorry, I didn't mean to say that to you. I know you're doing your best.*

They flew until nightfall, and then landed in a clearing in the Gravestone Woods. Shadowstalker's massive body trembled upon landing. His wings flopped to the side; the dragon huffed and groaned before dropping to the ground, sending a plume of dirt out from under him. His golden eyes struggled to stay open as moisture glistened on his thick, scaly brow.

Faye sat beside him and rubbed down his scales. "Poor thing."

A chill of guilt rolled through Tristan. *I feel horrible watching Shadowstalker push himself.* Blood roared in his ears—rage at Zokar for infecting Emerson, rage at Malice for creating the zombie king.

After a restless sleep, the wizards rose just as the sun's rays seeped over the horizon. Like the day before, Shadowstalker beat his wings hard. The dragon's sides rose in and out with each exerted breath. His scales were slippery with sweat against Tristan's legs.

The third morning, the vibrant blue sky was quickly clogged with clouds when they reached Skeletonia's outskirts. Rain began to pour as they flew over the forest.

Freezing droplets pelted Tristan's goggle lenses, and his breath came out in white puffs, but he didn't care. He'd walk through fire to save any of his friends.

The downpour only increased by the time Shadowstalker landed in the castle's rear. It was as though the weather was already mourning Emerson. Tristan choked back a sob, praying to the gods that his friend hadn't turned. Shadowstalker landed, his body trembling again, his sides heaving. Tristan, Zombia, and Tibia dismounted.

"Coming?" Tibia asked Faye.

The Dragonblood shook her head. "I have to rub down Shadowstalker; he's sore."

"I'll stay and help," said Cerys, sliding down Shadowstalker's shoulder. "We'll catch up."

Tristan nodded, and at the same moment, Radius pushed open the heavy oak door to greet them. The king pulled his goggles off his face. "Where's Emerson?"

"It's my displeasure to say he's been moved to the dungeons," said Radius with a frown.

Tristan swallowed and nodded. He didn't want to have Emerson locked away, but it was the safest option next to exile.

"Has he turned yet?" asked Zombia. She gripped her glaive until her knuckles were white.

Radius shook his head. "Not yet. But he will. Quick, through here." He held the door open.

Despite being back in his own castle, Tristan felt the walls closing in on him as though he were inside a giant monster's maw, destined to be consumed whole. Taking a familiar right, Radius greeted the two skeleton guards stationed outside the dungeon's entrance. They nodded to their commander and king before moving their spears and admitting them inside.

Fire crackled in the background as Tristan descended the winding staircase. Once at the bottom, the smell of musty air and soiled hay smacked Tristan in the nose. There were no instruments of torture present. No rack, no head crusher, or iron maiden; Tristan didn't believe in violence—even toward his enemies, it seemed inhumane. He passed cells containing dangerous brigands and warlords, but none of them mattered right now. He focused only on one person.

At the end of the hall, Cameron greeted them; his eyes were bloodshot and lined with red. Tristan whispered *Cweorth* and shifted to his skeleton form, anticipating the battle that was about to ensue. Emerson was lying motionless on the hay. Gods above, he looked horrible. His tan lost the battle with the zombie green. His clothes were covered in unsettling red splotches. Though the lighting was low, Tristan saw those evidently pointed ears peeking through disheveled brown locks.

"Open the door," said Tristan.

The metal door swung open with a click, and the king entered, kneeling by his friend's side. Emerson's chest wasn't rising and falling, sending panic through Tristan. Tibia and Zombia stood by the bars, weapons ready. Then, he pressed his ear to his chest, listening for a heartbeat. The king gulped.

"He has no heartbeat." Tristan pressed his fingers to Emerson's wrist. "No pulse either."

Zombia and Tibia backed away, weapons held higher.

"Get out of there," said Tibia in a harsh voice.

Tristan's mind reeled. He stared at his friend's stationary body. *No, no, this can't be.* Tears threatened to break free. Some did, blurring his vision. His throat closed, trapping a sob inside.

"Emerson—"

"Tristan! Get away from him!" shouted Tibia.

As she said this, Emerson's eyes shot open, revealing scarlet irises.

# Chapter Twenty-Five

Tristan barely had time to back away from a now-zombified Emerson. Green fingers swiped past his vision. The king landed on his backside outside the cell, and he clambered to his feet, scrambling for his sword.

Emerson growled. A sinister grin spread across his face.

Tristan's throat clenched as he faced the rest of his companions. "Our friend is gone." The zombified knight growled again, bearing serrated teeth. It was deep and guttural, filled with nothing but ire for the living.

Too many emotions pounded through Tristan's mind. Anger burnt at Zokar for biting Emerson. Sadness mixed with the anger, a deep knowing the friend they once knew was no more. Tristan swallowed the emotions and grasped his magic. All he could do was block Emerson's escape path. Reaching into his satchel, Tristan took out the elixir.

Emerson lunged out of his cell with a supernatural

strength Tristan was barely prepared for. He nearly knocked the elixir from the king's hand. Tristan fell against the wall but luckily his quick reflexes clutched the fragile bottle in his palm, close to his chest. Emerson feinted right then lunged but never touched the king. Tristan blasted him with a spell, sending the knight flying across the dungeon. He smacked into the wall, rattling empty chains.

A bloodthirsty grin spread across the knight's face that caused Tristan's insides to churn. It was as though Emerson felt no pain.

When Emerson ran at Zombia, Tristan summoned a couple clones and positioned them at the other end of the dungeon. This gave Emerson a diversion and bought Tristan the time he needed.

Emerson chased one of the clones, but when he went to chomp down on the decoy Tristan's arm, the clone vanished in a puff of golden smoke. He charged at the next clone and the same thing occurred.

Emerson brought his hands up, drawing a sloppy rune, and then muttered half of it. The spell formed but didn't finish.

*He absorbed a portion of Zokar's magic!*

"Stay still, Em," Zombia commanded; she had her

glaive angled at him, though her face was creased with regret. Her voice settled to a plea. "Take this potion, please. It'll help you."

Tibia shook her head. "He's not going to simply *drink* the elixir, Zombia. We have to force him to drink it." Her sapphire eyes flitted back to Emerson. "Even if I have to shove the whole thing down his throat."

"Good luck catching me." Emerson laughed. It was a deep laugh, but it didn't express joy or happiness; it expressed malice and thrill for blood. Radius and Tibia blocked Emerson's path, sword and crossbow drawn. Cracking a sinister smile, the knight dodged Tibia's bolt with better grace than Tristan expected from a zombie. Radius lunged, but didn't raise his sword to swing. Rather, he opted to intercept the knight's path instead of hurting him. Emerson easily ducked under Radius's sword and bound for the stairs.

"We can't let him into the castle's main floor!" shouted Tristan. Following his trail, Emerson had already passed the main chamber and was clambering up the stairs. The king, Zombia, and Tibia raced after him.

A roar echoed down the hall.

*He's not going to get away.*

Tristan recognized the roar and voice in his mind as Shadowstalker's. Zombie Emerson tumbled back down the steps. Given the sounds and angle he landed, Tristan guessed Emerson received a few bruises in his fall, maybe even a broken bone. But he didn't hear a yelp or cry of pain, even after falling face-first onto the wet stone floor. Emerson looked up and disturbingly cracked his neck at an abnormal angle.

Shadowstalker marched down the steps; smoke curled up from his nose. Faye and Cerys sat in the saddle between his wings. Emerson clambered to his feet and faced the dragon.

"I can take you." His green face stared fearlessly, not the usual behavior of someone standing before something ten times their size.

Shadowstalker swiped Emerson up in his claws. The knight growled and squirmed, slamming his fists on Shadowstalker's scales, but to no avail. He began another incantation but never finished as Cerys flung a rune to counteract the spell, sending it ricocheting off the damp walls and vanishing into thin air. Tristan silently thanked the gods his friend didn't receive Zokar's magic in full; Cerys might not have been as lucky.

"Stop resisting, Emerson!" Tristan shouted,

holding the elixir in front of him. "Drink this!"

Emerson pounded his fists on Shadowstalker's claws and snarled. Tristan had never thought he'd hear that sound from his knight.

"I have magic now!" shouted Emerson. His decaying face twisted into a sneer. "Once I return to the zombie kingdom, I'll learn all the dark magic I want!"

Tristan's body quaked. If he had been in human form, the dungeon's darkness and his friend's new demonic voice would have sent goosebumps down his arms and neck. Hearing such vehemence from his most trusted knight was uncanny.

"Please, Em, this isn't you," Cameron pleaded.

"Cameron, you moron. He's a *zombie*. He won't listen to you!" shouted Tibia. She kept her crossbow aimed at Emerson's forehead. Tristan watched a single tear escape from her eye.

The zombie groaned, still struggling against Shadowstalker's grip. "When are you going to stop addressing me by his name? I'm not him!"

Cameron clenched his fists. "This ends now!" He snatched the elixir from Tristan's hands and marched up to Shadowstalker.

"Cameron, wait—" Tristan said. He couldn't stop his voice from shaking.

It was too late. Cameron climbed onto the dragon's shoulder, down the length of his arm, and held the potion out to Emerson. "Drink this!" he shouted.

Emerson turned his head, evading the elixir. Shadowstalker's talons closed around the knight tighter, this time capturing his arms and halting all his movement. With his other talon, the dragon gingerly pried Emerson's bloodied maw open while Cameron poured the elixir in. Hope surged in Tristan's chest as he watched the neon-green potion spill over the glass vial's lip and into Emerson's mouth. Once the vial was drained of its contents, Cameron replaced the stopper and climbed down the dragon's shoulder.

Tristan's grip on his bow loosened as he watched Emerson cough and sputter, sending a few stray drops of elixir from his mouth.

"Is it working?" Tibia asked. Her grip on her crossbow hadn't loosened an inch.

"We have to wait," Cerys said calmly. Tristan noticed the mage's posture was a combination of rigid and hopeful.

Emerson's coughing suddenly stopped. His entire body went still as he stared off into the distance as though contemplating his next move. Tristan nearly leaped for joy when the green pigment in his skin receded. The redness in his eyes faded, leaving behind his natural eye colors. The points in his ears vanished, leaving a perfectly rounded helix.

Tristan's jaw hurt from leaving it agape. *Gods above, Blanchett's elixir worked!*

Shadowstalker gently set Emerson on the ground. The knight stretched his back and blinked before glancing down at his hands. He touched his ears and smiled. When his gaze turned to his friends, his smile broadened.

"Emerson!" shouted Cameron. He lunged forward and enveloped his friend into a warm embrace, burying his face into Emerson's chest.

"You're cured," Tristan breathed, hardly believing what he was seeing. He tentatively approached Emerson. Zombia, Cerys, and Tibia did the same. The king's sister kept her crossbow locked and loaded, still unsure whether Emerson was thoroughly cured or not.

"Why do I feel like I've been run over by ten chariots?" Emerson said with a weak smile.

Tristan couldn't resist anymore. He flung his arms around his friend. Tears of joy and solace poured from the king's eyes; he didn't think he'd ever get to hug

Emerson again. He noticed the smell of decomposition left him. More arms wrapped around Tristan and Emerson as Zombia, Cerys, and Faye joined in the embrace. Heat wafted off Shadowstalker's scales as he wrapped his muscular arms around the entire group.

"You did it," said Emerson, pulling away from Tristan. "You found a cure. I knew you could."

He lifted his arm and pushed back his nightshirt's sleeve. To Tristan's horror, the odious ring of toothmarks remained. They were scar tissue, but left an indelible print on his skin. *What a shame. I thought a potion that powerful would cure the physical abrasions. At least he's no longer a zombie.*

"The High Wizard, Ashley Blanchett, brewed it for us," said Zombia, with her arm still wrapped around Emerson. "She's been experimenting with potions in her absence and thank the Moon Goddess, she found one."

"I'm glad she did; it saved me from shooting you," said Tibia with a smirk.

The knight lowered his shoulders, moisture rimming his hetero-chromatic eyes.

"What's wrong, Em?" asked Cameron, placing a hand on his back.

Emerson's lips tightened as he wiped his eyes and remorsefully shook his head. "Just all the trouble I caused. If I had only told you sooner, it wouldn't have come to this." The knight let out a long sigh as though he was trying to breathe life into those around him. Arms held close to his sides, Emerson looked up through a curtain of unkempt chestnut-brown locks. "I'm sorry...for everything."

Tristan placed both hands on his companion's shoulders, granting him a compassionate smile. "There's nothing for you to be sorry for, Emerson. This was all Zokar's doing."

"He'll pay for what he's done." Tibia's gruff tone rang loud and clear. She tapped the point of her crossbow's bolt with her finger.

"What matters is you're okay." Tristan looked from Emerson to Zombia. Cameron handed her the empty vial in which the saving elixir was held. Shadowstalker even gave the king an affirmative nod. "And we have a cure."

# Chapter Twenty-Six

Emerson's head pounded incessantly. Cameron helped him from the dungeon to his quarters. Every muscle in the knight's body ached; when he reached his room, he collapsed on the bed. Cameron pulled the quilt over his shoulders and called for the apothecary to brew some more chamomile tea.

Minutes later, Cameron returned carrying a carpenter's mug with tendrils of steam drifting into the air. The sweet scent caressed Emerson's senses before the liquid even touched his lips. Taking the warm mug into his hands, he sipped at the tea and smiled at Cameron. Chamomile was the best thing Emerson tasted in days.

"Thanks, bud," said the knight.

Cameron nodded, a grin breaking out on his face. "It's so good to have you back!" He jumped on Emerson's bed and threw his arms around his friend, almost knocking over his tea.

"Careful," warned Emerson.

Cameron sat back as redness crept into his face. "Whoops."

A moment of silence skipped by. Emerson sipped some more tea while Cameron jumped off the bed.

The guild master walked toward the door. "Get some rest, my friend."

A grin tugged at the corners of the knight's mouth.

"Because once you've rested, I need you to help me with a few"—Cameron tapped his chin with a gloved hand in a mischievous manner—"projects."

A heaviness settled in Emerson's stomach; he knew what his friend's "projects" entailed. "What would those be?"

"Fixing a few chairs, forging a few swords, and maybe pranking Tibia later this week?"

Emerson's eyes widened as he nearly spat out his tea. "Cameron, she'll kill you."

The guild master smirked and shrugged. "Only if she can catch me."

Both he and Emerson dissolved into a fit of giggles before Cameron reached the door's threshold. "If you need anything, just ask."

After finishing his tea, Emerson curled up under

his quilted blankets, wincing a little from the bruises he received in his fall, and allowed the footsteps of castle guards to lull him into a dreamless sleep.

The following morning, Emerson woke up feeling...off. He couldn't explain it; it was a feeling that settled deep within. He expected the aches and pains to have vanished completely. He expected to feel brand new and ready to sprint around the castle's perimeter three times. But he didn't.

Heat flushed Emerson's face. Sweat trickled down his forehead; his nightshirt's collar clung to his neck. *What in the Underworld?*

Emerson climbed out of bed, pulled open the curtains to let sunlight in, then approached his mirror. A pit opened in the knight's stomach. Cold fingers of dread raked down his spine.

A splotch of green developed on the right side of his face, stretching from his temple to the bottom of his square chin. Pulling at his eyelids, Emerson inspected his irises. A scream trapped itself inside his throat.

Red crept through them.

Stepping back, the knight frantically yanked up his sleeve to see his bite mark was a reddish-purple. He gently touched the skin, finding it was inflamed.

Shallow breaths left Emerson's lungs as though there wasn't enough air in the world to breathe. *Blanchett's elixir isn't holding. I'm regressing into a zombie.* Pressing his hands to his temples, Emerson slid his back down the stone wall.

*We were so close,* thought Emerson. *But I'm not going to hide this.* He shot to his feet and headed for the door. *I'm not making the same mistakes I did last time. I'm going to alert my friends.*

Tristan, Zombia, Cerys, Faye, Tibia, and Shadowstalker were congregated in the apothecary's wing, sitting around a massive oak table. They were surrounded by shelves upon shelves of herbs, giving the room a nice earthy smell. Potted aloe and lavender plants were suspended from the ceiling while several mint plants sat on the window-sill absorbing all that rich sunlight. A desk rested in front of the window, covered in parchment papers and leather-bound books, packed with experiments and recipes. A quill rested in an almost-empty inkwell, telling Tristan they were used frequently.

The door swung open revealing a bedraggled,

tired Emerson. A pit gaped inside Tristan's chest; tears brimmed Emerson's eyes. Splotches of green covered his face, redness seeped through his irises, and sweat clung to his skin, adhering his nightshirt to his body.

"I don't think Blanchett's potion is working," said Emerson plaintively.

Everyone raced over to him. Tristan's gut coiled, an unbearable tightness settling within. *How can this be? Emerson was fine yesterday!* Tristan looked over his shoulder to Cerys.

"What's going on?" the king asked through a cracking voice.

The mage approached Emerson and pressed her palm to his forehead. "Blanchett feared this might happen."

"Feared what might happen?" asked Zombia, a frantic edge in her voice.

A somber look swirled in Cerys's eyes. "The night before we left Aramore, Blanchett and I discussed the effectiveness of the potion. She brought up a good point: this was a bite from Zokar. Since he is Malice's son, her evil spawn, Blanchett feared it might not work."

Tristan swallowed back bile. *I should've guessed. Zokar's sinister magic is what accelerated the zombie virus. No wonder it affected the efficacy of Blanchett's elixir.*

"What do we do now?" Tibia asked, pounding her fist against the table.

"I have an idea," said Zombia. All eyes turned to her.

Reaching into her jerkin pocket, she withdrew the shimmering magenta potion Ingrid gave her. "Here's a potion Ingrid made. Let's try this; she says it's a regeneration potion, which should reverse the zombification effects. The only problem is, it lacks dragon scales."

The dragon sidled up to Zombia and gently gripped her shoulders and spoke for the first time in Tristan's existence.

"I can help with that."

His voice was deep, but not guttural like a zombie's. It possessed an air of wisdom and deep knowledge.

Tristan's lips parted. Shadowstalker didn't even speak outwardly when the king visited Elandorr. He'd learned from his parents that dragons used to speak before the Cadre took power. Maybe even before the Apocalypse. Though Tristan didn't expect any dragon to utter a word until the magic-loathing faction lay in defeat, listening to a dragon's actual voice was as every bit astonishing as he hoped.

Shadowstalker handed Zombia one of his scales. "Here's one that molted off. Crush it up and put it into Ingrid's potion."

Zombia grabbed a mortar and pestle, dropped the scale in, and crushed it into a fine powder. Next, she opened the elixir, poured the powder in, replaced the stopper, and shook the vial.

"After Emerson drinks this potion, use your healing powers, Zombia," said Shadowstalker.

"I'll bond you to me so you'll have dragon magic too. That'll aid in the healing process."

Tristan's breath hitched in awe. *She'll have dragon magic like me.*

The knight smiled and nodded. "I'll take whatever I can get." He cast a nervous glance at his hands, which were starting to turn green. The knight looked from Shadowstalker to Faye.

"Trust him." The Dragonblood elf gave Emerson a stern look.

Zombia fiddled with the ends of her hair. "I'd be happy to, but I'm not sure I'm suitable for that kind of job. Don't you need someone more powerful like Tristan or Faye?"

"You're the only healer in our group," the dragon replied. He regarded Zombia with the reverence one would show a goddess. "The others don't have the magic Emerson needs."

"Don't all wizards have healing powers?" Zombia asked.

"To heal themselves, yes," said Cerys. "When it comes to healing others, they are few and far apart."

Tristan's chest swelled with pride for his friend as he touched her shoulder. "You're the one he needs."

"And it will expand your healing skills," added Faye.

Hazel eyes twinkling with confidence, Zombia nodded. "All right, I'll do it." She handed the potion to Emerson. Pulling out the stopper, he downed the liquid in one gulp.

"Zombia, place your hand over Emerson's bite mark," instructed Shadowstalker. She did as she was told, taking Emerson's wounded bicep into her small hands.

"Ready," she said to the dragon. Shadowstalker gave an affirmative nod.

Tristan prayed to the gods that this idea worked. He didn't want Emerson to devolve back into a zombie. He didn't want to exile his friend, or worse—kill him.

Shadowstalker pressed his forehead to Zombia's forehead, keeping his talons on her shoulders. The dragon began to chant in the elven tongue. His eyes glowed a bright purple, highlighting every surface in the apothecary's den. Tristan stepped back as Zombia's eyes, too, began glowing purple. Her entire body beamed a bright purple. From Tristan's vantage point, he could see a lavender light emitted from Emerson's bite mark and shining through Zombia's fingers.

Shadowstalker lifted his chin to the heavens as a purple mist curled out from his mouth in the shape of a dragon. It writhed in at the center of the vaulted ceiling of the apothecary's den for a moment like powerful ocean waves, before encasing Zombia like a gossamer cloak. An ancient elven rune followed, seeping into her very being. She was now part dragon.

At the end of the chant, Shadowstalker said in the common tongue, "In the name of the Dragonbloods, I, Shadowstalker, bond you unto me."

*Gods above,* thought Tristan. *This is what the bonding ritual looks like.*

The glow vanished in a puff, leaving zero trace. Zombia lifted her hand and stepped back.

"That was INCREDIBLE!" Emerson held up his arm and ran his fingers over the smooth, sleek black scales covering his bicep where Zokar's bite mark was. The green coloring vanished from his complexion, and his eyes returned to their normal hues. He was emancipated from zombification.

"So, does this mean Zombia's going to sprout horns and a tail?" asked Emerson with a smirk. Laughter filled the room.

"No," said Shadowstalker. "She'll have a minor

resistance to fire and increased strength, like him." The dragon cast a glance at Tristan.

Emerson wrapped his arms around Zombia. "Thank you," he whispered into her shoulder.

"What are friends for?" she responded.

Releasing his embrace, Emerson clasped Shadowstalker's talon. "Thank you, too."

The dragon flashed the knight a broad grin.

Tristan smiled, his heart feeling full. He gathered Zombia and Shadowstalker into an embrace.

The Hidden Wizard

A day passed and Emerson only improved. On day two, Emerson was well enough to don his full set of crystal armor and visit Tristan, Zombia, Faye, Shadowstalker, Cerys, and Tibia in the apothecary's den.

"Feeling good as new," Emerson said as he strutted into the room, chest out. Sunlight spilled through the window, making his armor shimmer like a thousand tiny teal suns.

"That's wonderful," said Tristan, turning around from his place at the table.

"Though I'm still getting used to these scales." Emerson ran his fingers over the scales and took a seat between Tristan and Zombia. She had a wooden mixing bowl before her, and, at her right, she had a mortar and pestle. "What are you working on?"

"Now that I have dragon magic, I'll brew the curing elixir by combining crushed dragon scales and Ingrid's potion." Zombia held up the glowing magenta potion the blind sorceress had given her. "Apparently, her potion combined with Shadowstalker's scales can withstand Zokar's dark magic." She rolled the bottle between her fingers, a soft smile adorning her face. "But I'll have to contact her for the recipe. If we're going to cure the entire Haunted Lands, we'll need a lot more.

"I can't believe I did it. I actually cured Emerson." Zombia's face beamed, her shoulders rolling back so her chest and chin jutted out with confidence. "I never thought I'd be capable of such things." Zombia's voice took on a somber tone. "My mother healed people, but not like this. I, with Shadowstalker"—Zombia looked up at the dragon sitting hunched behind her—"and Ingrid's help, cured the virus that's plagued the Haunted Lands since the Apocalypse began."

Tristan's heart soared with pride for his friend. He wrapped his arms around her and gave her a peck on the cheek. "You're the healer the world needs."

Zombia's green face reddened.

Shadowstalker winked at her and smiled. "The prowess in herbs and altruistic spirit can extend to other ailments as well, not only the zombie infection."

Setting the potion on the table, Zombia turned to Tristan. "Since discovering my magic, I always feared it'd always be weak and inferior to yours and Tibia's. I feared I'd be more of a burden than a help to the Wizards of the Apocalypse and that I'd let Blanchett down. But I guess I was wrong all along. My prowess lies in a *specific* type of magic—healing magic."

Tibia slapped her friend on the back. "You're

going to save a lot of people, Zombia. You're more than a big help; you're irreplaceable."

"Everyone has their strengths and weaknesses," said Cerys; she grinned and held her arms out, palms up. "Wizards included."

More redness crept through Zombia's cheeks, causing Tristan's heart to soar.

Reaching into her pocket, Zombia withdrew a few black scales and dropped them into the mortar before grinding them up into a fine powder.

"Now that we have a cure, let's talk distribution," said Emerson. He inclined his head.

"Simple: crush up dragon scales, brew the elixir, and distribute it to everyone," offered Tibia, drumming her fingers on the oak wood.

"It's not that easy, Tibia. We can't distribute any elixirs or tonics without the Cadre's approval," said Faye. She ran her long fingers through her lilac hair and leaned against Shadowstalker's leg. "The Cadre has massive influence over the Haunted Lands. They have everyone believing they 'saved' the people from the dangers of magic by only showing them its dark side. And the ratio of dragons to zombies is extremely low. It takes months to hatch a dozen new dragons. Hundreds of zombies can be amassed in days."

Cerys leaned against the table and got a wistful look in her eyes. "Blanchett told Ingrid and me bedtime stories of times when dragons from all tribes lived in harmony. They would fly through the skies as frequently as birds. Wizards could practice magic in peace without fear of being burnt. It's a period in time I hope isn't lost forever."

Tristan nodded. "I know, but we'll find a way. The truth will be revealed in the end. The Cadre's deception will only hold for so long." *I hope.*

Zombia placed her arms around Tibia and Tristan. "We can make it happen."

"Sounds like a plan," added Tibia. "First, we should focus on killing Malice and Zokar." She twirled her crossbow. "Then we focus on exposing Kieran and his goons for the liars they are."

"And we can work on brewing tons of the cure," Zombia said, tapping the vial with her nail. "Also, it needs a name."

Tristan pressed a finger to his chin. He dug through his mind, thinking of a name that would resonate power, but also hope and optimism. He locked eyes with Zombia as if reading her mind.

The Hidden Wizard

"Dragon's Cure!" Tristan and Zombia said simultaneously.

There was a lightness in the king's body. He and his friends had saved Emerson. They found a cure. He hadn't failed his duty as a king.

With his right hand, Tristan patted the dragon-claw dagger at his hip. Malice was still alive, and she'd return soon. The battle with the undead was far from over, but at least whatever lay ahead, Tristan would face it with his friends at his side. So, there was no time to waste. The Haunted Lands were counting on the Wizards of the Apocalypse.

DRAGON'S
CURE

# Chapter Twenty-Seven

Exhilaration. That's what Marcus felt right now. He couldn't suppress the emotion as it blossomed in his chest like flowers after a dreary winter. *So close. I'm so close to becoming king of the zombies.*

It was the following night and a full moon hovered in the sky, casting obscure shadows on the fern-green land. Trees surrounded the area in a small copse. Maeve led the way, her silver-trimmed robes billowing behind her; she and her sorceresses wanted to continue on foot once they arrived at the Dragon Isles—specifically the Moonlit Mountains. Zokar griped the whole way, but that didn't even bother Marcus. Not when Malice was about to return.

When the second-in-command heard waves crashing against solid surfaces, he realized the ritual site rested on the cliffside overlooking the Draconic Ocean. He often wondered what lay beyond. Were there other continents out there? Ones filled with survivors?

Dragons perhaps?

Cresting the hill, the icy wind bit through Marcus's wine-red doublet. Not only were they close to the Ice Queendom, but seeing the ritual site didn't stop goosebumps from rising on Marcus's skin. A circle of granite pillars jutted up and into the sky, their bases connected to form a platform. Now up close, the gray masses he saw earlier became monolithic ruins. Perhaps from an old temple?

Curiosity wound its way through the second-in-command. Marcus knew he wasn't magic, but he hoped someday Malice would teach him. He rarely left the outskirts of Zombieshire, save for Skeletonia and neighboring villages. His eye widened as he tried fathoming the existence of a whole magical world nesting inside the Haunted Lands.

While most of the columns were eroded, the stone floor was intact. So intact that Marcus could see sigils and runes scattered methodically, following the floor's round shape. The writings spiraled into the center, ending at a drawing of the Triple Goddess. In the full moon, a raven was etched.

Maeve turned to Marcus and Zokar. "These are called Portal Platforms. Like the Fortress of Portals, they allowed for easy transportation to the surface world."

Maeve drew her wand, a small book of spells, and sashayed to the center of the ruins. Her coven members spread out in a wide circle, covering the entire floor perimeter. Zokar looked at her dubiously.

"What now?" the zombie king asked, splaying his arms.

Marcus rolled his eye and sighed through his nose. *Can Zokar ever shut up?*

"We perform the ritual," said Maeve.

"And let me guess, you need blood, don't you?"

The sorceress shook her head. "Not from you."

Zokar bowed his head in relief, and Marcus pressed his hand to his mouth, suppressing a laugh. The zombie king anxiously rubbed his palm. The flesh was still rigid and raw from when Malice sliced his hand to get blood for the Fortress of Portals.

Taking a dagger, Maeve cut her palm and let a few red drops fall directly on the raven's eye. Following after, Maeve cracked open her book and began her incantation. The sorceresses surrounding her joined in, speaking in an ancient tongue Marcus had never heard.

Loose pebbles on the ground began bouncing. Zokar's throat bobbed, his face blanching; Marcus held back a snort.

"Are we supposed to help with the ritual or what?"

Marcus shook his head. He remained composed, even as the ground shook violently like it was ready to split at any second. Fear scrunched Zokar's brows together.

"This is a ritual only the Silver Flame Tribe can perform," said Marcus, his voice flat. The captain placed his arms behind his back, chest out, unafraid.

"I have more magic than all of them," growled Zokar. "My mother's the queen of the Shadowbloods, for Moon Goddess's sake."

Marcus rolled his eye but remained still. "That's not it, sire. Sorcerer magic is different from yours; they can work with the moon in ways you can't. And, of course, I don't have any magic." He showed the zombie king his empty hands for emphasis. "So, with all due respect, step back and be quiet."

The ground shook harder now; the trees and ruins vibrated with such force that Marcus and Zokar nearly fell over. They had to brace themselves on a thick tree trunk. The chanting grew louder; the sorceresses faced the sky, the moon, as though they were speaking directly to it.

Deep cracks formed in the stone floor, slithering along until the whole platform looked like a spider web. Then, the raven split open, and the ground parted, releasing the Otherworld's bright-red and orange light.

A hunched form rose out in a cloud of crimson smoke. She lifted higher and higher as the ground resealed itself and landed on two sturdy legs. Through the haze, Marcus could see four recognizable points atop her head. The demon's robes were tattered and caked in her black blood. Though she looked injured, her spirit definitely wasn't. Malice's eyes flitted from Zokar to Marcus.

The second-in-command dropped to one knee. "Welcome back, your Highness."

# Acknowledgements

I can't express how surreal it is having another book out in the world! Writing a sequel isn't easy, but after tons of time editing, drawing, and editing some more, here we are!

To my friends and family—thank you for sticking by my side as I plug through the many drafts and writing sessions, and your encouragement that kept me going, especially when impostor syndrome hit. Your kind words and uplifting words never fail to keep me motivated.

To my beta readers—thank you for your constructive criticism, feedback, and providing perspective to hone my story.

To my fellow writer/author friends—thank you for being there, being so encouraging and so generous in your support for me and my books. I wouldn't change our writing sessions, idea bouncing, or laughs for the world.

To my editors, Isobelle and Carly—thank you for giving me the feedback and constructive criticism my story needed, polishing it for the public. To everyone who helped with formatting, cover design, and proofreading, thank you!

Finally, to my readers—thank you for giving *The Hidden Wizard* a chance. Thank you for your encouragement and enthusiasm for my story and characters. You've made my dream of being an author come true, and for that, I am eternally grateful.

www.ingramcontent.com/pod-product-compliance
Lightning Source LLC
Chambersburg PA
CBHW071552150726
48000CB00004B/1433